I'LL MEET YOU
in Florence

ANGELA PEARSE

Set in Sabon and Futura
Cover art by Kostis Pavlou kostispavlou.com

ISBN 978-1-914531-88-0 Paperback (IS)
ISBN 978-1-914531-89-7 Paperback (KDP)

For Tanz and bella Italia

CHAPTER ONE

'Have you got that, Jenna?' Whipping my head around, I find India Carver staring at me—pointedly. Whoops.

I'm supposed to be listening to her quick-fire explanation about the solar power. But I've been distracted by a sweeping black marble staircase, the super high ceilings looming above and the sheer number of crystal chandeliers. I can count at least five from where I'm standing.

And the electronics. Oh my God. Nothing has a simple switch. The whole house is digitally operated from a phone app. No wonder I've spaced out.

'I'll text you the link to the app and you can download it,' India says. 'It's quite simple. But we should have a run-through before I go, otherwise you won't have electricity. And I don't want to have to field calls about it while I'm on holiday.'

I nod gratefully. 'Thanks.'

Erk. That's put me in my place.

This Victorian mansion in Hampstead is enormous and it's caught me off guard. The website listing didn't have any photos of the house, only the cat, so I was expecting an average-sized semi with the usual two or three bedrooms. Not a seven-bedroom, fifteen-foot ceiling, five chandelier affair.

The owners are just a couple rattling around in all this space. They must be either stonkingly rich from their day jobs or have inherited a lot of money. From the snippets of what India's been telling me, I've managed to piece together that Drew Carver, her husband, is a music producer and that she owns an organic skincare business. I haven't been able to place her age. She could be anywhere between thirty-five and fifty-five if botox injections are involved. There has been no mention of kids either—toddlers or teenagers—which would have been an instant age marker.

India leads the way up the marble staircase, then glides down the dark-wood parquet hallway in her pink leather house slippers. She's asked me to take my shoes off, so I'm skidding in my ankle socks. She gestures at doors right and left, announcing their purpose 'our room... main bathroom... Drew's study... media lounge... zoo room...'

Zoo room? That sounds worrying. As far as I know, there's just the cat to look after. My ears prick for any squeaks or squawks that might suggest a menagerie of exotic animals. Sometimes owners also try to slip in friends' dogs, so you have to be on your guard. But there are no suspicious noises that I can hear coming from the room.

We continue until she pauses outside a room at the far end of the hall and glances back at me to check if I'm keeping up.

Her blonde hair swishes across her cheekbone, then swings into place. We both have shoulder-length bobs with layered fringes. Unlike my straight golden-brown locks, which I trim myself because I can't afford a haircut at the moment, her cut is immaculate. Almost as if her stylist has used a ruler to make sure every hair on her head is the correct length.

'This is the largest of our guest rooms and the only one on the top floor. But you can choose one of the others downstairs if you'd like to be closer to the kitchen,' she says. I recall the earlier part of our grand tour in which five guest bedrooms were mentioned. At least I've remembered something.

India leads the way into the guest room, and I gape. The walls are pink. But not any old pink. Luscious strawberry gelato pink. An oak four-poster bed features white satin bedding and a gossamer canopy. On the floor is a faux zebra-skin rug. The black-and-white theme is matched by framed prints of iconic movie stars dotted around the walls; Audrey Hepburn, Marilyn Monroe, Grace Kelly. It's a Disney bedroom for grown-up princesses who go designer shopping in Knightsbridge.

'It's *fantastic*,' I breathe, forgetting it's gauche to show one's excitement when shown around an upmarket house sit. 'Like medieval meets modern with a nod to retro.'

'Yes, that's exactly what I was going for. Drew thought it was too much but I went with my instincts.'

'No, it totally works!'

India looks approving. 'What do you do again, Jenna? I don't think you said in your profile.'

'Oh, I'm an interior decorator,' I say, after a pause. I don't tend to mention this because then owners want to know why I'm house sitting and start asking awkward questions; and it's my foot-in-the-door system to win clients. This is how it works. I subtly rearrange the furniture or accessories in a room as if on a whim. Then, when the owners get back and exclaim 'Oh, this looks different but much better!' I casually mention I'm an interior decorator. If they say something like, 'I've been wanting to redecorate' or 'I have a friend who needs an interior decorator', then I have an in.

But advising someone on the best shade of beige carpet for a one-bedroom flat in Wandsworth is small fry. Taking on a room in a house like this is exactly what I'm after if I want to raise my profile.

However, India doesn't leap at the chance of hiring me or suggest she has a friend in need of my services. 'It has a nice outlook over the garden, much like our room,' she says, changing the subject. She flings opens the mullioned window and I peer over her shoulder. 'Wow!' I exclaim before I can stop myself.

The garden is at least an acre; landscaped lawn, clipped box hedges and raised flower beds full of pink roses. Methinks the lady of the manor has ordered a themed garden to be created in her honour. Over to the left, I spy a decent-sized swimming pool twinkling blue in the sunlight. There's also a lovely wooden cabana with a straw thatch roof and white lattice loungers. Situated behind the pool is a glossy black shipping container with a sliding door, windows and a little wooden deck. The garden shed, I assume. A property this size probably needs a lot of hoes and hedge clippers and other… implements.

I'm about to comment on it, but India says she'll show me the kitchen next so we can have a cup of tea and go over the app for the solar electrics. 'I need to order my taxi to meet Drew at his office in Hammersmith,' she remarks looking at her watch. 'We're going to Heathrow from there. Rush hour traffic will be positively hellish. I wish we had a private helicopter. I might ask him about getting one.' I almost let out an amused chuckle but then realise—she's not joking.

Downstairs, I'm greeted with yet another revelation, the kitchen of my dreams. It's a new extension, India tells me. Glass bi-fold doors open out onto an upper-level garden patio. There are three skylights. A polished brass mixer tap and an oversized sink are fitted into a white marble counter. The walls are lined with sleek high-gloss black cabinets. The glass-top kitchen table could seat twenty people. It's all a bit overwhelming.

India is dying to show me the chrome kettle. 'It's clever, we ordered it from the US,' she says. 'Watch this.'

She holds up her palms and claps twice. Soon, there's the sound of boiling water, and steam rises from the spout.

'You clap once to turn it off. That's the only drawback. If you forget, it boils dry, and it's game over for the kettle. When we first got it, we were clapping like mad things and ended up with cups of tea for Africa. Sephy thought we were potty, didn't you Sephy, darling?'

Sephy (aka Persephone) is their grey fluffy Persian and the reason they need a housesitter. She's just made an appearance in the kitchen through the cat door and chirrups at India, no doubt thinking she's going to get an early dinner. India picks her up and buries her face in the soft fur, causing the cat to squirm. 'Isn't she adorable?' says India to me. Sephy swipes a sharp-clawed paw, narrowly missing India's smooth unblemished cheek. I don't ask if I can have a cuddle, those claws look lethal.

After herbal tea and solar electrics 101, India shows me the garden. Stepping out through the doors and onto the red-brick patio, we stand there shading our eyes in the glare of the afternoon sun. 'You can get to the pool that way,' she says pointing to some concrete steps.

They lead onto a path which winds down through low shrubbery and ends at the pool. Hot rays beat down on my shoulders and the water looks cool and refreshing. I haven't been for a swim once this summer, so I'm glad I packed my bikini on the off-chance they had a pool.

'Your shipping container garden shed is on trend,' I comment, trying to sound in the know.

'Oh, it's not a garden shed. That's Seth's studio,' India says airily.

'Seth?' I echo. 'Is he the on-site gardener?'

She gives a short laugh. 'No, he's my stepson.'

What? I glower inside but am careful to make sure it doesn't show on my face. I hate it when house owners do this. You think you're going to be alone, then you find out you're also babysitting a teenager and their teenage friends. Before you know it, there's an all-night drinking session underway.

'Um, right. How old is Seth?'

'He's twenty-six.'

OK, so not a teenager.

'Why can't he look after Persephone? Is he going away too?' I ask, trying to sound unconcerned.

'Oh no, he's staying here, but he's got his own life and likely to forget.' India sniffs. 'Poor Sephy wouldn't survive if Seth was on cat duty.'

I push down a pang of annoyance.

'Does he come inside to eat?'

India shakes her head. 'It's a self-contained studio, and he's got his own private entrance in the adjoining lane. He nips out to M&S or orders takeaways,' she explains. 'Most of the time I forget he's around. Drew goes down there periodically to check on him to make sure he's still alive.'

'But don't worry,' she says, seeing my eyebrows raise, 'he likes to keep to himself. We've told him we're getting a house sitter. Even though he knows you're here, he won't bother you.'

Well, if that's the case, my shoulders relax and I breathe more easily. It's still fine. I don't have to worry about babysitting someone or having them walk in when I'm doing a bit of subtle knick-knack rearranging. And I can turn a blind eye to any all-night drinking sessions.

'That sounds perfect,' I say, smiling. Excitement bubbles up. *Living in Hampstead for two whole weeks!* I hug myself in glee. Figuratively, of course, India hasn't left the house just yet.

CHAPTER TWO

When I applied for this house sit, I didn't think I'd get chosen. The Hampstead listings always have a ton of applicants and get snapped up as soon as they're posted. But everyone catches a break eventually, and this is mine. A relaxing two-week escape in the world of posh people; I deserve it.

That's what I tell myself anyway as I help India and her silver shell suitcase into a black taxi, and wave them off in the direction of Hammersmith.

However, I know I'm sticking my head in the sand. The reality of my life is starting to pinch. I'm duly reminded of that when a message appears on my phone shortly after from Violet: *What's the house like? BTW, you left your hairdryer behind.*

Lugging my wheelie up to the Disney bedroom, I dig around in my clothes to check. Damn, she's right. Well, I'm not going back to Putney to collect it.

Me
House is nice. Yes, I did forget my hairdryer.

Violet
Is it posh? Is it right next to Hampstead Heath?

Me
Yes and yes.

Violet
Vid tour?

Me
Yes, later on. I have to figure stuff out.

Violet
What stuff?

Me
The microwave.

After India left, I noticed that the microwave had no control panel which worried me. I thought there might be something in the manual she emailed but when I checked, it was mainly about Persephone. Usually, I can live without a microwave except that India said she'd left some vegan heat-and-eat meals in the fridge. I'm not vegan, but if they're going free, I'll eat them to save some cash.

The microwave is also an excuse because I don't want to

show Violet the house. She tends to be overly critical and will burst my bubble.

I know what she'll say: 'Jesus, don't break your neck on that marble staircase' or 'the garden looks nice but what a hell of a lot of work'. I can do without her negativity right now. Yet, I don't want to piss her off. She lets me crash on the couch in her one-bedroom flat between house sits. I try to line them up, so I don't have to go there but often, there's a gap.

I head back down to the kitchen. The microwave is a black box inset above the induction hob and streamlined with the cabinets. The door opens easily with a tug. I press every inch of the front, run my hands over it, and nothing flashes or beeps to make it work. I even try clapping but only succeed in turning the kettle on. At least I know I can have a cup of tea if all else fails.

Think, Jenna, it can't be that hard.

Duh. The app. Everything is powered through the app so of course, the microwave must be on there.

I bring up the app on my phone and flick through the household items until I see "microwave". Clicking yields a list of times and cooking preferences. I click on "one minute express", and voilá, the microwave starts up. Yes!

I'm about to click out of the app when I see "Seth Studio" near the bottom. Curiously, I click in and see three icons: lighting, heating and microwave. Funny to think I can turn his microwave on too. I'm tempted to click "one minute express" to mess with him and make him think he has a ghost. But he may not get the joke. I've already formed a vivid picture of Seth based on what India told me about his takeaway-heavy lifestyle. Overweight, with greasy hair, thin lips, a scraggly beard and a bad case of chin acne which he's trying to cover up with said beard. Not my type at all.

Sephy lets out a plaintive meow reminding me that I have to sort out her dinner. India's specific instructions are one scoop of organic cat biscuits in the morning and one at night, so I'm careful to follow it to the letter. For all I know, she has special cat scales from the US that she'll weigh Sephy on afterwards. I can see the two-star review now: *Jenna was a lovely girl but too heavy-handed with the cat biscuits. My darling Sephy is now on a strict diet...*

But at least she hasn't requested a daily check-in which many owners do. I had one old dear who insisted on photos of her dog pooping to make sure she wasn't constipated. Ugh. Luckily for me, India's more of an out-of-sight, out-of-mind owner.

Once Sephy's fed, I heat my microwave vegan meal, grab a glass of juice and head through to the small lounge off the kitchen that I discovered on my self-guided nosey. It's like an afterthought, but I prefer it to the main lounge, which is impersonal and massive.

This one has a cosy vibe with plush white carpet, a soft

grey L-shaped sofa with bright pink scatter cushions, a wrought iron fireplace and a floor-to-ceiling bookcase. The bookcase is cluttered with vases, photos and objets d'art, so there's plenty of knick-knack rearranging potential. I thought the zoo room might be worth photographing too but the door is locked, and I couldn't see anything through the keyhole.

I'm about to message Violet to say I'll give her a video tour when my phone rings and "Stacey" flashes on the screen. I breathe a sigh of relief. Saved by my elder sister. She lives in Edinburgh, and we usually chat every few days. Except that she's fallen off the grid lately, and I haven't spoken to her for a couple of weeks.

'Hiya, stranger,' I say, settling back on the sofa.

'Hi, can you talk?'

'Yup. Just finished my sundried tomato and lentil ragu.'

'Ergh. Hopefully, it tasted better than it sounds.'

'It wasn't too bad actually.'

'Are you at Violet's? Don't tell me she's turned vegan.'

I laugh. 'No, God forbid. I'm doing a two-week house sit in Hampstead. A massive Victorian mansion. It's right posh—marble staircase, chandeliers, mod cons, pool—the works. The owners have gone to the French Riviera for a holiday.'

Stacey gives a murmur of approval. 'Lucky you. Has the dopamine kicked in yet?'

'Yeah, I'm on a house sit high. It's the nicest one I've done so far.'

'Animals?'

'One cat and she's pretty easy. Oh, and there's a stepson. But I won't meet him.'

'Why not?'

'He lives down the back of the property in a self-contained studio and doesn't come into the main house. A bit of a loner apparently, from what the owner said.'

'Ooh, mysterious. He might be cute.'

'I doubt it,' I scoff. 'More likely the Hunchback of Hampstead.'

Stacey chuckles at that. 'You must be a little curious though?'

'Maybe, but not enough to go down there and introduce myself. He's likely to tell me to piss off and stop bothering him.'

'Well, you never know until you try. Leave no stone unturned and all that. How old is he?'

'Twenty-six,' I reply reluctantly.

'There you go. He's the same age as you.' Once Stacey gets an idea in her head, it's hard for her to abandon it.

'I don't think so.'

'You have to move on from Gabe at some point, Jen.'

'Just because I'm single, it doesn't mean I haven't moved on from him!' I say, my hackles rising. Right, time to change the subject.

'Anyway, how's the biz?'

We chat for a bit longer about Stacey's latest purchases and how well her Etsy shop is doing. I try not to feel envious. She sells artwork and homewares made by local Edinburgh artisans and has built her business from scratch. It's her I can thank for encouraging me to try interior decorating on a freelance basis rather than work for another agency. She's given me lots of support and tips and even then, last year was a hard slog. I nearly gave up a few times, but she keeps telling me to stick with it since the first couple of years are the hardest. I'm not sure I have her tenacity. I have had projects, but not my "breakthrough client". The one that will put me on the map.

After hanging up from Stacey, I decide I need a cup of tea and some happy-clappy kettle distraction.

While I'm waiting for it to boil, I wander out onto the patio where it's cooler. The evening is still and quiet apart from a timed sprinkler spraying a jet of water over the thirsty roses with a shhhh-tik-tik-tik sound. The pool with its underwater lights looks even more inviting in the dusk.

Maybe I'll go for a swim tomorrow, I think, gazing at it. It is quite close to Seth's studio though, and my bikini is a bit skimpy. I'm not sure I want some loser guy perving at me from behind the curtains while eating his takeaway and getting his kicks. I watch for a little while to see if there's any movement from the studio. But there's nothing. Hopefully, he's out most of the day if he has a job or is too busy playing computer games if he's unemployed. I should've asked India more questions about him. What if he's a weirdo?

As if answering my question, a light blinks on inside the studio, making me jump. He's definitely in there. Perhaps I should be friendly and go down to introduce myself. But not tonight. I need to clap to turn the kettle off. Then I'm going to take my tea up to the Disney bedroom, unpack in a leisurely fashion and relax in a bubble bath. Even if nothing comes from it, I've been damn lucky to get this house sit, and I'm going to enjoy my good fortune while it lasts.

CHAPTER THREE

When everything blew up with Gabe, I considered taking my parents' offer to stay with them. It was the easiest option. Go back home and live with Mummy and Daddy. But even though their house has three bedrooms, the guest ones are tiny. I'd be sleeping in a single bed, surrounded by dressed-up teddies, sharing a bathroom and listening to my father read out the obituaries at the breakfast table every morning. Hardly inspiring.

Besides, they live in Camberley, a backwater town in Surrey, and I didn't think I'd be doing my career any favours. As Stacey said, I needed to be in London if I wanted to make a name for myself. So I decided to stay put and couch surf at Violet's in Putney. After a month, we were both getting on each other's nerves. On top of that, my back was so wrecked from her dilapidated couch I had to see a cheap chiropractor. Violet also lives under a Heathrow flight path. House sitting seemed like a brilliant idea under the circumstances.

Over the past year, I've done around thirty, mostly in London, but some out in the commuter towns as well. From those house sits, I've managed to land five projects and another few projects by word of mouth and my website. It's not bad, but it's not good either. And not consistent enough to be able to afford rent.

I read somewhere that you can have a great job, a great apartment and a great love life. But you can't have all three at the same time. Which is reassuring because at the moment I don't have any. I just have to keep on doing what I'm doing and hope that things will come right eventually. When you're at rock bottom, the only way is up.

Over the next few days, I settle into a routine. First thing in the morning, I feed Sephy who's meowing her head off and pawing her bowl by the time I walk into the kitchen. Then make myself a cup of tea and help myself to some organic cereal and oat milk, topping it off with a banana. Then generally laze around enjoying the house and pretending I'm lady of the manor.

India has been generous about the food situation, but I can't rely on her for the whole two weeks. So I start venturing out to the M&S in the Village to pick up some supplies. Only in the morning though, as London is in the grip of a heatwave and it's sweltering by the afternoon. Initially, I stay away from the pool because of Seth and take cool showers. But by the third day, I think, *this is ridiculous, I want to have a swim, so what if he perves?*

When I plunge into the icy water, I'm sure my shriek will prompt Seth to poke his head out the window and call 'Hello. You must be Jenna. Nice to meet you!' But there is no grand appearance. It's disappointingly uneventful.

Near the end of the week, he still hasn't shown his face, so I start having a swim in the morning and afternoon. I also do a little sunbathing after and have a doze in the shade of the cabana. Heat shimmers over the garden, and I'm lulled by the persistent drone of bumblebees flying around the roses. On Friday, I bring down a jug of iced water and some magazines I found in the small lounge. *This is heavenly, I could get used to this,* I think, gently guiding a stray bee away with a rolled-up Vogue from my bare thigh.

At the weekend, the temperature shoots higher. I notice that all the windows of the shipping container have been flung open. The sliding door is ajar but the net curtain is still drawn. *He must be boiling in there,* I think, and feel guilty because I've been swimming a lot. But surely, we can share the pool?

It occurs to me that Seth *may* be using the pool, just not when I'm around. It is possible. I am pretty consistent with my timing. What if he's worked out my schedule and is avoiding me? Is he really that anti-social? No man is an island, for God's sake. It's not healthy to shut yourself away like that. I tell myself this is me being concerned about Seth's state of mind, but it's more likely I'm lonely since I haven't spoken to anyone for a while.

In my mind, Seth's appearance has changed as well. Now I'm starting to picture him as more like Mellors, the gamekeeper in Lady Chatterley's Lover. Big, brawny and dressed in fawn breeches, a white blousy shirt and braces. It's probably the whole garden shed thing or maybe Stacey's comment about leaving no stone unturned. It's getting a bit ridiculous. I need to rein it in and stop speculating about what he looks like. Even if I do see him, I know the reality won't be nearly as good as my imagination.

On Monday morning, when I go outside to get rid of the kitchen rubbish, I notice the bin is filled with several Uber Eats paper bags with stapled receipts stuffed in at the top. They must be Seth's.

Curiously, I flick the nearest receipt towards me to check what he ordered: bruschetta, caprese, gorgonzola salad, pesto rigatoni and a bottle of San Pellegrino sparkling water. Huh, intriguing. Not too unhealthy. Not even a dessert. There are a couple more bags. I sneak a glance at the shipping container to make sure he's not actually standing there watching me, then check those out too.

The other receipts show the same Italian restaurant, Luigi's, and show a slight variation of the order. He's swapped out the pasta and chosen a different salad. Fair enough. He must like Italian food a lot to order it so much. I don't blame him, I'm partial to pasta myself. But what does a twenty-six-year-old guy that loves pasta and San Pellegrino look like?

I'm about to close the bin lid when I spot M&M's in the bottom of one of the Uber Eats bags. I shuffle the bag and see there's a ripped packet at the bottom with them spilling out. I stare down at it for a moment then realise with a start that there aren't any green M&M's. I upend the packet. There's not even one green M&M. A zing of unease runs through me. I shut the bin lid with a bang and scuttle back to the house feeling like I've discovered something I shouldn't.

Green M&M's. Why the hell would he only eat green M&M's? That's weirdo behaviour. I pace around the lounge disconcerted, trying to figure it out. Finally, I grab my phone and type "why would someone eat only green M&M's?" into Google not expecting to get any answers. But sentences start jumping out at me... *there's a rumour that the green ones are an aphrodisiac... they pick the green ones out to feed to objects of their desire... green is associated with healing and fertility...* Erk. Maybe I'm not too far off the mark with Lady Chatterley's Lover!

By late afternoon, I can't stand it anymore. The mystery of Seth and the green M&M's is mucking with my head. I'm going down there. Not to interrogate him, just purely for information gathering to see what he's like... And determine if he's a serial killer.

Seth's probably not cute, but I change into one of my nicer summer dresses, brush my hair and slick on some lip gloss… just in case. Halfway down the path, I get an attack of nerves. What if he tells me to piss off? *Well, then you'll know he's a fuckwit,* says the voice of reason in my head, *and you'll never have to see him again.* I take a deep breath. Exactly.

When I reach the shipping container, there's no sound from within, but he must be in there otherwise the sliding door wouldn't be ajar. I slap across the deck in my flip-flops, making a decent amount of noise to let him know he's got a visitor.

A slight breeze ruffles the net curtain and I pause, my throat dry. *I really hope he's not a fuckwit or a serial killer.* I wipe my clammy palms on my dress before rapping on the glass with a knuckle. My heart pumps uncomfortably in my chest. There's nothing for at least ten seconds, then a low 'Yes?'

'Uh, Seth? I'm Jenna, the house sitter. I thought I'd introduce myself and say hi. So, er, hi.' My voice squeaks at the end.

There's a creaking as if he's getting up off a chair, and then silence, as if he's contemplating me through the net curtain. Is he coming to the door, or not? My heart rate increases, and I take a step back. But he doesn't appear. 'I know who you are,' he says.

Woah, his voice is really nice, with a hint of private school, but not too plummy. Deep and melodious. Kind of sexy. Green M&M's sexy.

I plough on, trying to get some kind of conversation going. 'Great. Well, I hope I haven't been disturbing you with my ah… pool usage.'

But annoyingly he doesn't reply, and I cast around in vain for something else to say, other than a sarcastic, 'Goodbye Seth, thanks for the chat.'

'Um, do you want to have dinner at the house tonight? I'll cook.' *What?* Why the hell did I go and say that?! I brace myself for rejection.

There's a long silence as if he's pondering. Then he says, 'What's on the menu?' *Good question, Seth, very good question.*

'Uh…' Shit, what will I cook? I panic and pick something at random, 'Lamb rissoles.'

'That's quite specific.' He sounds amused. 'What if I'm vegetarian?'

'Are you?'

'No, but it's polite to ask first.'

OK, touchy. I wait for a bit without saying anything.

'Fine.' He sounds resigned. 'What time?'

'Six forty-eight,' I say, to be pedantic.

'Again. Oddly specific.'

'I'm a specific person,' I say haughtily. 'See you then.'

There's a muffled hmph in reply that I assume is

agreement.

Walking back across the deck and up to the house, I get a strong sense of being watched. Only when I step into the kitchen, I let out the breath I've been holding the entire way. I sit down at the dining table feeling shaken by the encounter. The hairs on my arms are standing on end. Wow, that was scary. But I did it. I met him. Kind of.

Then I realise I haven't actually seen Seth, and I still don't know what kind of weird he is. Instead, I said I'd cook him dinner, it's five o'clock and I have no ingredients for lamb rissoles.

CHAPTER FOUR

According to BBC Food, lamb rissoles are pretty easy to make. I've noticed a small herb garden growing near the kitchen, so I poke around in there and yank out some parsley and rosemary. I then hotfoot it to M&S Food to buy the rest of the ingredients. As I'm in the meat section, it occurs to me that inviting Seth to dinner could be construed as a date. Erk. Not exactly what I was wanting.

To prove how not like a date this is, back at the house, I don't change out of the sun dress I'm wearing and keep my flip-flops on. And only retouch my lip gloss. No other makeup. When Seth sees me, he'll know by my lack of effort this is purely a casual dinner. Nothing more.

I set to work mixing the ingredients in a large bowl, then divide it into six and roll it into balls. That's three rissoles each. Is that enough? I'll halve them again and make it twelve, so he can have eight and I'll have four. I'm totally overthinking this. I've also bought some potatoes and peas to go with them. Operating the induction stove to cook it all means using the app. Which turns out to be a nightmare.

It's like India's tried to make it easier, so she can control the temperature while sitting at the kitchen table leafing through a magazine. But if you're doing proper cooking, it makes things overly complicated.

Since the rissoles are only going to take ten minutes to fry, I'll have to cook them when he's here. Great. Now I'm operating a stove via an app, for a dish I've never cooked, in front of a guy I've never seen. No wonder my stomach is clenching in a tight painful knot.

By the time six-thirty creeps around, I'm absurdly nervous, to the point that I open one of the bottles of red I bought and pour myself a large glass. It helps a bit. I put the potatoes on to boil using the app, feeling like I'm in the Matrix. The heatwave hasn't abated, if anything, it's worse. I find a spray bottle of Evian in the fridge and mist myself liberally. Water drips down my face, so I have to wipe it with a tea towel. My hair is wet now too and dragging around my face, so I scoop it up into a ponytail. Thank God I didn't put on any make-up. This whole thing was such a bad idea. I wish I could spend the evening on Hampstead Heath with a takeaway salad and get an ice cream for afters. Should I leave a note and say 'I'm sorry but I had to go and visit a sick friend, so we'll do it another time'?

But it's quarter to seven. I gulp. Too late to find note paper and a pen, let alone write a note. Two minutes to go. I stand there frozen and watch the minutes tick over on my phone with my heart going great guns... 6:47... 6:48... I can't hear footsteps coming up the path and no one appears in the kitchen from the patio.

I turn back to the stove and let out a sigh of relief. He's not coming. I'm off the hook. I pick up the glass decanter of oil to return it to the pantry. I'll put the rissoles in the fridge and cook them tomorrow night. I can have a simple salad on Hampstead Heath and relax.

But then the back of my neck starts prickling, and I get that being-watched feeling again. Slowly, I turn around to see a guy standing in the kitchen, inside the bi-fold door, gazing at me with an inscrutable expression. I'm so startled, the decanter of oil slips through my sweaty fingers and falls onto the counter with a loud thunk.

'Fuck!' I say, quickly righting it as the top falls off and oil dribbles out.

Seth still hasn't moved. We stare at each other. I know I've been making things up in my head about what he looks like since day one, but I wasn't expecting this. Tall, slim, moonlight pale skin with dark spiky hair, dressed completely in black.

He's giving off a cool, sophisticated vibe, and I fervently wish I wasn't wearing a red sundress. With my flushed face, I'm sure I look like a tomato. I'm also kicking myself for deciding not to wear any makeup other than lip gloss. He's definitely the kind of guy you want to make an effort for.

Damn. It's too late now. My only consolation is that I washed my hair this morning.

I feel like I need to say something since he hasn't. 'Hi, you're uh…'

A Goth, emo, freakin' hot

'…alive,' I say, grasping at one of the words my mind is throwing at me, which may not be appropriate seeing as he looks like he frequents graveyards. His sculpted lips curve. 'I am indeed alive,' he says, and I get the shivers again from his voice. If he narrated horror audiobooks, he'd make a mint.

'Dinner will be ready soon. I just have to do a bit of frying.' I turn to the induction hob and fiddle about with the app, cursing India under my breath. When I've got it working, I turn back to retrieve the rissoles and get another shock. Seth's now leaning on the other side of the island counter right across from me. I didn't even hear him move. 'Lamb rissoles. An interesting choice,' he says, looking at them nestled in flour on the plate.

'They're supposed to be made from cold lamb. I didn't have any of that, so I'm using lamb mince. I haven't actually cooked this before, but I'm hoping it will taste OK. I also bought ketchup so if it doesn't you can smother it in that,' I say. Oh, lord. The wine and nerves are starting to make me gabble. But Seth says 'Ah' in a serious tone.

I try to calm down. The worst is over. He turned up. He seems OK. Now we can have a nice meal together. Easy peasy. Especially if we're both drinking to loosen things up.

'Have some wine if you want.' I push the bottle and a glass towards him. He eyes it, then his eyes shift to my wine glass which is half full.

He looks like he's going to say something but nods. 'Thanks.' He pours out some wine and takes a sip.

I expect him to sit at the table. When he props himself on a bar stool, I realise he's going to watch me cook. Awkward.

'Don't mind me,' he says.

But it's like having a large bat hovering behind me. I wish he'd scroll on his phone or something. Every time I turn to the island to get more rissoles to add to the pan, we lock eyes and then look away. And every time I notice new things about him. He has a facial piercing; a silver barbell at the end of his right eyebrow. The top of his shirt is unbuttoned and there's a tattoo of something written on his collarbone. His fingers grasping the wine glass are long and slender, tapered at the ends.

I manage to cook the rissoles without burning them, which is a miracle because my concentration is completely shot.

Finally, I serve up. I then grab some cutlery and the ketchup. Seth collects the other bottle of red wine and both of our glasses too before I can ask him.

But when I put his plate down in front of him on the table,

he stares at it without saying anything.

'Is it OK?'

'It is. But why did you place the peas in a circle like that?'

'Oh. I don't know, it's something I do… To make them look neat and tidy. I've done it since I was little.'

He gives me an odd look. *You can talk Mr Green M&M's.*

We concentrate on our food for a while. It actually doesn't taste too bad. The rissoles could use some more salt, but on the whole, I'm pleased with the result. Not that I'm hungry anyway. It's so hot in here, I feel like I'm melting. I have to keep blotting my sweaty face with a paper towel. Seth doesn't seem at all concerned by the heat. There's not a bead of sweat on him, even though he's wearing a long-sleeved shirt and jeans. I don't know how he can handle it. Is he cold-blooded?

After consuming half the meal in silence, apart from Sephy meowing under the table because she's come in hoping for a titbit, I attempt to make conversation. 'So, Seth. What do you do?'

'I'm a musician.'

'Oh, in your spare time?'

'No, in my main time.'

He's a full-time musician?

'Are you in a band then?' I know I'm starting to sound nosey, but he's not exactly being forthcoming.

He nods.

'Would I have heard of you?'

Seth flicks me the briefest of glances. 'Probably not.'

'Why?'

'You're not our target audience.'

'Too happy?' I say blithely before I can resist.

He gives a low grunt which could contain amusement, but I'm not sure. 'Something like that.'

Sephy's tail brushes my leg as she goes off out to the garden, and we fall silent again. I'm eating pea by pea by this stage, and drinking wine, not sure what else to say. It's obvious we have nothing in common.

Then Seth clears his throat and makes me jump.

'So, what do you do in your main time?' he asks.

'Interior decorating.' I wave a hand dismissively. 'It's not really paying the bills. That's why I'm house sitting.'

Erk, why did I go and say that? Now I sound like a loser. But it seems I've given Seth something to latch onto.

'What did you think of the zoo room?' He tilts his head to indicate upstairs. 'Did India show you?'

'No. I got the impression it was off limits because the door's locked.'

'Hah.' His shoulders hunch. 'That used to be my room.'

'What's in there?' I ask.

Seth snorts derisively. 'She read about Victorians keeping exotic animals in their homes, so she decided to do her own take on it based on Avatar. There's a jungle in there. She's even got wild animals.'

I laugh uncertainly. 'Are they stuffed?'

'I hope for your sake that they are.'

I can't tell by his tone if he's joking or not.

I'm getting the impression that India isn't his favourite person. Hmm, so it's not that he doesn't want to come into the house but that she turfed him out? Curiosity must show on my face because he says quickly, 'Anyway, I prefer being outside. It's more private.'

'I *was* starting to think Mellors was living in the garden,' I say to lighten the mood. He stares at me blankly.

'The gamekeeper from Lady Chatterley's Lover.'

'Ah. Don't worry, I won't do any naked frolicking in the sprinklers while you're here,' he says dryly, and I stifle a giggle.

We do that weird eye-locking thing again and I drag my gaze away. 'At least you've got your own space.'

Seth sighs. 'Yeah, it's fine. We generally keep out of each other's way. And I'd rather be around, because of Dad.' I wait for him to elaborate, but he doesn't.

He pours himself some more wine and indicates the bottle toward me. I nod and he fills my glass.

'So, what about you? Where's your fixed abode?' he asks.

'I don't have one. I'm a serial house sitter at the moment. I stay with a friend between house sits.'

'Intriguing. Are you a gypsy?'

'Perhaps.' I smile, warming to him a little for giving a

romantic spin to my situation. 'My last name is "Freeborn" after all. It had to come from somewhere.'

Seth nods and I drink some more. Then he says casually, 'Seeing anyone special?' I almost choke on my mouthful of wine. My heart gives a little flutter. Well, he is gorgeous, even if he's not exactly my type.

'Uh, no. The last relationship I had was a year ago when I dumped my long-term boyfriend Gabe in a spectacular fashion.'

I bite my lip. Erk, that came out of nowhere. I stare suspiciously at my wine glass which, I'm certain, was a quarter full but is now full again. Did he sneakily top me up?

'I'm sure you don't want to hear about all that,' I say hastily.

But Seth is sitting up straighter. 'How come you ended it?'

I shift uncomfortably in my chair. 'Well, I found out from a friend he was going to propose. It freaked me out. I guess it opened my eyes to some things in our relationship and what I wanted from life. So, we parted ways. He cried. I felt like the world's biggest bitch, but it was for the best.'

A glimmer of sympathy crosses Seth's face, and I suck in my breath. He's actually affected by my story. It makes him even more attractive if that's possible. If I were a Goth groupie, my black knickers would be getting damp right about now.

'Tell me more,' he says softly. Of course, hearing about someone else's pain is how he gets his kicks. I guess he has to get his inspiration from somewhere.

I plough on with my tale of woe, seeing as I now have a captivated audience.

'I feel bad that I didn't really give Gabe a proper answer as to why I was breaking up with him. He was hurt enough as it was so I didn't want to make it worse by saying all the things about him that I couldn't stand. But breaking up with him ended up being worse for me as it also meant not only having to move out of our flat but losing my job too.'

'How come?'

'We both worked at the same design agency in Islington. It was a great job, I cut my interior decorating teeth on it. But Gabe played the guilt card. After I broke up with him, he said he couldn't tolerate working with me, and I should leave since he'd been there longer and was the dumpee. I've been struggling to make ends meet ever since.

'Now I'm doing house sits and sleeping on my friend Violet's couch. Do I wish I was still with Gabe? No. But I do wish I'd stayed until I'd found another job instead of letting him push me out. I thought it would be easy enough to strike out on my own. Serves me right for being overconfident. I'm paying for it now.'

I run out of steam and take a deep breath of sultry kitchen air. Seth is staring at me thoughtfully in the half-light and I give a shaky laugh. 'So there you go. Are you going to write about it now? The gypsy girl who's lost everything—boyfriend, job, flat—it could make a great song for your fans to get depressed about.'

'No, probably not,' he says evenly. 'Writing songs… There's a small issue with that.'

'What issue?'

Seth's eyes glitter like black jewels in the semi-darkness. 'I've lost my muse.'

We stare at each other and I can't tear my gaze away, I'm captivated. He's so good-looking and *nice,* it's difficult not to be. A droplet of sweat runs down between my breasts like a finger, and I shiver. Unless the heat is warping my brain, I'm getting the distinct feeling we've moved from complete strangers to I-could-quite-happily-shag-you mode.

'I should go…' he says, breaking the silence. Yet he doesn't move. Like he's waiting for me to determine what happens next.

I open my mouth to reply 'Or you could stay…' but a blood-curdling yowl sounds from the garden propelling Seth into action. He moves soundlessly across the kitchen and slips out through the patio door like a shadow.

I fumble for my phone, turn on the kitchen lights from the app and run out onto the patio. At first, I can't see anything, since the garden is almost dark now. Then a figure materialises in front of me, and I give a little yelp.

'Sorry. It's me. That was Sephy, she has fights with the neighbour's tom. He's on the prowl and he loves terrorising her. Here, you better take her inside and lock the cat door for tonight.'

He gives me a bundle of fur and his hand brushes against mine. His skin feels like cool silk on my hot palm and a tremor runs through my body. Oh God, I think I am turning into a Goth groupie. I'm glad it's dark because I'm sure what I'm wanting is written all over my face.

'Goodnight then,' I say, trying not to sound expectant. Possibility hangs in the air between us fleetingly, but he says, 'Night. Thanks for dinner and the talk,' and melts away into the darkness.

I stand there with Sephy squirming in my arms, listening. But I can't hear him walking down the path, and he doesn't turn on his phone torch. It's like he has bat vision. A few moments later, a light winks on in the studio.

So that's that, I think, going inside with Sephy. She runs off as soon as I set her down on the floor. I know I should feel relief that the meeting with Seth went OK, but I don't. Now the intrigue has changed into a yearning for more of him. Surely, it wasn't just me feeling it?

I lock the cat flap and start clearing the table. When I pick up Seth's plate, I look at it in confusion. What the?

I didn't notice when we were sitting down, because I was too busy ogling him, but he's left three green peas on his plate, arranged in an upside-down triangle. I know instantly it's not random but a deliberate thing. Like he's left me a message. But what on earth does it mean?

CHAPTER FIVE

After doing a cursory clean-up of the kitchen, I head upstairs and flop onto the princess bed, feeling strung out. It's too hot to even think about sleep. Besides, Seth's face is invading my mind. I can't stop thinking about him. He was so different to what I imagined. Not only the way he looked but his whole persona. He was so beguiling and charming and… sexy. I groan. God, yes, so freaking sexy! I hope tonight isn't the only time I'll see him. I have more questions than ever now. Who was his muse? A girlfriend? Why does he need to be here for his Dad? Where's his Mum?

After a while, when my head feels like it's going to explode, I decide to ring Violet. She's into the Goth scene, so she might have heard of his band.

Violet answers with a 'Hi, Jenna' she sounds grumpy. Whoops, I forgot she's an early-to-bed person. If she doesn't get her ten hours a night, she turns into "Violent Violet", the nickname I privately use when she's in a sleep-deprived mood.

'Are you still up?'

'Yes, but it's a bit late for a video tour. I'm about to go to bed.'

'Ah, sorry. It's not for a tour, there's another reason I'm calling. Have you heard of a Goth muso called Seth Carver?'

'Oh, yeah!' she says sounding perkier. 'He's the lead singer of Sublime Misery—they put out an EP last year, and there's another album in the pipeline apparently. It's dark stuff but really good. He's dreamy. Why do you ask?'

'Because he's living in a shipping container at the bottom of the garden, and I just cooked him dinner,' I say deadpan.

Violet lets out a strangled scream. 'No fucking way! Oh, oh, I'm coming over tomorrow. I have to meet him!'

Wow, OK, he's got adoring fans. Well, one anyway, if Violet's reaction is anything to go by.

'No, you can't,' I tell her rather too quickly. 'He wouldn't like it.'

'But you're allowed to meet him though?' she says accusingly.

'That's different. I didn't know who he was. I'm not a Goth groupie.'

Violet humphs. 'How do you know he wouldn't like it?'

'A vibe I got. He's an introvert.'

'But... but... This is my only chance to meet Seth Carver!'

'Sorry.' I feel a bit guilty, but it's better to shut down any ideas she has about that right now. She's likely to turn up and demand I take her down to the shipping container to meet

Seth. The thought of it makes me feel nauseous. It was nerve-wracking enough to go down there in the first place, let alone with Violet in tow. But luckily she moves on. 'So what did you cook for him anyway?'

'Lamb rissoles.'

Violet guffaws. 'Oh my God. Classic. Lamb rissoles!'

'It was a random decision. It turned out OK. He ate them. There were also vegetables,' I say defensively. *And three random leftover peas…*

Violet laughs even harder, and I interrupt her to get to the point of the call. 'I'm glad you find it amusing. But since we're on the subject, can you look him up on Google? Is there a band website? I can't look at my phone since I'm talking to you. And my laptop needs charging.'

That's a massive fib. It doesn't at all, but I'm too afraid of discovering a photo of Seth with his arm draped around a gorgeous Goth girl. If he's seeing someone, it's better coming from a middlewoman.

'Uh, sure bear with. I'll get my laptop.' I hear her sniggering away to herself and I roll my eyes.

'Right,' she says shortly. 'Being serious now. So, there's a website but nothing much on it. Just a home page and an About page.'

'Can you describe it for me?' I ask.

'Uh, sure,' she says, sounding a bit surprised. 'The home page is black and there's the name of the band across the top in silver letters. There's a one-liner underneath saying an album is coming out in spring, and beneath that is a silver door and the keyhole is a blue eye. You click on the eye and it opens to reveal the EP songs. That's pretty cool.'

'And the About page?'

'Yup, getting to that.' I wait, then hear Violet making a choking sound.

'What is it?'

'Sooo… There are black and white profile photos of each band member. There are four of them. Seth is at the top since he's the lead singer. It's an awesome photo, very atmospheric. He's sitting on a park bench in winter with his legs apart leaning forward looking intently at the camera. Urgh, it's like he's staring into my soul. *Shivers down the spine material!* There's a white sky with the black branches of trees above him and his hair is inky and spiked up. It looks like it's merging with the trees. He's wearing a long black coat, tall black boots with chains, possibly eyeliner, and his milky skin is flawless. Fuck, he looks *phenomenal*. I'll send you the link.'

'No *don't*, er, I mean, I'll look it up tomorrow,' I say hastily. I forgot that Violet is writing a Gothic horror novella and tends to love describing things to the n-th degree. I could have done with a little less detail. Now the image is burnt into my brain in all its monochrome glory, and I can picture Seth exactly. Especially the intense eyes staring into the soul part, I had a taste of that tonight.

'I can't believe you sat across a table from *him* and managed a conversation,' she continues, 'I'd be catatonic.'

'There was some wine involved.' I'm regretting drinking so much now and spilling my guts. What if he finds his muse and writes a song about a loser gypsy girl without a life? Cringe.

'I don't suppose Google says anything about him having a girlfriend?' I ask Violet hesitantly.

'Hmmm, she would be one lucky girl.' I hear her typing and muttering under her breath "Does Seth Carver have a girlfriend?" 'Nope. Well, he may do but unfortunately, Google doesn't have that particular information. Why? Surely you're not interested?'

'No, just curious,' I say.

'I wouldn't get your hopes up about him,' she warns. 'You're not really the type a Goth would go for. Your clothes are far too colourful and you don't mope enough.'

'Hah.' *Thanks, Violet.*

'What did you talk about anyway?' she asks.

'We managed to find some common ground,' I say evasively.

'Really? God. You're so lucky. What are the chances? I might start house sitting myself if guys like him live in the garden.'

'Haha, yes. Anyway, I should let you get to bed. Thanks for the chat. I'll take a vid of the house for you before I go,' I say. I'm eager to get off the phone. I feel like I've found out everything—and nothing.

'No problem. Are you still coming to mine on Saturday after the house sit?'

'Yes.' My back twinges at the thought of having to sleep on Violet's couch. I don't want to think about it. But I've still got several days left, so maybe I'll run into Seth again.

As if Violet reads my mind, she says archly, 'If you see gorgeous Goth boy before you go, say hi from me.'

Despite Violet's warning not to get my hopes up, over the next few days, I'm in a state of anticipation. To say I'm on tenterhooks is using the barest literal meaning of the word. Every time I go into the kitchen, which has become ground zero, I feel sick with nerves. To the point where I can't bear to go into the room, yet I can't bear not to, in case he pops in. The energy required to keep up this level of expectation is exhausting.

The intense heat isn't helping. Despite having the window wide open and only a thin Egyptian cotton sheet, I toss and turn at night, sweating profusely and analysing our conversation to death. His cryptic pea arrangement is also fucking with my brain. Is he trying to say "I Pea You" as in "I See You" like from Avatar? Is it an invitation to go down to his studio? I don't really want to assume that and make a fool of myself.

Then again, it may not mean anything deep and meaningful at all. He could be saying "Thanks For Dinner" or "Nice Meeting You" or any multitude of three-word phrases. It's driving me crazy. Maybe that was his intention. I imagine him smiling wryly to himself, knowing that I'll never figure it out. It's a cruel thing to do to a nosey person with a vivid imagination.

On Thursday morning, after another nearly sleepless night, I drag myself down to the kitchen to feed Sephy who's meowing pitifully. I know how she feels, I have a strong urge to do a few yowls of my own. *Will that bring him running?* I make myself a strong cup of coffee and decide to take it out onto the patio to do a sneaky reconnaissance. The dew-laden air is fresh and cool. It's so early, a tinge of pink is still colouring the clouds. There are no signs of life in the shipping container except an open window. I'm not sure what to do. I want to see him again and time is running out. The Carvers are back on Saturday.

Perhaps he's been biding his time, playing it cool, and he'll show up at the eleventh hour. *Or maybe he's just not interested,* says a little voice in my head.

Around Friday lunchtime, when he still hasn't appeared, I have to face the facts. No matter how sure I was that we connected or that we had serious chemistry going on, Seth's not going to pursue it. I'm not going to see him again.

When I think about it, I'm actually relieved. I didn't come to this house sit looking for anything except a respite from Violet's flat. It's been a relaxing stay in a flash house, with a brief interlude where I met a hot but extremely unsuitable guy. Monday night now feels hazy and insubstantial, like it was a dream. Not reality. Reality is sorting out my fledgling career, so I can earn enough to pay rent. If I want to meet someone, I'd be better off online dating, even if the thought of that isn't appealing after hearing Stacey's horror stories.

I've been off the market for five years when I was with Gabe, and then another year, because I was "getting over him". But I was the dumper, so I can't exactly use my unbroken heart as an excuse for much longer. Maybe my random meeting with Seth was a sign to get back out there and start dating again; nothing more than that.

CHAPTER SIX

To keep my mind off Seth, I decide to do an aesthetic arrangement of bookcase knick-knacks in the small lounge. That will make my followers go gaga. There's nothing Instagrammers love more than a photo of a beautifully arranged bookcase. I've got my eye on a lemon-yellow vase, a white horse statuette and a gold lizard.

First, though, I have to remove all the framed photos. They are mostly of India in various stages of her life—as a knobbly knee teenager, as a young woman smiling broadly with her arms around two friends in a field of tulips, another with the same friends posing with cocktails in skimpy bikinis. There's also a large photo on a higher shelf. I reach up on tip-toes to collect it and inhale sharply when I see it. It's India, dressed in a simple white satin and lace wedding gown, holding a large bunch of white roses. But that's not what caught my attention. She's laughing up at a tall dark-haired man who's grasping her around the waist from behind and smiling down at her affectionately. Drew obviously, but he looks so much like Seth, it takes my breath away. He's an older version and he isn't a Goth, but I can see where Seth gets his good looks from. They have the same dark soulful eyes and chiselled cheekbones.

Carefully, I place it on the couch, my heart thumping. *Get a grip, Jenna, it's just a photo, and it's not even of him.* Lower down, there are a few smaller ones of babies, so I take them off too and give all the shelves a good dust with a soft cloth. Then I notice an unframed photo lying on the floor. It's of a family in front of an amusement arcade which looks like the one in Brighton. A couple standing behind two children, a boy and a girl. The smiling husband is a younger handsome Drew, but the wife isn't India, she's similar-looking, yet she has wavy brown hair and is curvy.

At first glance, I don't recognise the boy. But when I look closer, I realise it's Seth. He's gangly, wearing black ripped jeans and a black t-shirt. He also has a bad fringe and teenage acne. It's definitely him though. His arms are folded and he's scowling so ferociously it makes me laugh; like he'd rather be anywhere else at that particular moment than have his photo taken. The girl is about the same age; blonde, pretty. She's wearing a pink party dress and smiling brightly at the camera.

I gently touch Seth's face with my finger, then the girl's. Is this his sister? They're like night and day. I tuck the photo behind one of the frames and continue my arranging. But my mind keeps wandering to it. Judging from Seth's attitude towards India the other night, and now seeing the photo of a different woman with Drew, I'm pretty sure something's gone down. But what?

I'm still thinking about it a couple of hours later while I'm packing my wheelie case. So far, I'm on scenario six. It's the one where India had a steamy affair with Drew, the wife walked in on them and India threatened to kill her, unless Drew married her instead. To save his wife, Drew was forced to marry India, and buy her a house in Hampstead to keep her happy. It makes perfect sense. Sort of. I giggle self-consciously.

Zipping up my bag, I hear the guttural purr of a motorbike coming up the lane on the left side of the house. It sounds like it's right outside. Then again, the air is so still, it's amplifying even small noises. It could be several miles away. The engine cuts off and then there's silence.

Intrigued, I peek out the window and then duck down. A dark-haired figure dressed in black exits the shipping container and disappears through a gate in the fence. There's the sound of voices. Then the motorbike starts up again and heads off down the lane.

I sit back on my heels. So, Seth makes an appearance, albeit fleetingly. Off for a motorbike jaunt with a band-member mate to do whatever Goths do on a Friday afternoon?

Seeing him in the daylight breaks the mystique a little. I've been thinking of him as a creature of the shadows. But he's just a guy. One I won't even remember in a week from now, I'm sure. The good thing is, now he's gone out, I can have a swim.

When I step outside onto the patio, I'm startled to see the sky is roiling with monstrous black clouds and the air is thick with humidity. *I'll have a quick swim to cool off before the rain comes.*

I do a few laps, then float on my back staring at the angry sky. A fat raindrop lands on my cheek, then another on my forehead. Typical, I've only just got in! Well, at least I'm already wet. I hope Seth gets to wherever he's going in time. Being on the back of a motorbike during this won't be fun. A few more drops land on my chest. Heavier this time. Actually, a little stinging. I stop floating and swim over to the side unsettled. A lone bird tweets, then takes off flapping from a nearby tree and the world seems to hold its breath. Then the heavens open. I don't even have time to think, it's a deluge of biblical proportions. The rain beats down so heavily, the pool looks like it's steaming.

Dragging myself out, I collect my towel in the cabana, which is already sodden, but I wrap it around my torso anyway. I jam my feet into my flip-flops and am about to dash up the path when I see that Seth has left his window and sliding door wide open. His stuff is going to get drenched. Shit. The idiot. I hunker down under the force of the rain and squelch over the muddy grass and onto the deck with the intention of closing the door from the outside. But there's a crack of lightning and the rain intensifies. It feels like needles are piercing my skin. I shriek and without thinking about it, I dash inside and slide the door shut with a whump.

Thunder rolls ominously overhead as I shiver and drip on the floor. The shipping container has one of those living grass roofs so at least it's mercifully soundproof. But rivers of rain are pouring off over the door. The guttering can't be that effective. I slam the window shut over Seth's desk. It is already getting spotted with rain. Seth's desk. Oh my God. I'm actually in his studio.

I turn around, half-expecting to see him standing there with his arms folded and a scowl. But it's empty. Despite knowing I'm invading his privacy, and that if he found out, he'd probably be livid, I'm a teensy bit curious. OK, I'm immensely curious. I'll have a quick look around, then leave. He'll never know I was here.

I was expecting it to look like a bat cave, but it's actually quite cosy, in a masculine way. There's a kitchen nook with a microwave and sink, a leather chair with a red cushion angled towards the sliding door. He must've been sitting in that when I knocked. A sizeable black sheepskin rug covers the floor and there's a well-stocked wooden bookcase. The double bed has a rumpled black and red duvet, like he's recently been in it or still is. I eye it nervously in case he's hiding underneath and will spring out at me. *Don't be ridiculous,* I tell myself, *you saw him go out!*

I wander over to the bookcase and check out the spines. You can learn a lot about a person from the books they read. Plenty of Stephen King, to be expected, I guess, and a lot of high fantasy. I pull out a couple, but they're by authors I've never heard of. Hah, there are some Harry Potter books too. I crouch and survey the bottom shelf. Italian language books and a Rome guidebook. Oh, was he or is he learning Italian? He definitely likes eating it.

I stand up and notice my flip-flops have made muddy prints on the wooden floorboards. Yikes. I'm going to have to get a dry towel or some toilet paper to wipe those up.

The bathroom is in a separate section of the container. It's tiny, with a shower stall, toilet and a sink with a toothbrush and toothpaste. There's a dark blue towel on the railing. I grab it, but it's damp. My stomach flips knowing that Seth's rubbed the towel over his naked body. I gulp. My gaze drifts to the shower and I spot a bottle of expensive shower gel by a company I can never afford. Gingerly, I crack the door open and pour a drop into my palm. Mmm, it smells heavenly, like citrus and musk. I'm tempted to hop in and have a hot shower. But what if he happened to come back? How mortifying—though the look on his face would be almost worth it.

It won't hurt to have a quick peek in his cabinet though.

I'm hoping to find something juicy, like condoms or

haemorrhoid cream, but there are only towels, spare toothpaste, toilet cleaner and a tub of extra-hold hair gel. His bathroom cabinet is as elusive as he is. Hmm, I should steal his toilet roll, then if he gets super famous I can sell it on Ebay for thousands. TOILET ROLL KNICKED FROM SETH CARVER'S BATHROOM - THIS IS NO LIE.

The thought makes me giggle. There's no way I'd do that! He only has one toilet roll anyway, if I took that, he'd know I'd been in here. I tear off a length and wipe up my flip-flop prints like I've committed a crime and am erasing the evidence. The rain has let up. I'm about to open the sliding door and leave, when I see it. An open journal with writing on it poking out from under the pillow.

A warning voice sounds in my head *'Don't, Jenna'*, but I push it away impatiently. This is the real core of him, the songwriting bit that I want to know more about. What's the harm in having a quick look and then pushing it back under? He'll never know.

I sidle over to the bed, tug at the edge of the journal and take a cursory upside-down glance. There are a couple of verses. One has a line through it and then has been written again like he changed his mind and decided it was OK. Half a sentence has been crossed out emphatically several times. FUCK!!! is written underneath the whole thing in large black capitals. Intriguing. I draw out the journal and read the lyrics properly.

It's eyebrow-raising stuff. Hearts imploding from pain, souls cracking open with grief, someone never able to move on and thinking what's the point. Angst city. I let out a slow breath. I really hope this isn't about me and Gabe. My soul didn't crack open from grief, it was merely nudged. I did cry a bit at the beginning. But I was mostly feeling sorry for myself.

My eyes flick to the crossed out sentence. He seems to be having a lot of trouble with that one. I can barely make out the words, he's scribbled over it so much. Is that why he went out, to clear his head? I read the lyrics again. It's definitely morose but there's some interesting imagery. Even if it's not to my taste (Lana Del Rey is about as angsty as I get), I can see he's a good writer. I read it once more, then notice it's barely raining now. I need to go. Imagine if he suddenly came home and found me standing here reading his song lyrics! I place the journal back under the pillow, making sure it's in the exact same spot.

I check there's no trace of footprints on the floor, the books are aligned in the bookcase and the bathroom door is closed. Opening the sliding door, I slip out onto the deck. The air has that earthy just-rained scent and a triangle of blue sky peeks through the remnants of clouds above the house. I'm walking across the deck towards the sodden grass area by the pool when something strange happens. The line of a song pops into my head, no music, just words. Then another. Fully formed. It's a momentary flash, but it's enough to make me freeze in surprise. What the? Probably something I've been listening to on Spotify. But I haven't been listening to Spotify. I've been doing my knick-knack arranging and packing. Oh, well.

I continue across the deck, but the words get more insistent, pulsating in my brain until it actually becomes quite painful. I freak out that I'm having some kind of aneurysm. Seth's going to come back and find me lying dead on his deck, in a bikini and flip-flops. That will give him some good inspiration. He could write a whole album about that.

Then it clicks. The lines I'm getting in my head complement the song he's writing. They're all about wandering lost in the darkness and neverending pain. I almost laugh out loud. It's kind of funny but also incredibly weird. I'm not a songwriter. Or any kind of writer for that matter. I've never even written a poem. OK, I did when I was a teenager and was depressed because I liked a boy who didn't like me back. The results were dire. I distinctly remember tearing the page out of my diary in embarrassment and ripping it to shreds.

This must all be happening because I read Seth's unfinished song a few times and my brain has somehow produced the missing lyrics. A fresh set of eyes and all that. But I can't exactly WhatsApp it to him, I don't even have his number. Besides, how do I explain it? He'll have to figure it out for himself. But the thought of Seth sitting there on the bed with his head in his hands, wracking his brain, makes me feel sorry for him. I try to take a step onto the grass. My foot hovers in mid-air. I can't let it go.

CHAPTER SEVEN

When I get back to the house, I don't feel guilty about what I did in the slightest. I'm on a high and feeling a little chuffed. My lyrics totally make the song work. Maybe I'm a songwriter after all. This could be a new career for me.

But when I'm in the shower washing the mud off my shins and trying to warm up, I have a mild panic attack. Shit, am I completely mental? I tried to copy his handwriting and make it look like he'd written it, but unless Seth takes mind-altering drugs that make him forget what he does—he's going to know it was me.

I groan inwardly. *Jenna, you've done some cringeworthy things in your time, but this takes the cake.* Now he's not going to come up to the house because he wants to chat or get my number. He's going to come up to the house because he's fucking pissed I've been in his studio and tampered with his song. I whimper a little.

By the time I'm dressed, I've gained perspective. So what if I did? I was only helping out. It was harmless! If there's going to be a showdown, bring it on!

When early evening rolls around and Seth still hasn't

appeared to tear a strip off me, I'm relieved. My bravado has faded. I'm not good with confrontation, I tend to clam up and get tongue-tied. The worst that may happen is that he'll tell India and she might give me a one-star review. *"Jenna seemed trustworthy but, for the love of God, don't leave any private papers lying around".*

I go to bed feeling slightly anxious but with a plan in place for tomorrow. I'm packed. The Carvers are returning at noon and not expecting me to be here. All I have to do is feed Sephy and leave as early as possible. Simple.

But around two in the morning, I wake with a jolt when the gate in the fence slams shut. Shit, he's back. My heart drops out of my knickers. He must've gone into his studio by now. I'm half expecting to hear a howl of indignation, but when nothing comes, I get up and peer out the window. The shipping container is shrouded in darkness. It looks like he's gone straight to bed. He probably hasn't even looked at the journal. A feeling of relief washes over me. *I'm going to get away with it.*

The next morning, I'm awake at six sharp thanks to the alarm on my phone and my active conscience. I dress and give my face a cursory wash in the bathroom. I don't put on make-up since it'll waste precious minutes. I'm not having breakfast either, I'll grab something en route or go without. There's something furtive about my actions. I'm not exactly scared of encountering Seth. I just don't want there to be any *unpleasantness*. I want to leave with the good memories of my visit intact—Sephy, the Disney bedroom, the luxury of the place. I can sift through the other stuff—the intense attraction, the cryptic peas, Seth not appearing after the dinner, my snooping in his studio—later on when I've gained some objectivity.

Wheelie case waiting in the hallway, all I need to do now is feed Sephy. Then, I'm out of here. She's not around, but I put biscuits in her bowl and top up her water. I unlock the patio door, poke my head out and give a low whistle to see if she comes. It would be nice to give her a pat before I go. But she doesn't. Ah, well. Then out of the corner of my eye, I see a flash of movement which I assume is her. But it's not. To my horror, I spot Seth. He's wearing a long-sleeved black t-shirt and jeans and is halfway up the path on approach to the house. His face is determined and his hair wild. Oh, shit! Instinctively, I lock the patio door and back away. I have about ten seconds before he reaches the house.

I scurry into the hallway and grab my wheelie. Where the hell did I put the house keys? I rummage in my handbag, but they're not there. Fuck. I hear the sound of the patio door rattling then stop. Yikes, he might come round the side since he probably has a main door key. Arrrggh, think! Then I remember I put the house keys in the back pocket of my jeans for safekeeping. I whirl out the front door, slam it shut and poke the keys through the mail slot where they fall with a loud clatter on the parquet floor.

Hefting my wheelie, I take off at a fast trot down the front path, keeping an eye on my right where the gate by the bins is. Thankfully, Seth doesn't appear. I reach the footpath and take off at full tilt, dragging my wheelie behind me. When I reach the Overground, I still can't breathe freely until I'm on the first train and speeding down to Putney.

$$\triangledown \quad \triangledown \quad \triangledown$$

Violet's flat is on the second floor of a tan brick building over a Sainsbury's. Being so close to the supermarket is a blessing and a curse. You can nip down and buy bacon and eggs for breakfast, but you have to put up with teenage louts hanging around on Friday and Saturday nights. Well, I do, since the lounge overlooks the street where they stand and yell at each other. Violet's bedroom is in the back, looking out onto a neighbour's narrow strip of lawn, so she misses the worst of it.

Sometimes, she goes away for the weekend to visit her parents in Cornwall, and I get to sleep in her bed. But it doesn't happen that often. As she says, 'Porthcurno is a bitch to get to if you don't have a car.'

As I'm walking to her flat from East Putney station, I remind myself that I'm grateful I have someone who doesn't mind me crashing on their couch indefinitely. I do have other girlfriends in London, but they're all married with toddlers. They'd put me up if I asked, but I wouldn't be able to come and go as freely as I do here. Violet's even had a key cut for me. I can't immediately locate it in my frazzled state though, so I have to press the buzzer for her to let me in.

She opens the door blearily, dressed in an old black t-shirt and with a bad case of bed hair. 'It's seven o'clock on a Saturday,' she mumbles. 'You'd better have a bloody good excuse for waking me up.'

Dark circles, à la Alice Cooper, are smudged under her eyes from the black eyeliner she wears but never bothers to remove before bed. Along with her pale skin and lank ebony hair, she looks like she could be Seth's sister. I'm running from one Goth to another.

'Hello to you too. Sorry about the early arrival. I had to leave in a hurry.'

Violet opens the door wider so I can come in. 'Did Seth Carver kick you out of bed?' She smirks as if she's thinking *Jenna having sex with him would never happen in a million years!*

I decide right then to keep the rest of the story to myself. Violet is a bilingual PA for a senior partner in an international law firm, and the girls she works with are terrible gossips. It's fun listening to the stories she comes home with, but I don't particularly want to be the subject du jour on Monday. Plus, her office is in Hammersmith and since Drew's is too, it's a bit close for comfort.

'Hah. I just hate being there when owners come back, I always feel like I'm in the way,' I reply casually wheeling my bag through to the lounge.

'Fair enough. Did you see him again though?' she persists following behind.

'No, but I wasn't expecting to,' I say to put her off the scent.

It's true, I didn't see him in the way she's meaning. Storming up the path to have my guts for garters doesn't count.

Her mouth turns down at the corners. 'Pity. I still can't believe you met him.'

I don't say anything.

'Well, there's breakfast stuff in the kitchen if you're hungry. Nothing fancy, just cereal and toast. The jam's run out, but there's marmite.'

'OK. I'll go down and do a shop shortly.'

'Great, thanks. Can you also get some more loo rolls? Oh, and I need some rubbish bags. There's a list on the fridge.' She yawns and rubs her eyes, smearing the eyeliner further. 'I think I'll go back to bed for a bit.'

Violet and I have an arrangement that I buy the food and incidentals when I stay here. It makes me feel like I'm contributing and saves us from having to work out what I owe her in the way of bills. Sometimes I'm only here for a couple of days, sometimes it's a week. This lifestyle has its benefits; like being able to stay in posh houses in Hampstead, but the instability is starting to wear me down. I want a place of my own. Unfortunately, I can't see that happening anytime soon unless I give up the freelancing and go back to a nine to five job. But since I've had a taste of being my own boss, I don't want to do that. I feel like I'm in a catch-22.

After she goes back to her room, I stow my suitcase in the corner of the room so it's out of the way and unpack a little. There's a cubby-hole bookcase and Violet has cleared out one corner as a makeshift dresser, so I can at least have somewhere to stow my clothes.

The lounge is merged with the kitchen and dining area in an open-plan design. Although the space is small, it's cheerful enough with clean white walls, a cream woven rug with a black geometric pattern, an easy chair and a coffee table made from a cross-section of a tree trunk. There are a couple of prints on the wall: a ubiquitous Banksy and *Ophelia* by John Everett Millais. Ophelia's expression of despair is precisely how I feel after more than two nights of sleeping on the couch, a purple velvet roll-armed affair Violet bought from a charity shop.

I'm sure it was comfortable in its heyday, but now the saggy middle is the bane of my existence. I try not to think of the princess bed in Hampstead and how it was like sleeping on a firm but fluffy cloud. In the distance, I hear something that makes my heart sink—the faint rumble of a jet engine. Hmmm, time to open my laptop. Being underneath a Heathrow flight path is great motivation to search for another house sit.

A couple of days later, my back is killing me and Violet's work stories are starting to grate. I'm also not sure how much longer I can endure her evening rants about her new boss who, by her reckoning, has a "Goth prejudice".

'I can't believe his narrow-minded attitude. Today he said my presence was "disconcerting",' she says shaking her head as we're watching TV.

'What did he mean by that?'

She snorts. 'It means he hates Goths.'

'If it's that bad, why not quit and look for another job?'

Violet raises her eyebrows, as if to say *And end up homeless like you, no thanks.*

'Or... ooh, why not go to Paris for a bit? Have an adventure!' I suggest enthusiastically since she speaks French fluently. 'I think that would be amazing. If I were you, I'd be there right now scoffing pastries and conversing with locals.' But Violet just screws up her nose and I drop the subject before she can launch into all the reasons why it's a bad idea. She always has a ready excuse as to why she can't do something. I honestly think she'd rather complain about her life than take action and do something positive.

Unlike me. Action is my middle name at the moment. I'm going mad from lack of sleep and the number of planes flying over. I've applied for five house sits and am currently in conversations with two of the owners.

India gave me a five-star review and a brief one-liner for my profile: *"Jenna was a lovely house sitter and looked after our Sephy very well"*.

I'm relieved; it looks like Seth hasn't said anything to her. I've calmed down about it all and am now in a completely rational state of mind. Although I enjoyed staying at the house, it was good I left when I did and didn't have any further entanglements with him. Imagine if I'd stayed another week—I think I would've been in serious trouble. By that, I mean emotional trouble, rather than trouble with the police. What with wondering about his family, spying on him out the window, creeping around in his studio and writing lyrics for his songs, I feel like I was getting way too involved; and I suspect Seth Carver could be a bit of a heartbreaker.

There's another thing too. I've gone over our conversation from dinner and realised that although he asked me if I was 'seeing anyone special', it doesn't mean he was actually interested, or even single. He could've been testing the water for a band member and thinking 'oh well, I've got a girlfriend but Zack hasn't and he likes blue-eyed brunettes who can cook meat and two veg.'

So really, I'm much better off not having anything to do with him. Though Violet keeps bringing up his photo from the website on her phone, shaking her head and saying 'Seth Carver, mmm, il est magnifique' just to get a reaction. I'm doing my best to ignore her, but that photo she described is burning my brain.

I need to get another house sit soon, otherwise I might grab her phone and throw it out the window.

CHAPTER EIGHT

The next day, I'm about to agree to a week-long house sit in West Acton when I get a message via the house sitting site. It's from a woman called Cathy Morris who's based in Florence. She's coming to London to visit her ageing parents and urgently needs an experienced house sitter to look after her cat, Filippo. This happens sometimes, you get random offers from overseas which are completely unsuitable. But there are a couple of things about her message that make me take notice. Firstly, she says she'll pay for a return flight since the request is last minute, and secondly, the house sit is for two weeks.

I lean back on the couch and consider the possibility. Two weeks in Florence. A place I've not visited but have always wanted to. It would give me masses of awesome Instagram photos, and I wouldn't have to try and cobble a number of short house sits together. It also means I can bypass the headache of staying at Violet's. But it seems too good to be true. There must be a catch.

Cathy's profile on the site says she's fifty-three, a sculptor, and an expat Londoner. Her artsy black-and-white photo shows she's quite attractive. With a long dark plait draped over one shoulder, she looks like she could be part Italian. There is nothing indicating she has a partner, only an accompanying photo of Filippo asleep on a patchwork coverlet. He's a tabby who looks a little grizzled. There are no photos of the apartment. In her message she says it's "centrally located". However, that could be a stretch to make it sound more appealing.

I send her a friendly but casual message saying I'm interested, as well as asking for Filippo's age and the street the apartment is located on. She replies almost immediately:

Hi Jenna!
Thanks for getting back to me so quickly. Filippo is nearly seventeen, he's a little cranky, but he shouldn't be too much trouble as he sleeps most of the time. Even though he's not on a special diet, I mainly feed him fish - he has trouble digesting meat. I saw you'd looked after some older cats in one of your reviews, so I took a chance that you were available. My apartment is in Via de' Bardi, I'll send you some photos. Can you let me know asap if it's suitable and we can sort out flights?

OK, so that's the catch, a cranky old cat. I waver. I have looked after older cats before, yet it wasn't that successful as one of them died immediately after I left. The owners were really nice about it, but I got the feeling they blamed me. I felt so bad. But he was twenty-two years old and barely clinging to life. He also had no teeth and was on a diet of mashed boiled eggs which he refused to eat. Poor thing. I think he took his chance and carked it while they were out of the country because they were so intent on keeping him alive.

But if Filippo is seventeen and not on a special diet, it should be OK. There's a ping and another message from Cathy arrives. This time with four photos attached. The first one is of an arched double window which has been opened out to reveal a view of the Ponte Vecchio. Oh my God, it's right on the Arno. The second reveals a living room with an L-shaped couch in soft grey leather and adjoining mustard yellow modern chairs. I can see the edge of an abstract artwork on the wall. The third is of a bedroom, plainly furnished but with a double bed. I recognise the patchwork coverlet as the one Filippo was sleeping on. Through the open window, I can see a sliver of the Arno. The last is of the bathroom. It's decorated in an old-fashioned 1950s style but has spotless white subway tiles with dark green edging and gold fittings. Also, there's a full-length bathtub... OK, it's a no-brainer.

My fingers fly over the keyboard: *Hi Cathy, it looks great! I'm keen to do the house sit. Let's organise flights.*

After that, things happen quickly. Cathy books me a flight,

leaving in two days, from Gatwick to Pisa from where I'll catch the train to Santa Maria Novella station. Apparently, Florence does have an airport, but it's cheaper to fly into Pisa. I'm due to arrive in the afternoon so we can do a handover before she leaves.

It's all very exciting, especially as it's so soon. I'm dying to tell Violet. The minute she steps through the door, I blurt 'Guess what! I got a house sit in Florence, for two weeks! The apartment is right on the Arno!'

'No way.' Her eyes widen and her mouth forms an O-shape. 'Have you got photos?'

'Yes, check it out.' I proffer my laptop so she can see.

'Fuck, I hate you,' she says flatly and I laugh, delighted at my good fortune. Suddenly, this gypsy lifestyle is the best thing ever. Florence, here I come!

That evening I fall back down to earth with a resounding thump. What the hell am I doing? I can't afford to live in Florence for two weeks, even if the accommodation is free. I'm barely managing to get by on savings and what meagre amount clients have paid me. By going to Florence, I'm off the grid, so there'll be no chance of picking up new business. On top of that, I'm going to want to do some sightseeing and eat out, otherwise what's the point in going? I can't very well nab Filippo's fish to save cash.

In a panic, I ring Stacey to see if she can lend me some

money. I catch her walking to the pub about to meet some guy for a first date. They've been messaging for a couple of weeks. It's not great timing as I have to soothe her nerves and tell her that he's not going to be like Simon, her ex. Then, when I think she's suitably emotionally prepared, I drop my clanger.

'I hate to ask this but I'm doing an overseas house sit and I need some money as a buffer.' I wince inwardly at the silent pause. 'I might not use all of it, but I don't want to be on the bare bones of my arse while I'm there.'

There's the sound of muffled breathing, and I can hear her footsteps ringing on the cobblestones.

'How much?' she asks.

'Five hundred?'

'Where are you going?'

'Florence, it's a last-minute thing. I'll pay you back. You know I will,' I say, feeling guilty. I *think* I've paid her back the last lot I borrowed. It took ages, and it was all in dribs and drabs. God, I hate being poor.

'OK. I'll transfer it to your account tonight when I get home.' Stacey sighs and I feel slightly less of a person. But she's the only one I trust enough to ask. I don't want to bother my parents with my money troubles if I can help it. As far as they know, I'm doing OK.

'Thanks, Stace, I really appreciate it. Tell your date that I said you're bloody brilliant and he needs to snap you up immediately. In fact, give me his number and I'll ring him and tell him personally.'

Stacey laughs. 'No need for that. I don't even know if I'll be seeing him again after tonight. He may be awful.'

'I'm sure he's lovely,' I say adamantly, hoping he is. If anyone deserves to get her Prince Charming, it's Stacey. She's had a hell of a time with Simon. He turned nasty when she said she wanted a divorce, and he tried to take her for every penny she had. He even alleged she'd been having an affair, which she hadn't. Luckily she found a great female lawyer who whipped his arse and sent him packing. The last time I heard, he was living on the outskirts of Glasgow which is the kind of place he belongs.

On Thursday morning, having been woken at the crack of dawn by at least three overhead flights, I'm packed and ready to leave for the airport. My flight isn't until eleven but I'm eager to get going. Violet and I went out last night to La Casa Mia to celebrate my impending departure; her treat. She made me promise to send her videos of the flat and photos of any Italian men I meet.

'It's not like I have anything else to look forward to,' she said despondently, stabbing at her gnocchi alla fiorentina. I bit my tongue. There are only so many times you can tell someone to change their life. It has to come from her.

At Gatwick, I post a "Where am I going?" photo of the

departure board on Instagram to arouse follower curiosity, then head to WHSmith to buy a chocolate bar and peruse the books. I have that blah-I'm-never-going-to-have-a-boyfriend feeling so some chick lit might perk me up. I randomly select one with a cheery cover and read the blurb on the back. The romantic plot sounds completely implausible yet something I wish would happen to me. Perfect. That's what I need right now. A romance of my own seems to be too much trouble for the Universe to provide, so thank God for escapist fiction.

Then again, who knows? Maybe I'll meet a hunky Italian billionaire in Florence and end up redecorating his Tuscan villa. I trundle up to the counter to pay for my chocolate and novel. Well, dreams are free.

I'm in the queue to board and reading the first chapter of the novel when I hear a faint bleep in my handbag. It's probably Violet, telling me I've left my hair dryer behind again. I'll message her when I get to Pisa; the novel is starting to hook me in and I don't want to stop reading. A minute later, there's another bleep. Huh, only texts sound twice like that. And Violet usually messages me on WhatsApp. It could be a client. I rummage for my phone, and an electric shock goes through me when I see the text message on the screen.

It's Seth Carver. I got your number from India.
Can we talk?

I stand there with my mouth hanging open until a lady behind me says 'queue's moving' in a sharp tone. In a daze, I drop my phone back in my bag and shuffle along until my passport and boarding pass are checked, and I'm in the air bridge. I feel like I'm having an out-of-body experience. Maybe it's not real and I imagined it?

I take my phone out and open my text messages properly. Seth's text is sitting there in my feed. It is bloody real. A mixture of excitement and apprehension floods through me. What does he want to talk about? Is he pissed off? I can't function or think straight after that. On the plane, I discover I'm squished in between two beefy Italian guys around the same age as me. Even though both of them are good-looking, I'm not even perving.

All I can think is: *Woah, Seth messaged me!*

CHAPTER NINE

What the hell am I going to say? My text needs to be the perfect mix of nonchalant yet open, unassuming yet approachable.

I sense the guy on my left trying to make eye contact, but I ignore him. I need my full concentration. Right, I think I've come up with something suitable. I reach down and get my phone out of my handbag, ready to send my reply. 'Uh uh, no mobile,' the guy on my right says immediately, shaking his head.

'Huh?'

'Flight mode only.' He points to the window and I see the plane has pulled out and is starting to make its way to the runway.

'I just have to send a text.'

He shrugs and looks pissy. 'Go ahead. But if we crash, I will blame you.'

'Oh.' He's watching me with beady brown eyes, so I turn my phone to flight mode and put it away. Dammit, now I have to wait until we land!

The next two hours are excruciating. All I want to do is

text Seth. I can't concentrate on my novel because the guy on my left keeps trying to read it too. I feel like saying 'for God's sake, take it!' In the end, I shut the book and lie back with my eyes closed, trying to control my impatience.

As soon as the plane touches down, I take my phone off flight mode and wait for the signal. Jesus, *come on*. Everyone else is busily sending and receiving messages, there's a chatter of Italian. Even the guys next to me are tapping away on their phones. Soooo slow. Eventually, the WELCOME TO ITALY text message appears. But now everyone is retrieving their bags from the overhead lockers. It's chaos.

Once off the plane, I'm carried along on a sea of people with no chance to stop. When I get to customs, there's a "no cellphones" sign. There's only one official man in the booth and he's stamping passports at a snail-like pace. It will be at least a half-hour wait. By this point, I'm so agitated I can barely stand still. When I reach the Arrivals hall, I don't even bother with my carefully worded reply. I pull off to the side by a wall, away from the enthusiastic Italian reunions, and send:

What do you want to talk about?

He messages back instantly:

I think you know.

Shit.

It was pissing down and your door and window were open. I only went in to shut them. I'm sorry.

My phone starts ringing. He's calling me? Seth Carver is calling me in Pisa Airport! I want to fling my phone away, but I force myself to answer.

'Hello?'

'Not that. I don't care that you went in—what you did with the song,' Seth says. My knees start trembling at the sound of his voice. Is he angry? I can't tell. I go for nonchalant.

'Yeah, sorry about that, too. I know it was an invasion of your privacy. I was just curious and you seemed to be having trouble so I, er, tried to help. Please, just scribble them out.'

'But they're perfect.' His tone lowers on the word "perfect" and my stomach dips; it feels like he's saying that about me.

I clutch my phone tightly. 'Really?'

'I've been trying to write that song for over a week. I was tearing my hair out. What you wrote was exactly what I wanted to say, but I couldn't word it properly. Does that make sense?'

'I guess,' I say doubtfully. Were the lyrics really that good?

I thought so at the time, but I can't even remember now.

'Can we meet up? I'd like to discuss it some more.' My insides quail, but I try to maintain an air of indifferent approachability. *You can so lose it afterwards Jenna, right now you need to be cool.*

'Ah, I'd like to but that might be difficult. I'm not in London.'

'Where are you?'

'Um, Pisa Airport. I'm just about to catch a train to Florence to do a two-week house sit.'

'Florence?' He sounds surprised. There's a thoughtful silence that goes on for so long that I think he's hung up.

'Hello?'

'I'll come to you,' he says finally.

'Huh?'

'I'll meet you in Florence. Speak soon.'

He hangs up and I stare at my phone in disbelief. That surely doesn't mean what I think it means. That's mad. He can't do that.

Suddenly, I feel lightheaded and my vision narrows. I slide down the wall until I'm sitting cross-legged, hunched over with my fingers pressing against my eyes.

Next thing I know, a hand is on my shoulder and a woman is saying something that sounds like 'are you OK?' But then I realise she's saying something else 'Che cos'è?' I shake my head to show her I don't understand. A water bottle is proffered, and I gratefully take a few sips. She rattles off something in Italian and I say 'English. No Italiano.'

'A man?'

I nod, and she sniffs. 'Ragazzo?'

'No.' I think that means boyfriend. 'He's, he's…'

'Amante?'

'No, no—a friend.' Whatever it means, amante sounds too intimate.

But the woman nods as if she's already decided what my problem is. And pats my shoulder and says firmly, 'Si. Amante. Don't worry, he'll come.'

Which is pretty perceptive of her under the circumstances.

After I recover my senses and reassure the woman I'm OK, I manage to get myself from the airport into Pisa and catch a train to Florence. It's an hour-long trip. By the time I get there, I've gone backwards and forwards in my head so many times, I've got brain whiplash. He's coming, oh my God, he's coming! Surely he's not, that's ridiculous. Why would he fly here to meet me, he hardly knows me? It doesn't make sense. Our fates are aligned, *I knew it wasn't over*.

Florence is bathed in early afternoon sunlight when I come out of the train station. I follow a network of narrow streets catching glimpses of ornate tiled churches, piazzas, and rows of shops with all manner of goods. I don't stop to explore, knowing Cathy is waiting for me. I keep walking with my wheelie until I pop out next to the Arno. I've seen photos, but it's so much better in person. I drink in the glorious sight of the Ponte Vecchio, shops hanging over the emerald water, flanked on either side by golden stone buildings. In one of these is the apartment I'll be staying in for the next two weeks. It hardly seems real.

Soon, I'm pressing a buzzer next to an arched wooden door and climbing a flight of stairs to a first-floor landing. Cathy has come out of her apartment and is peering over the balcony. 'Ciao, Jenna! You made it,' she calls down to me in a lilting British accent.

'Ciao,' I say, hefting my bag up the stairs.

When I get to the landing, I see her properly. She's just like her photo but taller than I expected. She's dressed in an elegant dark-blue shift dress with her signature plait.

'How was the flight?' she asks smiling.

I think about Seth's message and my stomach lurches. 'It was fine, uneventful.'

'Come in. I'll give you the tour, and you can meet Filippo. He's in the lounge.'

I stash my bag by the door, and I follow her down a short hallway, then through an open door. The lounge is larger and grander than the photo Cathy sent. There's a faint scent of vanilla, wafting on the breeze from the open window. The view of the Ponte Vecchio is overwhelming. I try not to let it show on my face. I'll do a victory dance and some silent screaming when she's gone.

Filippo has staked out one of the mustard yellow chairs and is curled in a ball, fast asleep. Cathy picks him up. 'Wakey, wakey, Mister,' she says and cradles him like a baby. He yawns and fixes me with a green-eyed stare.

'Hi Filippo,' I say, hoping he's going to like me. We're stuck together for two weeks whether he likes it or not.

'I named him after Filippo Brunelleschi,' she says. I look at her blankly. *Who's he when he's at home?*

'Florence's famous Renaissance architect? He designed the dome on the cathedral.'

'Ah. I haven't been to Florence before so I'm not up on its history. I didn't have time to read anything.'

She laughs. 'Yes, it was a bit of a quick arrangement. I wasn't sure if you had been, so I've left a list of must-dos in the kitchen. As well as some good restaurants that are off the tourist track.'

'Oh, thanks.' Hmm, I doubt I'll be hanging out too much at good restaurants thanks to my pitiful bank account, but it's nice of her all the same.

Cathy shows me around the rest of the apartment and gives me the rundown on Filippo's food when we get to the kitchen. 'I normally buy him fish from the Mercato Centrale and freeze bits in separate plastic bags. Then, it can be defrosted and chopped as needed. You can mix it up with some tinned cat food to make it go further, anything fishy, not the meat kind. I've left some cash in the sugar pot for all that. I went shopping the other day, so he's fine for now, but you'll need to stock up again in a couple of days. I've put the address on the list.'

'OK, thanks. So is there a supermarket nearby?'

'Yes, there's one just up the road before the bridge.'

'Cool.'

'Well, I think that's about it. Here's the spare key, I put it on a key ring for you.' She hands me a cheap plastic key ring with a photo of the Duomo. It's a reminder that I'm a tourist and not here for the long haul. Two weeks, that's all I get.

'If you want some company, there's a girl around your age living next door. Antonella. She's American, from LA, and has been here for six months now, learning Italian and discovering her roots. She's very obliging and friendly. I mentioned you were house sitting for me, and she was keen to meet you. She's usually home in the late afternoon, so just knock on her door.'

'Thanks, I will.' I don't particularly want to knock on her door, but it would be nice to have someone to chat or hang out with. Maybe I'll bump into her in the hallway.

'Right, I'd better head off. Send me an email if you need to know anything about the flat or call if it's an emergency. I gave you my number, didn't I?'

'Yes, you did.'

'Well, arrivederci and divertiti, Jenna'. She gives me a

wink. 'That means "goodbye and enjoy yourself"'.

I feel my cheeks flushing. Hopefully, she means in general, not in a sexual way. Cringe. Luckily, she doesn't know about the hot Goth possibly winging his way to Florence as we speak.

CHAPTER TEN

He doesn't call. I know because I've put his name in my contacts and I'm glued to my phone for the next two days. I've hardly left the apartment. It's like being back in Hampstead, waiting for him to appear in the kitchen. As well as draining, the whole situation is now making me angry to the point that I start having conversations with him in my head. They usually go: 'How dare you ruin my nice time in Florence—you fucker.' 'I was doing fine until you came along.' 'What makes you think I want to see you anyway?'

Seth is always very silent during these one-sided conversations, it's as if he knows it's better to let me have my rant and stay out of it.

On the third day, I wake up and lie there thinking, *I'm sick of this. The sun is shining, I'm going to go out and do something lovely today.* In the end, *something lovely* turns out to be buying fish for Filippo and a few food items at the Mercato Centrale. It's a relief to be outside and interacting with people, even if I can't understand what they're saying. My Italian so far consists of being able to say hello, goodbye and thank you, and I did learn the word for fish (pesce) from Google translate before I went out. I have visions of myself pulling a guppy face and flapping my fins to make myself understood. But it all goes smoothly, and I feel proud of my first purchase. Even if it is a stinky one.

The market is bustling, lively and full of delicious smells. I'm tempted to hang out there longer and try some of the food, but I have a bag of fish that needs to go in the freezer. When I get back to the apartment, I see another door down the hallway. That must be Antonella's apartment. I wonder if hers is as nice as Cathy's and how she can afford it. I feel a frisson of envy that she's able to live here and learn Italian and generally swan around. It sounds stress-free and idyllic, the kind of life I wish I had. I know that everyone has problems and their lives aren't as good as their Instagram feed makes out, but often it feels like some people have a great life, while others just get the shitty end of the stick through no fault of their own. Nevertheless, that sounds like something Violet would think and I don't want to take on her attitude.

No, I'm going to bomb my Instagram feed with photos of Florence and make it look like I'm living a charmed life. I take a photo of the view out the window of the Ponte Vecchio and post it with the caption: "Living the dream in Florence!" with suitable hashtags. When I check back half an hour later, I'm shocked to see the photo has forty likes, ten comments and I've got twenty new followers. Whoop. Right, this is my chance to boost my profile, I'm going to milk this view for all its worth.

I've taken half a dozen arty shots from out the window, which on closer inspection are actually all pretty much the same. Then it occurs to me that Seth might be on Instagram and he might have posted something about coming to Florence. It won't hurt to take a quick peek, and it's not like I'm going to follow him or anything.

I do a search for a profile under his name, then variations of his name, and then the band's name, but come up with nothing. The only thing I can find is a photo of a black motorbike parked outside a brick semi-detached house taken a couple of weeks ago by @_calypso_. There's no caption, just Seth's name as the hashtag. There's also no information about the poster, no profile pic and it's their only photo. It's like they deleted everything in a hurry but forgot that one. Or they deliberately left it for some reason.

I screw up my nose. Why would someone take a photo of a motorbike and hashtag him? Was Seth actually there? Is Calypso his girlfriend? The whole thing is weird. And why doesn't he have his own Instagram account? It's like he's trying to shroud himself in a cloak of mystery to titillate fans. But really, who does he think he is? It's not like Sublime Misery are that famous. I'd never even heard of them before I spoke to Violet about it. All this deliberate secrecy is bloody irritating.

I'm partly aware that I'm thinking withering thoughts about Seth to gain control over the situation. Every time I imagine him being in the city, within walking distance, my stomach churns with anxiety. But being annoyed at him gives me a feeling of self-righteousness which is quite satisfying.

In the afternoon, I'm sitting on the loo, updating Facebook, and thinking my morally superior thoughts when I get an incoming call.

For a moment, I gaze at "Seth Carver" flashing on the screen uncomprehendingly, then let out a yelp. My blood runs hot. Then cold. Fuck, he's calling. I stare at the screen helplessly. There's no way I can answer it, I'm on the loo with my knickers down! He's going to have to leave a voicemail. The call ends, and I quickly finish up and wait impatiently for the voicemail message, but it doesn't come. I don't believe it. He finally rings *and I'm on the blooming loo!*

After half an hour, he hasn't called back, and I'm getting a headache from urging my phone to ring. I feel like throwing it out the window. I could always ring him, I suppose. Get it over and done with. Be bright and breezy; like a friend would. 'Hey Seth, just missed your call. What's up? Are you in Florence yet?' But I know I'll never pull it off. I'm too into him to act like a friend. So I do the only thing I can. Go out for a gelato. And leave my phone behind.

Cathy has put the names of a couple of gelato places on

her must-do list. One of them is Gelateria Santa Trinita, a five-minute walk from the apartment, next to the bridge of the same name. 'THE BEST' she's written. 'Try the stracciatella and the sesame!' But when I get there, I spend so long looking at all the mouthwatering flavours that I can't decide. A queue of impatient people builds behind me.

'How many flavours do I get for the largest cup?' I ask the girl serving behind the counter.

'Six,' she replies. Erk, that's a lot of gelato. But it all looks so good.

'I'll have that then, please,' I say and start pointing out what I want. 'The stracchey one, sesame, blueberry, caramel cookie, raspberry and pistachio.'

The gigantic cup she hands me is a colourful work of art. A girl nudges her friend and they stare open-mouthed. 'I'm sharing it,' I say to the queue as people start giving me looks like I'm a piggy porker. But really, I'm going to gobble it all up myself and enjoy every mouthful. I haven't been eating much because of the Seth stress and I'm starving.

I'm standing on the bridge, enjoying the sunshine, the views of the Ponte Vecchio and my gelato, when a tour guide walks past leading a group of people to the gelato shop. He's middle-aged with a beard and beer belly and doesn't look the slightest bit Italian. More like Ernest Hemmingway with a side gig. Out of the corner of my eye, I see his name badge "Seth" and almost drop my cup. Then as they pause to cross the road, people start asking loudly in American accents "Seth, is this good gelato?" "How much is it, Seth?" "Seth, what are the best flavours?" It's like a chorus of Seth's going off. Some of the stragglers at the back are looking at my massive cup enviously. Then they all crowd into the shop.

I dig my spoon into the blueberry and take a mouthful, but I've lost my appetite. That was weird. I'm trying to forget about him, and I'm still getting reminded. It makes me feel nervous like he's around somewhere and is going to pop out at me unexpectedly. If he was ringing because he's in Florence, then it's entirely likely that he could head towards this gelato shop. There are tour groups coming here, so it must be quite well known. He could appear any second.

The thought makes me move off the bridge. I start walking back to the apartment at a rapid pace. I don't particularly want him to catch me chowing down on a huge cup of gelato. I'll put it in the freezer and finish it off later.

I'm making my way up the stairs when a pretty girl with light brown hair comes bouncing down. She stops when she sees me.

'Oh, ciao!' she exclaims with an American twang. 'Are you Jenna? Cathy's house sitter?'

'Yes, that's me. Are you Antonella?'

'Si, but please call me Nella if you want. Less of a mouthful.' She grins and eyes the cup in my hand. 'Speaking of mouthfuls, I see you've been sampling the local gelato.

Good stuff, isn't it?' She peers at me closely for a moment.

I feel like I should explain why I've got so much. 'Yeah, I couldn't choose, so I went a bit crazy.'

Antonella chuckles. 'I know, it's so good! I have it at least once a day. I think I'm addicted. Anyway, I have to rush. I'm meeting a friend. But we should definitely do something. Have you been up the Duomo?'

I shake my head.

'We should do that, the views at sunset are incredible.'

'Sounds good, I'm free any time really.'

'Excellento. What about this later on this afternoon?'

I nod and say that would be great. So we exchange numbers, and Antonella says she'll message me to arrange a time.

Wonderful, another person I'm waiting on to get in touch with me. But she seems nice, and I'm sure she'll keep her word.

It's only when I look in the bathroom mirror that I realise why she was staring at me. Oh God, my lips and tongue are stained blue. And I'm wearing a white sundress. I look like Smurfette.

CHAPTER ELEVEN

Antonella turns out to be extremely knowledgeable about Brunelleschi's dome. She gives me a running commentary when we're climbing up. How he won a competition and designed all these crazy cranes to build it and how he was way ahead of his time with his architecture.

This is good in one respect—I'm learning stuff. It also distracts me from the pain in my calves and quads, my burning lungs and the dizziness I'm experiencing from being in an airless, narrow passageway. Thank the lord I'm not that tall, otherwise, I'd be in trouble. A guy ahead of us is in the six-foot range, and he's struggling, hunched over with his neck at a weird angle.

Antonella doesn't seem to mind being in the tight, dark airless space. 'I've done it a few times now with different people. It's a good way to keep fit too,' she told me when we were waiting in line. 'You're not claustrophobic, are you?'

I shook my head. 'I don't think so.'

'I guess we'll find out,' she said with a grin.

Little did I know what was in store. A heart-thumping, gasping slog with sweat pouring off me. At least I can tick it off Cathy's list and burn some calories from the ginormous gelato.

'Did you know that there aren't any plans or sketches of how Bruneschelli actually constructed it?' Antonella remarks, now breathing heavily behind me. I'm glad she's starting to feel it because my lungs are on fire.

'Putting in a lift would've been good,' I gasp.

Antonella gives a breathy laugh. 'These steps were built for the workers, they weren't meant for the public. So yeah, it's not tourist friendly.'

'Remind me again how many there are to the top?'

'Four hundred and sixty-three. Keep going. We're nearly halfway, then you'll see the interior dome up close. The frescoes are amazing. It's the Last Judgement!'

I feel like I'm experiencing the Last Judgement personally, but I press my lips together, wipe the sweat off my forehead and keep trudging.

Eventually, we pop out onto a narrow pathway bordered by a high plexiglass screen that runs along the side of the cupola. Above us float the most exquisite colourful paintings I've ever laid eyes on. I have to admit it's stunning and worth the effort. 'We're forty metres above the church floor,' says Antonella 'Check it out.'

Far below is the central nave of the cathedral, with ant figures moving around and brown matchstick pew seating.

We hang around on the balcony for at least fifteen

minutes. I give the excuse that I need a breather, and I want to take lots of photos for Instagram. Antonella doesn't seem to mind and takes some too. 'The frescoes were designed by Giorgio Vasari, but they were actually mostly painted by his less-talented student Frederico Zuccari.'

I nod, trying to take it all in. Gosh, she's such a fountain of knowledge, it's like having my own personal tour guide.

It's lovely being out in the open dome rather than the enclosed airless space. I almost suggest that we don't bother going to the top. But we've paid for the tickets to get there and I don't want to look like a wimp.

'Right—onto the next section,' Antonella says decisively pointing to a rectangular opening cut into the stone.

'OK,' I say. Surely, it'll be fine.

Not far in, we get stuck behind a group waiting for people to come down, then we move forward again, and the passageway narrows and steepens. I gulp nervously. I feel like I'm being squashed on all sides by solid stone. The cathedral has been standing since 1436, I remind myself, it probably won't choose this particular moment to collapse.

As if she's cottoned onto my discomfort, Antonella comments, 'It's even more stifling in the height of summer, a hundred times hotter. Like slowly being cooked alive.'

That's a pleasant thought. After another hundred steps and another gallon of sweat, through one of the windows cut into the stone, I catch a glimpse of terracotta roofs. We're quite high up. It can't be that much longer. We stop for a breather and a well-earned drink of water Antonella's been carrying in a small backpack. My heart is going like the clappers.

'We're heading up there.' She points to a flight of steep narrow stairs, which seem to be stretching up endlessly.

'It gets worse before it gets better,' she says. 'But it's so worth it. Then, we can check out the view before we head back down.' I groan a little. Going back down! I forgot about that.

Just when I think I can't take much more, and I'm going to have to be taken down on a stretcher, we reach the top. The terracotta-tiled roofs of Florence spread out before us and, in the distance, the green smudge of the Tuscan hills with the sun sinking behind them, bathing everything in golden light. Church bells toll solemnly in the hazy stillness. The view is so beautiful, it takes my breath away. And I don't have much of that in my possession at the moment.

I hang onto the railing to steady myself while trying not to look down. The drop to the streets far below is dizzying. A slight breeze cools the sweat drenching my skin. Antonella hands me a wet wipe, and I pass it over my face and under my armpits gratefully. She's so well prepared, she even has snacks in a small plastic tub: a mix of salted nuts, dried cranberries and dark chocolate.

'Well done. It's a workout and a half, huh?' she says as we

lean against the cupola wall gulping water, munching on snacks, and generally trying to recover.

'Yeah, I wasn't expecting it to be quite so tough.'

'Going down will be easier.'

'That's good to know. I thought I was reasonably fit. I was wrong.'

She smiles kindly. 'Do you want to do a loop around the platform to get the full viewing experience and take some photos? It would be good to keep moving so our legs don't seize up.'

'Right. I think that's already happening,' I say with a laugh. My knees feel strange. I really need to do more exercise.

There were a few other people at the top, but they've dispersed, so we almost have the platform to ourselves. I'm getting some amazing shots and selfies.

Antonella is busily pointing out landmarks. 'That's Giotto's Bell Tower right in front. And that smaller round domed building is the Medici Chapel, where the Medici family are buried. It's also an art museum.'

'Who are the Medici?'

'Um, they were like only *the* most important rulers of Florence.' She looks at me in bemusement. 'Don't you know about the history of the city?'

'Not really, I came over on a whim to do the house sit. The name sounds familiar though.'

'You should do a walking tour and get informazione.'

'I will, definitely.'

'We can go out and do some exploring if you like. I'll teach you some Italian, it will be a good way for me to practice.'

'That would be amazing, thank you.' Having Antonella next door is definitely going to be fun, as long as she doesn't want to do expensive stuff or shop at Gucci. But I suppose looking is free.

'That's Santa Croce where Michelangelo and Galileo are buried,' she continues, pointing out a white-and-green tiled church. 'That's Palazzo Pitti...'

I'm just raising my phone to zoom in on it when I get a text:

Ciao, Jenna, I'm in Florence at the Relais Villa Medici. Can we meet? There's a bar here. 7:30 OK? Text me back if you can make it.

Then another one immediately after:

BTW, it's Seth Carver.

I squeal and almost drop my phone over the edge of the Duomo. I grip it and the railing for dear life. Antonella stares at me. 'Are you OK? You've gone really pale.'

I take a deep breath. 'I... I'm fine. Could I have some

water?'

'Here.' She hands me a bottle. 'Do you want to sit down?'

I shake my head and take a swig.

Now he chooses to text me, Jesus!

'I'm OK, really. I just felt a bit faint.'

'Phew, I thought you might need a defibrillator. We'll take it easy on the way down.'

I can't help looking at the messages again. He sent them an hour ago and I've only got them now. There must've been dodgy reception inside the Duomo... "BTW, it's Seth Carver"—as if I would've bloody forgotten!

'Is it bad news?' I can tell Antonella is curious but not wanting to pry.

A wave of relief, immediately followed by unbridled joy, washes over me. 'It's actually great news,' I say grinning at her. Then I realise, Seth's wanting to meet up tonight. I check the time. It's six forty-five. I need to get down to ground level, walk to the apartment, shower, dress, do my make-up and turn up at the hotel looking halfway decent. All in forty-five minutes. Shit.

'Um... I kind of have to go.'

'Oh, OK.' Antonella looks confused. I feel I should explain. 'It's just... I'm meeting a guy.'

She brightens. 'Oh! Well done, that was quick work. Though, the way the men are so forward here, I'm not surprised.'

I smile cagily. 'Ah yes. He's not from Florence though.' I edge towards the stairwell. We really have to get moving. 'Do you think we can make it back to the apartment by seven fifteen?'

Antonella grimaces. 'No way Jose, we'd have to run at breakneck speed down the Duomo. What time does he want to meet?'

'Seven-thirty.'

She shrugs. 'Just tell him you'll be there at nine.'

'Nine!'

'He can wait, can't he? You'll get there when you get there.'

The possibility of telling Seth Carver that he can bloody well wait hadn't occurred to me. It feels shocking but also powerful. I've been moping around like Ophelia, why not make him stress a little?

'What should I say?'

'Say you'd like to meet up but you can't until nine o'clock.' With shaking thumbs, I type:

Hi Seth, sure sounds great but can we make it 9 pm? I'm busy early evening. Jenna.

'Done! Thanks!' It's perfect. Cool, casual, yet mysterious, like I've got stuff going on, but I can also fit him into my schedule in a pinch. He doesn't need to know that in reality, I'm going to be navigating a narrow space between two domes as fast as humanly possible without doing myself an injury.

'No problem.' Antonella shrugs nonchalantly. God, I wish I could be like that. I'm so out of practice with talking to guys. Maybe we can jack up some kind of earpiece, so she can feed me the right things to say. I'm not kidding.

'Do you want to take some more photos or...' she says, gesturing at the view, but I'm already hurrying towards the stairwell as if I'm a speed walker in the Olympics.

CHAPTER TWELVE

We arrive back at my apartment an hour later. Antonella comes in too, and we head to the kitchen to gulp copious amounts of water while Filippo yowls at us. I'm a little over anyone called Filippo at the moment after the Duomo ordeal, but Antonella picks him up and strokes him which quietens him down. He's already been fed, so I assume he just wants attention.

'I'm going to quickly jump in the shower,' I say. 'Hang out if you want though. There's some food in the pantry. I did a shop this morning. There's nothing too exciting, but see what you can find.'

'Thanks, I should go and do some study, but my brain is fried after that expedition. I'll stand in the lounge by the window and cool down, so I don't sweat on the seats.'

I giggle. 'OK.'

This is good, I think in the shower. I'm keeping busy and focusing on getting ready, not worrying about how it's going to go tonight. If I let myself think about seeing Seth, I'm going to unravel.

I received a text reply from him somewhere inside the

Duomo, but I couldn't check until we were outside and heading back to the Arno. It was brief:

OK, see you then. I'll be in the bar.

Whether that means he's going to be rolling drunk by the time I get there, I'm not sure. I wish I'd bought some alcohol when I did a shop this morning. Maybe Cathy has a liquor stash and I can take a few sneaky swigs to give me Dutch courage.

When I come out into the lounge wrapped in my cotton robe and combing my wet hair, I see Antonella has set up a tray on the window seat filled with prosciutto, olives, cheese, bread and grapes. She's opened the windows wide, letting in the night air and floating up from below are the ambient sounds of footsteps, and the occasional snatch of conversation from passersby. The Arno is a shimmering black mirror reflecting the yellow lights along its edge and the shops of the Ponte Vecchio.

I take an olive and pop it in my mouth sighing at the salty flavour. 'I'm starving.'

'Have more.'

'I can't, I have to get ready. It's nearly eight.'

'You should eat something. Drinking on an empty stomach could lead to all sorts of trouble.'

She waggles her eyebrows knowingly, and I dutifully make myself an impromptu sandwich and take a massive bite to avoid replying. She's right, I need to be in control of my faculties.

'So, is this guy from London?' she asks casually, helping herself to cheese and grapes.

I nod with my mouth full.

'Good-looking?'

I chew silently, not sure how to reply. Good-looking doesn't even begin to describe Seth. I do a version of the Italian shrug, but my cheeks are on fire.

Antonella grins. 'Delicioso?'

I swallow and nod slowly. 'Very delicioso.'

'You may not be back tonight then,' she says casually.

I swallow bread and stare at her. 'Huh?'

'You know, if you're getting on well.'

I laugh nervously. 'I don't think that's going to happen.'

Antonella tilts her head to one side. 'Why not? He's come to Florence, he's invited you to the bar in his hotel.'

'Because...' *I've only just accepted he's messaged me, let alone contemplated sex.* 'Because I... I think it might be just business,' I stutter.

'Whatever,' scoffs Antonella. 'It's never *just business* when a guy hops on a plane to see a girl. No matter how much he says it is. What hotel is it?'

'The Relais Villa Medici.'

Antonella whistles. 'Nice, that's a five-star. Is he rich?'

'Um, possibly. He comes from a wealthy family at least.' I

don't want to get into the whole 'he's in a band' thing, otherwise Antonella is going to insist on looking them up, and then I'm going to have to endure her exclaiming about his profile photo on the website (which I still haven't looked at). It's going to be Violet all over again.

'I really need to get ready.'

'What are you wearing?'

'Uh, a dress?'

'Show me.'

She follows me into the bedroom where I've laid out my nicest dress on the bed. It's knee-length, light-blue with short sleeves. I used to wear it in the office to meet with clients. I think I look quite smart in it, and I always used to get compliments whenever I wore it.

But Antonella doesn't look impressed. 'Hmm, it's a bit corporate. What else have you got?'

Twenty minutes later, she's raided my wheelie bag, and her own wardrobe from next door. I've tried on multiple outfits but nothing is working, and time is marching ever closer to Seth hour. My stomach keeps squeezing uncomfortably with nervous tension. But between fashion consultations, I've managed to blow-dry my hair and put some makeup and underwear on. If not actual clothes. At this rate, I'll be meeting him in my bra and knickers.

Antonella lounges on the bed with Filippo curled up next to her. She's changed into a clean t-shirt and track pants and doesn't look like she should be giving out high-fashion advice. But she has lived here for six months, so she probably knows what she's talking about.

'You want to look effortlessly put together like Italian women do. Like you've thrown on your clothes and waltzed out the door looking like a sex goddess. It's a real knack.'

'For an effortless look it seems like we are going to an awful lot of effort. I think it's easier if I just wear my dress, at least I feel comfortable in it.'

'But you're going to a five-star hotel, to meet a gorgeous guy. Don't you want him to drool?'

It's shameless, but I can't help it. 'I do,' I admit. 'I want him to look at me like there's no one else on earth, and he'll do anything to have me.' Why lie to myself?

'Right, put this on, and this.' Antonella hands me a short black leather skirt that's more like a belt and a sheer white blouse that's practically see-through.

'I can't wear that, you can see my bra.'

'Who said anything about wearing a bra?' she smirks mischievously.

'No way, I'm not meeting him with my boobs on show!'

'You wear the Gucci jacket on top but with some of the domes undone, and then it's just a hint of boob when you move. He'll think, did I see that? Is she braless or isn't she? It will drive him wild.'

'Hmm.'

'Trust me, it's as sexy as hell.'

I'm not convinced, but what do I know?

Finally, I'm ready. Antonella has redone my makeup so it's more alluring, complete with smoky eyes and top-lid liquid eyeliner which I can never do. She's tousled my hair using product into a sexy bedhead style that suggests I've come from a wild love-making session. I'm braless under the blouse, but I have on her white Gucci jacket with most of the domes done up, 'you can undo some more during the night depending on how the evening's progressing,' she says with a wink. The little leather skirt barely covers my thighs but at least my legs are sporting a tan from sunbathing at the Hampstead house sit. Antonella eyed them critically but she said they were 'passably brown' like there was a standard level of brownness before they could be exposed in Florence.

Overall, the effect is definitely wow. I look edgier, sophisticated and, dare I say it, hotter than hell. But it's getting so late, I've had to order a taxi on the app Cathy suggested.

'It's best you do,' says Antonella, 'If you walk the streets looking like that, you might turn up with a trail of Italian men behind you. Which isn't a bad thing,' she muses, 'At least he'll know he has competition.'

I check my phone. 'The taxi is five minutes away and I need to get down the stairs in these heels. But thanks so much for the makeover.'

'No sweat. But three more things before you go. First.' She reaches into the pink quilted Moschino toiletry bag she's brought from her apartment and pulls out a bottle of perfume. She squirts it into the air above my head. A light scent of jasmine and lemon mists over me; it smells divine. 'Mmm, what's that?'

'Giorgio Armani's Acqua di Gioia.'

While I'm still revelling in the gorgeous fragrance, Antonella says 'Second' and reaches under the skirt and tugs down my knickers.

'What the hell?' I splutter. 'I'm not meeting him without knickers!'

'Take them with you in your handbag then. If you really feel uncomfortable, then nip to the restroom and put them on. If you do end up in his hotel room, trust me, there's nothing sexier for a guy in the heat of passion discovering a woman is knickerless.'

I can't even imagine shaking hands with Seth, let alone being in the heat of passion with him. And now I seem to be meeting him practically naked. I don't think I could be any more obvious if I had FUCK ME written on my forehead in marker pen. But Antonella seems to know what she's talking about and when it comes to attracting guys like Seth Carver, I'm clueless.

'Third. Drink this.' She hands me a small bottle of mini-bar vodka. 'For Dutch courage.'

Quickly, I unscrew the cap and gulp the bottle down in one. A pleasant warmth soothes the knots in my stomach. 'You read my mind. I so needed that. I think you might be my fairy godmother.'

She blows me a kiss and waves an invisible magic wand. 'My pleasure, Cinders. Have fun with your handsome prince.'

The Relais Villa Medici is on the other side of the Arno. It's actually not too far from the train station, I would've walked quite close to it when I arrived. But it's out of the way from the main centre in a less touristy area. Then again, Seth is an off-the-beaten-track kind of guy. My stomach flips as the taxi pulls up outside the hotel, a three-storey beige and brick building with shutters and flags over the top of the entrance. In exactly five minutes, maybe less, I'll be seeing him. I don't think I've ever been this nervous in my life. It's all a bit surreal—*I'm in Florence and meeting a guy I had dinner with once.* Especially since Antonella's enthusiasm and the hit of vodka have worn off, and I'm sans underwear. What the hell was I thinking? But it's too late now. Hopefully, I can just wander in and find him without anyone taking too much notice of me.

But that doesn't quite go to plan when I enter the reception area. The guy behind the front desk immediately jerks to attention, and says 'Can I help you, madam?' He's an Italian guy, in his forties and immaculately dressed in a black suit, white shirt and tie. His name badge says "Giacomo".

'Ah yes, I'm meeting a friend in the bar. If you could just point me in that direction?'

I notice Giacomo's eyes flick discreetly over me and his eyebrows lift a smidgeon.

'The Jockey Bar or Harry's Bar?' he enquires, now staring openly.

I teeter on my heels uncomfortably. 'Um, I'm not sure. One of those.'

His eyes shift down to my legs and I realise it looks dodgy to be coming to a hotel dressed like this and saying I'm meeting "a friend". Isn't that code for "prostitute"?

Giacomo's eyebrows knit together, and I have a bad feeling that he's going to say I can't go in. That it's against hotel policy for me to be meeting "a friend". Oh no, surely not. Suddenly, my fear of meeting Seth morphs into a fear of not being able to see him at all.

I give Giacomo a confident smile and start walking through the ornate foyer before he can do anything to stop me. As I veer towards the left, he calls out sharply 'Wait! Madam!' Oh, God. I look back expecting him to be marching towards me ready to turf me out on my ear. But he's come out from behind the counter and is gesturing to the right to show me the way. Phew. I take a deep breath and change direction. First hurdle over. Now to find Seth.

The hotel is deceptively large. I peek into various empty rooms with high ceilings and antique furniture that seem to lead nowhere. There's nothing even remotely resembling a bar. I check my phone, it's ten minutes after nine, no messages from Seth. Should I text him? But I don't know exactly where I am, so he can't even come to find me. We could wander around for hours in this place and not bump into each other. Then, he'll just give up and go to bed. And there's no way I'm asking Giacamo which room he's in so I can "visit".

I turn into a long, carpeted corridor with windows along the righthand side and low couches with tables in between. Through the windows, a kidney-shaped pool glows blue with underwater lights and set around it are tables with candles, where people are having drinks. Tinkling piano music is playing from a hidden speaker. This looks more promising. But there's still no sign of Seth.

I keep walking until I see a white arched door. There's a sign next to it that says "Jockey Bar", and I can hear talking inside. I breathe out in relief, hopefully he's in here. I do a quick fluff of my hair, an under-eye mascara check and make sure the domes are done up on the jacket so I'm not showing any boob. With a shaking hand, I push open the door and go in.

A short flight of stairs leads down to a wood-panelled room which is crammed full of people. They're either sitting on caramel-coloured leather couches or huddled in small groups having murmured conversations. Everyone's dressed in bright cocktail dresses and tuxedos and holding slim glasses of bubbles. The instant I enter, all heads swivel, conversation hushes and everyone stares at me. It's like I am indeed Cinderella arriving late at the ball and standing at the top of the stairs. I freeze, taken aback. Have I interrupted a private party or something? I'm sure I must look goggle-eyed. Then after a beat, everyone loses interest and goes back to their conversations, and I'm released from the spotlight. What the fuck was that about?

Then I see Seth off to the side. He's sitting on a stool with his back to the bar, long legs stretched out, and looking at me with an unreadable but not unfriendly expression. He's dressed in a black shirt and trousers, his dark hair gel-spiked. My nerves drop away and I'm grateful to see a familiar face in a sea of strangers, even if that face is so attractive it's intimidating. He draws me across the room to him like a tractor beam. My feet start moving and I have no choice in the matter.

CHAPTER THIRTEEN

'Jenna?' Seth says when I'm standing next to him, 'I wasn't sure if it was you. You look… different.'

'It's me,' I say, trying not to shiver upon hearing his voice. Up close he's all smooth pale skin, killer cheekbones, blood-red lips. It's like the fuzzy monochrome Seth in my mind is now in crystal clear focus and the technicolour version is hurting my eyes. 'Sorry I'm late, I got a bit lost. I wasn't sure where you were.'

His pierced eyebrow lifts. 'You should've texted.' *Is that allowed?* I stand up straighter. *Be confident, Jenna, he's not a vampire, he's not going to bite you.*

'Next time I will,' I say firmly. Next time? *Oh, dear. A bit overeager.*

But Seth doesn't seem to mind, and asks, 'What do you want to drink?'

'What are you having?' I eye his nearly empty glass of orange fizz. 'Is that Fanta?'

'No, it's a Bellini—prosecco and peach juice.'

Hmm, I've had vodka and mixing bubbles with spirits isn't a good idea.

'I'll have a vodka tonic, thanks.' *See, I'm thinking ahead, I'm in control. Oh God, I wish I was wearing a bra and knickers.*

'Sure.' Seth turns to the barman and orders my drink and gets another Bellini for himself.

I take a deep breath and look around at the room. 'So this is all a bit weird.'

'What's weird?'

'Um, you. Being here. In Florence. Not that I mind. It's just a bit sudden. That you've turned up like this.' I can't seem to speak in full sentences.

Seth grunts. 'Well, you did go into my studio. You started it.'

I gulp. 'Oh, that.'

'Yeah, that.' We stare at each other unspeaking.

'Hah,' I say, dropping my gaze to the creamy skin of his collarbone instead. That doesn't help because I can see the edge of his tattoo peeking out and I find that sexy as hell. To my relief, the barman puts the drinks on the counter and proffers a receipt with a pen and Seth turns away from me to deal with it. 'Please, add it to my room,' he says, signing it with a flourish. '312.'

'Certo.'

'Can we move to a table out in the hall where it's a bit quieter?' he says to me when he's facing back around. 'I'm starting to get a headache from all these people.'

'Who are they?'

'I think they've been, or are going, to the opera. They all piled in at once. It was a bit overwhelming.' He grimaces and I get the feeling he doesn't do too well in groups.

'That's fine. I got a bit of a shock when they all stared at me en masse.'

'There's a reason for that,' he says in a playful tone. His eyes touch mine again, and I'm enveloped in two dark fathomless pools. My stomach fizzes like his Bellini and I feel a bit swoony. Oooh, I thought that only happened in Mills & Boon novels. Nope, in real life too.

'Shall we? After you,' he says in a low voice that causes goosebumps to stud my arms. I pick up my drink and start walking towards the door, Seth's presence a dark shadow behind me. I feel like I'm about to get interrogated. But at least I know his room number—312, 312, 312—*stop it, Jenna!*

When we reach the hall, I choose the nearest couch slash table ensemble. As I'm about to sit down, I realise a) the couch is low; b) my knees are going to be higher than my hips; c) I'm going to give him an eyeful à la Basic Instinct every time I move if he sits opposite me. Why did I let Antonella talk me into this? I sink down in a regal fashion, keeping my legs tightly together and tucking them to the side. That seems to work. But then the top two domes of my jacket pop open and won't stay closed because my boobs are now pushing them out. Jesus. I'll have to sit as still as a statue and not move a muscle.

Seth, in the meantime, has decided to sit next to me on the couch rather than opposite and is unaware of my dilemma. He seems more interested in my fingernails. I painted them pink before I met Antonella to go up the Duomo this afternoon. Apart from the little fingernails on each hand which I've done in green. Seth gently touches a green fingernail resting on my leg, which is near his own, and I catch my breath.

'Why did you paint that one green?'

I shrug. 'I don't know. It's fun. Otherwise, it looks too perfect. It catches attention. I like to do that with rooms as well. Add a surprising pop of colour.'

'Can you work with your clients while you're in Florence?'

'Not really,' I say, unwilling to admit I don't actually have any at the moment. 'I'm just taking photos for Instagram and trying to boost my profile. Hopefully, I can pick up some more work when I get back to London.' So I can pay off Stacey…

'I see.' Seth takes a sip of his Bellini, then says, 'So, the reason I wanted to meet up was that I've got a proposition for you.'

I almost say 'yes, I'll do it' on the spot but manage to bite my tongue. I better find out what it is first, in case it involves drug dealing.

'What is it?' I ask warily.

'You really helped me with that song. I was wondering if I could pick your brain a little.'

'You came all the way to Florence to pick my brain?'

He sighs. 'OK, it's more than that. I'm under pressure,' Seth says, his voice sounding strained. 'We've got a new album coming out in spring, and I need to write ten songs by the end of September. I seem to have lost my creativity, my spark of inspiration, whatever you want to call it. I'm getting desperate. The band is relying on me, and I can't deliver.'

'Oh.' I consider this. That's kind of serious. 'How many songs have you written so far?'

'Two and a half.'

'Can't the other band members help?'

He shakes his head. 'I'm the main lyricist. Kyle can write at a pinch, but he's better at music composition.'

'Two and a half,' I say, 'You've got a few to go then.'

He nods. 'I know. I'm starting to have panic attacks. And I'm not sleeping well.' He rubs his hand over his cheek, and I notice he does have a faint bluish tinge under his eyes.

I laugh shakily. 'I'm not sure how I can help. I'm not a songwriter. The most I've written is some angsty poetry when I was a teenager.'

'But you wrote those perfect lines.'

'I don't know how that happened though, they just popped into my head.'

'You seem like a really creative person. Maybe you subconsciously tapped into my psyche.' He leans towards me, and the atmosphere thickens around us. 'I felt some kind of energy from you that night at dinner. I started writing the next morning, but I got stuck. Then I found those lyrics, and I guessed it was you. I came up to the house the next morning to see if we could vibe off each other, but you'd gone.'

I slump a little at hearing his side of it, thinking about the way I raced out of the house because I thought he was mad at me. If I'd stuck around a bit longer, who knows what would've happened if we'd started *vibing off each other?*

'So, anyway, I didn't know what else to do, so I came here,' he continues. 'I know it looks odd. It was a bit impulsive, but I thought if we could just hang out, I might start writing again...' he trails off looking at me as if he's unsure of how that's going to be received.

'Yes,' I say breathily. 'Of course. I'd be happy to hang out. I'm just looking after a cat and doing some sightseeing.'

'Really?' He looks relieved. 'That would be brilliant. I'm not sure how long I'll stay, but a week at least. I'll try not to make a pest of myself. Let me know if you get sick of me. Hopefully, I can shake this block.'

I clamp my lips shut to keep from screaming. *Seth Carver's here for a week, and I'm going to get to hang out with him! But surely he's not going to stay at a five-star hotel?*

'Are you going to stay here the whole time?'

He shrugs, 'Why not?'

'It just seems… expensive.'

'My Dad is helping out. He knows I've been having trouble. Besides, he's our producer, so he has a vested interest in how well this album does. He seems to think from the reception of the EP that we're on the verge of breaking through. I don't know. The fans seem to like us anyway.'

Fans. Like Violet. She would *die* if she could hear this conversation. 'Ah,' I say nonchalantly, 'I should probably listen to a few of your songs if I'm going to provide creative inspiration.' Though he still hasn't told me exactly how.

'Yes, that would be ideal. It will get you in my headspace. Although you may not want to delve too deep, it's pretty dark in there.' He gives a wry smile, and I gulp thinking of the lyrics I saw in his journal; the stuff of nightmares.

During this conversation, Seth has been pressing the back of his hand against mine in a distracted fashion. Like he doesn't seem to realise he's doing it. I move my hand away slightly, feeling like maybe it's a bit too intimate, and he notices.

'Sorry.'

'It's OK,' I say, not wanting him to think I don't want him to touch me.

'You just have inspiring hands.'

'Do I?'

'Yeah,' he says, taking my hand in his and looking at it

intently. Then he turns it over and peers at the lines on my palm. OK, this is... odd. 'I'm into the whole palm reading thing,' he explains.

'Oh.' That makes more sense I guess?

He traces the two lines on my palm that meet under my index finger. It tingles, and my body arches towards him in response. Seth touching me is pretty nice actually, I'm not complaining.

'See how the head line and life line are joined? It means you're highly sensitive and cautious. Though a cautious gypsy girl sounds like an oxymoron. I'm not sure I believe it. From what I've seen, you seem like a risk-taker.'

'Hah. What about yours?'

He shows me his palm which has a large gap between the two lines. 'That means I'm impulsive and I like breaking the rules.'

'Right.' I must sound nervous as Seth flashes a grin at me.

'Don't worry, I'm not dangerous. Well, not too much.'

He puts his larger palm against my smaller one and I start in surprise at the contact. Lordy, this is getting kind of full on. His palm feels cool and smooth against my hot one. My body temperature rises, even though his hand is like ice and should be cooling me down. Suddenly the hotel hallway is sweltering and I start overheating in the Gucci jacket. I remove my hand from his with the excuse of reaching for my vodka tonic, of which I take a large gulp. *Cool your jets.*

Think snow, Iceland, hot springs, Seth and me naked in a hot spring… Sweat breaks out along my hairline. I turn my head and try to wipe my top lip discreetly on my shoulder but Seth notices. 'Aren't you hot in that jacket? You should take it off…'

'*No!*' I exclaim rather sharply. Boobs on display; that's not a good look.

'Ah, OK,' he says, sounding taken aback, and I feel like I've yelled at a puppy. He's so different from other guys, like his sensitivity meter is turned up to full volume.

'I mean, I'll keep it on for now, thanks. I might just need some air,' I say gently.

'We can go out by the pool if you want?'

'OK,' I agree, and down the rest of my drink. He leads the way through a nearby side door. Outside, the air is cool and smells like roses. I take off my heels and walk barefoot across the soft grass to the side of the water. It looks so inviting, I wish I could go for a swim. But instead, I settle for awkwardly manoeuvring down by the side of the pool and dangling my feet in. The water feels really refreshing. Seth stands off to the side and stares in, the blue light of the pool reflected in his eyes. I wonder what he's thinking. Maybe he's writing a song already. *About me. Yeah, right.*

'Are you going to put your feet in?' I ask.

'No, it's OK.'

'Oh, go on,' I urge. 'Just for a bit.'

'Fine.' He rolls up his pant legs and takes off his shoes and sits down beside me and puts his feet in. He sighs. 'That does feel good. I was missing the pool at home.'

'Huh? You used the pool?' This is news to me. 'I never once saw you or heard you in it.'

'I only swim at night,' he says, 'Then I don't have to bother with a swimming costume.'

I swallow. 'Oh. That, er, makes sense.' I swish my legs in the water, trying not to imagine Seth skinny dipping in the moonlight while I was asleep. We're silent for a bit, and I start getting nervous that I'm boring him. I clear my throat. 'So, I don't know how much thought you've given to what our hanging out entails. But the woman I'm house sitting for left a list of activities and one of them was a bike tour. We could do that? It sounds like fun and it's only for a couple of hours around the city centre.'

'Riding a bike?' Seth says, sounding unsure. 'I haven't ridden one in years. I only usually go on motorbikes.' *I know*, I almost say but that would be a giveaway that I was spying on him.

'Maybe I should try and write something after tonight.' He sounds reluctant. 'Also, I can't be outside in the sun for long periods. The last thing Dad said to me before I left was, "For God's sake, don't go getting a tan, we need you pale."'

I snort. 'That's silly. If anything's going to help your creativity, it will be fresh air and exercise. You could probably write five songs after that.'

'Really?' He seems slightly more open to the idea.

'You could also wear SPF50, I've got some, we'll whack a decent amount on you. Trust me, no UV is getting through that.'

'Well, OK then. Do you want to book it and text me the details?'

'Sure.' I lean back feeling triumphant that I've got Seth to go on the bike ride. Then realise more domes on my jacket have popped open. Shit, this bloody jacket. Maybe I will undo all of them. It's pretty dark out here and he's not going to see anything. I pop them open and cool air rushes over my chest. I sigh in relief, *that's better*.

Seth turns to say something to me, but at that moment, the moon comes out from behind a cloud and I'm illuminated by its glow. I look down and realise he can see everything. My boobs are fully on display, covered only by sheer white fabric. He dips his head and looks away.

I hastily dome up the jacket.

'I should go,' I say, thinking *shit shit, I just flashed Seth Carver*.

'Yes, it's getting late.' I can tell he's trying to act like he didn't see anything, but I know he did.

'Um, I'll order a taxi.' I take my phone out of my bag. I can feel my face flaming. Bloody hell, that's exactly what I didn't want to happen. Now he knows I came to meet him braless, like I was expecting something. I was meant to give him a hint of boob, not the full mammary experience. I'm so flustered I have to put in my PIN number three times before I can get my phone to unlock. I order a taxi on the app and it says it's ten minutes away.

'Uh, are those yours?'

My eyes follow his gaze and spy my skimpy black g-string knickers lying by the side of the pool. They've somehow flopped out of my handbag.

Jesus!

'While you've got your phone out, can you text me your email?' Seth says studiously not looking as I stuff my knickers back in my bag.

'Ah, sure.' *I'm going to die, right now.*

'I need to send you a contract outlining your muse duties.'

Muse duties?

'Oh, and an NDA.'

'NDA?'

'Yes, I don't want anything that I discuss with you being leaked at any point. And no social media when we're in creation mode.'

'Oh, right.' Acidic disappointment churns through my gut as I take the hint. So much for the palm reading session. I've taken it the wrong way. He's only interested in me so he can write songs for the album. Nothing more than that.

CHAPTER FOURTEEN

I can be Seth's friend. I have male friends. Not ones I like this much, but that's OK. I just have to make a small mental adjustment, plus, a large physical and emotional adjustment…

I'm trying to convince myself our arrangement is going to work as I wait for him to show up at the Tourist Point near the Duomo. When I got back to the apartment last night, I booked us onto an e-bike tour. Then, slightly despairing, consoled myself with the dregs from the vodka bottle and a chunk of frozen sesame gelato.

'Allora! Who's here for the eleven o'clock city e-bike tour?' A sprightly Italian guy in his thirties wearing lycra bike shorts, a yellow activewear t-shirt and a red bike helmet comes out of the shop. He looks around expectantly. Hands shoot up. 'Si, excellent, a full group! My name's Stefano. The sun is shining. It will be a good day. We're going to have fun!'

I hang around at the back hoping that it takes a while to sort out the bikes and that Seth arrives during the process. I thought this would be a small group as the description said it was an "intimate tour", but there are at least ten people, which isn't ideal since Seth doesn't like groups. I'm sure it will be fine. He'll show. He seemed keen when I texted him the details. Well, he texted back with a thumbs-up, so I assumed he was. After the underwear fiasco, I'm relieved he's still interested in hanging out with me.

Stefano finishes helping a couple of girls and looks around the group. 'Who hasn't got a bike?' I raise my hand tentatively.

'Are you by yourself?' he asks, giving me a not-so-subtle once-over. Uh oh. Seth better get here quick, otherwise Stefano's going to recruit me as his wing-woman.

'No, my friend is doing the tour too, but he's not here yet.'

Stefano frowns, glances at his watch and grunts. 'He might miss out. We're going soon.'

'It's only ten minutes after eleven,' I protest. 'Can't you wait five more minutes?'

He sighs. 'Si.' But I get the feeling he's annoyed at the delay.

'I'll call him,' I say hastily, getting my mobile out of my shorts pocket. But when I bring up Seth's number, I catch sight of the girl next to me leaning forward over her bike handles and poking her friend on the shoulder. 'Two o'clock,' she says in a whisper loud enough for me to hear. They both turn to look down the street, and I follow their line of sight thinking it must be some Italian hunk they're gawping at. But no, the object of desire is Seth, sauntering towards us looking like he's stepped out of Rolling Stone magazine. I gawp too, unable to help myself. He's dressed in skinny black jeans, a tight black t-shirt, and mirrored sunglasses. His skin glows luminescent like it's been scrubbed with moon rock, and the tattoo I've previously seen peeking out from his collarbone is longer than I thought. Inky words elongate down his exposed upper arm and coil around it like a snake. His hair glints blue-black in the sunlight and is perfectly gelled into spikes. Time seems to slow, the street sounds fade away, and all I hear is the pump of my blood beating in time with his footsteps.

No one is more surprised than me when Seth pauses at the Tourist Point and searches the group of cyclists. Then I realise, *The sex god is looking for me.* He catches my eye and nods, then strolls over, seemingly oblivious to everyone staring. There's a collective silence as if everyone senses there's a famous person in their midst, but they have no idea who the hell he is.

The girls shoot me an envious glance and start googling madly on their phones, probably using the search term "celebrity hot Goth Florence". They won't find him, I know, I've done it myself.

'Hey, you made it,' I reply weakly and give a small welcoming wave. I need to pull myself together, so I can talk to him like a normal person.

Stefano comes out of the shop and makes a beeline for us. 'Is this your friend?' he says to me. He looks Seth over unimpressed. 'You're not exactly dressed for biking. Not like your girlfriend.' He nods at my cream shorts and sky-blue tank top; my hair is up out of the way in a high ponytail. Stefano glances between us curiously. I know Seth and I look like chalk and cheese.

'Oh, he's not my...' I say, but he interjects and asks Seth 'How tall are you?'

'Uh, six-two.'

He turns to me. 'And you?'

'Five-four,' I reply huffily. I'm not liking his attitude. The sunny facade seems to have gone behind a cloud now that Seth's turned up and is giving him hot guy competition.

'I'll see if there are any bikes for you, there may not be since you're so late.' He gives us a pointed look and stomps off.

I pull a face at Seth and he smiles benignly. 'Sorry I'm late, I was writing a song.'

'Oh!' A little thrill goes through me as he gives me a private knowing look. 'A song?'

'Yeah, being around you must've inspired me last night. I stayed up a few more hours writing. Then this morning too. I was getting into it.'

'That's great,' I breathe. I don't know why, but it feels really good to help him with this. Like it's my calling in life to unlock his psyche or something. 'Is it...' *About me?* 'Er, dark?'

Seth's eyes glitter in amusement. 'Not as much as my usual stuff. I don't know if that's a good thing or not.'

'Yikes, you might start churning out happy little ditties because of me,' I quip. 'That would be funny.'

'I think it would be the end of my music career,' Seth says soberly.

'Oh,' I say. 'I should probably think depressing thoughts then, to give you a more mournful vibe.'

'Maybe. I don't want to bring you down though,' he frowns and flexes the fingers on his left hand which is so close to mine it's almost touching. He looks down at my hand, and I sense him wanting some kind of physical connection with me. God, if he starts holding my hand so he can get into "creation mode", I might melt into a puddle.

Thinking about holding hands with Seth and the intensity of his presence, makes me start gabbling. 'Don't worry, I'm a veritable Pollyanna. Nothing usually gets me down. Well, that's not to say I don't feel a bit low from time to time, but it's probably not on your level.' I bite my lip. *Shut up, Jenna, you make it sound like he's related to The Addams Family.*

Seth looks like he's going to say something to refute that, but Stefano comes out of the shop wheeling two e-bikes. I sigh in relief. It looks like we're going to be biking after all. The rest of the group is getting antsy by this stage. People are looking at their watches and grimacing at Seth. I feel like yelling 'Just sod off the lot of you, he was *writing!*'

The e-bike Stefano hands Seth is lime green and large, but it's in proportion to his lanky frame at least. Mine is extremely small. 'Um, are there no larger bikes than this one?' I ask, worried my knees are going to hit my ears.

'No, sorry. We only had a child's bike left. It's either that or nothing.'

'Great,' I mutter, hopping on it. I bet he did it on purpose so I look like a right idiot. Seth gives me a sympathetic look which makes me feel a bit better. At least I'm not going to fall off because the bike is so small, I can put my feet flat on the ground on either side of it.

As we start riding off, I'm more grateful. It's not easy navigating the busy street, even though it's pedestrianised. There are tourists everywhere, and the e-bike brakes aren't too efficient. Several times I pull up short when someone steps in front of me, and I have to squeeze the brake mightily hard before the bike actually halts.

Seth is riding ahead. I grudgingly admit to myself he makes it look effortlessly cool. I get the feeling he'd look cool no matter what he did, even if he was on his knees cleaning a toilet with pink rubber gloves on. The plan, that Stefano outlined briefly, is to ride the short distance to the Duomo, where we'll stop and he'll do a spiel. Then we'll ride another short way to Piazza della Signoria, where we'll have another break and more spiel.

When we reach the Duomo, we park in a semi-circle

around Stefano. He gives us a ten-minute history lesson on its construction and the major architects involved, of course, Mr Bruneschelli's name pops up again. I'm starting to feel like I know him well. Stefano suggests that we definitely do the climb to the top as it's well worth it, though we need to be fit since it's heart-attack inducing. Everyone chuckles as if he's joking. But I shudder, remembering the endless steps, the tight passageways, plus, the gasping and the sweat pouring off me in rivers. The photos I took from the top are doing well on Instagram though and are attracting lots of likes and comments.

Stefano directs our attention towards Giotto's Bell Tower and the group moves off to the side. Seth and I hang out at the back, away from the others. When Stefano starts reeling off dates, I tune out. I tend to find historical facts go in one ear and out the other. Unless it's anchored to something more personal, like the architect having a juicy affair with his friend's wife, it probably won't stick in my head.

Seth nudges his wheel against mine. 'You been up the Duomo yet?'

'Yeah, yesterday.' It seems like yonks ago, getting his text and then careening down the inside of the cupola to make the date in time. I smile to myself wondering what he'd think of that.

'By yourself?' he asks, settling back on his bike seat.

'Oh, no, with my next-door neighbour, Antonella, from

the US. She's learning Italian and has been here for six months. She was pretty knowledgeable, it was like having my own personal tour guide.'

'Anything more than Stefano said?'

Oh, a test, erk.

'Uh, the frescoes on the ceiling inside are pretty cool. It's the Last Judgement. They were designed by, er… some guy called Vasari, but then Zucchini painted most of it.'

Seth raises his eyebrows. 'Zucchini?'

'Yeah.'

'I think you mean Zuccari.'

'Oh, yeah, hah,' I say, mentally kicking myself. Damn, he obviously knows historical shit, I'm not going to fall into that trap again. I might just plead ignorance from now on. 'By the way, did you want some SPF50?' I say to change the subject. 'Your face is going a bit pink.'

He rubs it looking concerned. 'Shit, yeah, I forgot about that, thanks.'

I get the tube out of my cross-body bag and hand it to him. He rubs a dollop on his arms and then massages some into his face. I try not to stare but it's kind of sensuous, especially when he runs his hands down the side of his neck and over his tattoo.

'If we were in Venice, you could wear a mask,' I quip. 'That would stop you from getting a tan and it might stop the adoring fans gawping.'

'Adoring fans?'

I do a side-eye gesture to the two girls from earlier who have given up listening to Stefano and are now unabashedly watching Seth with barely-contained drools. When he looks over, they quickly turn away, and I hear them giggling and whispering.

Seth grunts but I notice he's gone even pinker in the cheeks. 'Yeah, that's annoying.'

'Oh?'

'The music is the only thing that matters,' he explains. 'I'm not interested in the other stuff that goes along with it. They don't even know who I am.'

'You're a mystery wrapped in an enigma,' I say in a joking tone.

'Ah, I need the right person to unwrap me then,' Seth responds seriously. He leaves that comment hanging in the air between us and pushes his sunglasses up on top of his head. His dark eyes search mine and I catch my breath. There's nothing I want more than to unwrap him, lay him out before me and study him minutely like he's some kind of exotic creature until I know every inch of him. He hands me back the sunscreen and our fingers touch briefly sending zooms of fire up my arms. 'You might want some for your nose,' he says 'It's like a little strawberry.'

'Uh huh,' I say dazedly. Some of what I'm thinking about wanting to unwrap him must show on my face because he leans closer. I think he's going to touch me, how or where I don't know, I just sense an urgency in him to be near me. I lean in towards him too, but with both of us sitting on bikes, it's difficult to manoeuvre and our handlebars clash.

'Ahem.'

I look around and Stefano and the rest of the group are eyeballing at us.

'I hate to interrupt, lovebirds,' Stefano says with thinly veiled sarcasm, 'but we're heading to the next stop now. Please, do join us. Andiamo!' he commands to the rest of the group.

Seth flicks his sunglasses back down and gives me a conspiratorial smile. 'Let's go, then'. At this moment, I'd quite happily bike to the moon with him, even if my knees were hitting my ears.

CHAPTER FIFTEEN

We ride in single file, down wide streets lined with shops, dodging pedestrians, dogs and baby prams, until we reach Piazza della Signoria. It's a sizeable open square, dotted with statues and bordered by an assortment of buildings. The largest is made of light-brown stone, with crenellations and a tower poking out the top. I imagine the piazza would be serene early in the morning when there are no tourists. But at this time of day, it's clogged. Our group weaves its way over to a massive statue of a naked man with an impressive physique. I try to avoid eye contact with his privates, but they're kind of in your face.

'David,' says Seth nodding at the statue. 'It's a copy though. Michelangelo's original is in the Accademia. The building behind him is the Palazzo Vecchio, the city hall.'

'Ah.' I'm beginning to think Seth is pretty clued up on Florence. Either he's been here before or he read Wikipedia before he came out.

Stefano tells the group that the seventeen-foot-tall statue is considered the embodiment of male beauty, a Calvin Klein-like model of physical perfection. And that when he was sculpting it, Michelangelo crashed his hammer into the marble shouting 'Why will you not speak?'

I snort, that's funny to imagine. I turn to see if Seth is listening, but he's not there. Where the hell is he? I scan the piazza and spy him riding towards some other statues in a portico a little way off. Should I go after him or stay here?

While I'm deliberating, Stefano wheels his bike over to me with a stern look on his face. 'Where is your boyfriend going? He needs to stay with the group!'

'He's not my…' I repeat, but Stefano seems to have a bone to pick with Seth and interrupts. He checks off on his fingers. 'First, he makes us wait, then, he holds up the group flirting with you, and now, he rides off. He is a troublemaker.'

'Hey, hang on a minute, there's no need for name-calling,' I say indignantly, trying to keep my temper, but this guy's attitude is starting to annoy me. 'If he wants to look at some of the other statues, what's the harm? He'll be back shortly. Just chill. Why can't we see them anyway? Your itinerary is a bit limited if it only includes David.'

Stefano grunts, but doesn't have anything to say to that except, 'We go in cinque minuti.' He holds up five fingers in front of my face in case I don't understand. When he wheels off again, I take a deep breath in and exhale slowly. What the hell is his problem? This is supposed to be a fun bike ride, and he's treating it like a military operation.

Shortly after, Seth pulls up next to me. 'What was all that

about?' He jerks his chin towards Stefano. 'I saw him interrogating you.'

'Oh, it was nothing,' I say, trying to make light of it. 'He just got a bee in his bonnet about you riding off. I told him to take a chill pill.'

Seth purses his lips and frowns at Stefano's rigid back. 'Sorry, I didn't realise I'd be court-marshalled if I nipped off.'

I giggle. 'It is a bit like that. Perhaps he's worried you're going to steal the e-bike and it'll be docked from his wages.'

'Maybe, though, if he wants good reviews, he'd be better off not antagonising us. Thanks for covering for me, corporal.' Seth slips his cool hand into mine and squeezes. I try to brush it off as a friendly gesture, but a host of butterflies soars in my solar plexus. Even my feet and wheels levitate off the ground a little. Then Stefano looks over. His lips twist when he sees us holding hands. 'Andiamo!' he growls.

I think I'd rather stay here and hold hands with Seth under the watchful gaze of beautiful David than carry on. But I squeeze his hand back and say, 'At least I didn't book the full-day tour.'

So we're off again riding towards the Ponte Vecchio. From there we'll cross over the Arno to Oltrano, my neighbourhood. Then we're cycling up to Piazzale Michelangelo for one of the best views of Florence.

As we approach the bridge, the streets become narrower, the stone on the buildings more roughly hewn. A delicious garlicky pepperoni smell wafts from a self-serve pizzeria, and my stomach growls. I feel like stopping and buying a slice, but I don't want to piss off Stefano by lagging behind. Plus, riding and eating pizza might be messy. Seth is ahead of me, looking in the shop windows and doesn't seem too fussed about keeping up with the group. It's funny to me that he's oblivious of the appraising looks he's getting from women, even from some of the men too. He does have a bit of a princely air about him.

We catch up with the rest of the group at the entrance to the Ponte Vecchio, where we find a bottleneck of locals and tourists.

'We'll have to push our bikes across. It's busy this time of day,' Stefano says. He tells us the fourteenth-century bridge covered with shops used to be the domain of blacksmiths and tanners. But they made too much noise and stunk the place out. The Medici duke of the time raised the rent to get rid of them, and they were replaced by jewellers and goldsmiths. As we start crossing the bridge, my eyes widen. I've never seen so many jewellers in a condensed space.

When we reach the middle of the bridge, there are three arches on each side that afford unobstructed views of the Arno. It's a great shot from this angle, so everyone stops to take some photos, including me. Seth seems more interested in what's above.

'What are you looking at?' I ask and he points at six

mullioned windows. 'There's a secret passage that runs right across the top of the bridge. It connects the Palazzo Vecchio, where we just came from, to Pitti Palace.'

Stefano overhears. 'Si, I was going to mention that,' he interjects, 'It's the Corridoio Vasariano, designed by Giorgio Vasari.'

'It was so the Medici family could move between the two palaces in private without being seen by people,' adds Seth.

'Oh, cool!' I say, with interest. 'How long is it?'

'A kilometre,' they say in unison. Stefano frowns viciously at Seth, who stares back with an insolent glint in his eye.

'Stop riling him,' I say when Stefano's gone to round up the others who are taking photos.

'He's the one acting like a supreme arsehole. I'm not sure why, but I think it might be because he set his sights on you. And I'm in the way. I'm getting a distinct whiff of eau de jealousy.'

'He doesn't like me, that's absurd. I've done nothing to make him think I'm one iota interested.'

'Did you look in the mirror before you came out?'

'Er, not really. I just got dressed, put my hair in a ponytail and slapped on some neutral lippy.'

'Your lips definitely aren't neutral.'

I swipe a finger across my bottom lip, and it comes away scarlet. Uh oh, I must have mistaken "Everyday Nude" for "Firebrand Red" since they're both in gold tubes. What is it with me at the moment? I'm either looking like Smurfette or a Vixen. But still, can't a woman wear red lipstick without a guy thinking they're on the pull? Obviously not in Italy.

I dig in my bag for a tissue and scrub at my lips. 'There—is it all gone?'

Seth looks at me critically. 'Almost.' He props his bike wheel against mine and rubs the corner of my mouth gently with his thumb. 'You didn't have to take it off, I kinda liked it.'

Jeez, I can't win.

We wheel our bikes to the end of the bridge, where the crowd dissipates. Hopping back on his black turbo model, Stefano does a chopping motion with his arm to direct us along the river 'Andiamo!'

Obediently, we follow him in single file, but even with the e-bike, my legs are starting to get tired. It's hot and my energy levels are flagging. Seth keeps pace with me, and we drop to the back of the group again. 'Do you think there's gelato at the Michelangelo whatsit place?' I ask wistfully.

'Definitely, let's have a big one,' says Seth. 'I think we deserve it.'

I cheer up at that. The thought of tucking into a big creamy gelato, maybe even three flavours, motivates me to pedal faster. Just then, we pass by Cathy's apartment on the right. I point it out to Seth.

'Hey, that's where I'm staying!'

He gives the building a glance. 'Looks nice. Good view?'

'Yeah, right over the Arno. You'll have to come and see it, and meet Filippo, the pussy cat.'

He nods and doesn't say anything. Yikes, did I just invite Seth to my apartment to meet my pussy? I feel hysterical laughter brewing. *Keep it together, Jenna!* At least until the gelato.

It takes another quarter of an hour to reach Piazzale Michelangelo. Or as I've started thinking of it, *Michelangelo's Pizza.* We ride alongside the river. The road veers off to the right and starts gently climbing up a hill. Luckily, there's a dedicated cycle path because there are cars whizzing down. I'm puffing and blowing, I thought e-bikes were meant to make riding easier? Maybe mine's broken? I fiddle around with the gears and the pedals suddenly move more easily. Oh, I've been riding on a low gear—whoops! The sudden freedom makes me zoom past Seth, who was slightly ahead because I'm so slow.

'Hey, speedy gonzalez.'

'You snooze, you lose,' I call back.

'Lose what?'

'Your place in line for the gelato!'

Seth rises to the challenge, and we end up racing. At one point, he swerves his wheel into mine accidentally on purpose, causing me to wobble precariously, but he quickly grabs my arm to steady me. This playful side of him is fun, and I'm definitely enjoying the touchy-feely side of things, though it's making it difficult to consider him a friend.

We reach the top out of breath to find the panoramic terrace buzzing with tourists.

'I can't see Stefano and the others,' I say to Seth, shading my eyes with my hand.

He shrugs and points. 'If you want gelato, there's a stand with seating on the far side. We'll keep an eye out for them.'

We ride over to the west side of the terrace, and he's right, there's a cute little stand with pink and blue chairs. It's not too busy either. We prop the bikes up near the stand and I plop down into a pink chair.

Seth rests a hand on my shoulder and I look up at him. 'What do you want?'

'I don't mind, just a lot of it.'

'OK, a lot of something coming up.' He smiles down at me. His face is cool, calm and collected, unlike mine, which I'm sure, is a sweaty mess. I fish out another tissue from my bag and wipe my skin. The tissue comes away orange-brown. Gone is my carefully applied foundation over the top of my sunscreen. No lipstick, and now my foundation has come off. I'm doing the make-up-free look for Seth. Lovely.

I put on my sunglasses and look around for Stefano. I spy them over by the balustrade taking photos. It is a stunning view. I can see the Duomo and, in front of it, Giotto's Bell Tower, and some of the other buildings Antonella pointed out but I've forgotten. From this height you get a real sense of how the city is cradled by the hills. Huh, she did tell me Florence was known as 'The Cradle of the Renaissance'. It makes me think of a whole lot of cots with squalling babies in them and I smirk to myself.

Seth breaks my reverie by handing me a large dripping cone of white soft-serve ice cream. 'Sorry, they didn't have the real stuff, but at least it's cold.' He sits down in a blue chair next to me and sips on something that looks like a lime slushy. It's giving his lips a faint greenish glow.

'Thanks. The others are over there.' I nod to the group.

'We could join them. Better here though,' he says grazing his knee against mine.

'Much.' I smile at him. And a better view, I think, since I get to now gaze at Seth's front rather than his back from the bike.

'Your lips are starting to look frog-like,' I comment watching him suck up the slushy at speed. 'What's in that?'

'God knows. Is my tongue green too?' He pokes it out and I crack up.

'It's luminescent!' Then I notice a flash of silver.

'Hey, do you have a tongue stud?'

'Yeah.' He pokes his tongue out further to show me.

I peer at it. 'I didn't notice that before. Did it hurt?'

'Not really.'

'Do you have any others?'

'Perhaps,' he says cryptically, which causes a thrill low down in the pit of my stomach. What else does he have pierced?

As fascinating as Seth's piercings are to contemplate, I see Stefano gesturing to the group to get them moving. I crunch the last of my cone and sigh. 'Looks like we're going back now. God, he's militant. It's amazing he hasn't come marching over here to tell us off.'

Reluctantly, I get up from my chair, put my hands on my hips and arch backwards, feeling my spine and hamstring muscles protest. Seth doesn't seem in any hurry and opens the top of his slushy to drink the melted contents.

'At least it's downhill on the way back,' I remark, hopping back on my bike, wincing as my butt hits the seat.

'Yeah.' He sighs and gets on his bike.

Assuming that Seth is following me, I start pedalling towards Stefano, who is looking around, obviously trying to spot us. He sees me and points sharply over to the others, so I start veering off in that direction. But then he looks past me and his brows knit together. Stopping, I twist my head to see what he's getting agitated about. Oh, crap. Seth is determinedly riding in the opposite direction. Where to, I have no clue. When he reaches the road, he pulls his sunglasses down and looks at me enquiringly. It's like he's issuing a challenge. Stefano or me? I don't hesitate. It was never even a competition as far as I'm concerned. Plus, I'm not leaving my wingman.

I ride in a circle and head back over to Seth. Stefano goes ballistic behind me, yelling loudly 'Ritorno! Ritorno!' and letting loose with a fast stream of Italian that I can't understand. People all around are staring. I don't know where Seth is taking me, but if he's there, I'm in.

When I reach Seth, I look back and Stefano is glaring at us while talking animatedly on his mobile phone. 'We've done it now!' I say, 'He's probably calling the polizia.'

Seth grunts. 'For going left instead of right? This way is much quicker and more scenic. Come on, andiamo!'

CHAPTER SIXTEEN

That lime slushy must've given him a sugar boost because Seth speeds off. I have to pedal furiously to keep up with him. He's right about this route being more scenic. The glimpses of the view between the trees are breathtaking, but the road is narrower and there's no bike path, so I'm too busy navigating the hairpin bends to pay much attention to it. When I catch up with him, he's sitting back on his bike seat, coasting along, with a contented look on his face that I can only assume is because we've gone rogue. *Mr Rulebreaker.*

'You're enjoying leading me astray,' I puff.

He shrugs. 'You could've gone with the others.'

'I didn't want to.'

'How come?'

Because I want to be with you, every minute of every hour, of every day…

'Because it's my credit card I booked the tour under, and if you wreck the bike, they'll charge me for it.'

'Right.' A loaded silence ensues.

'And… And because I wanted to be with you,' I admit,

giving him a sideways glance. He acts like he hasn't heard me, but suddenly, the energy between us feels sexually charged. There's a side street coming up. Seth points to it and says, 'Let's take a short cut.' He swerves abruptly into what turns out to be a shady side alley and jerks to a stop. I have to pull up quickly to avoid crashing into him.

'Hey, what are you...?' Before I can say another word, Seth steadies me with an arm around my waist, tilts my face towards his and kisses me squarely on the lips. I'm so surprised, at first I don't react, then my brain kicks in—*yikes, he's kissing you, do something!*—and I kiss him back tentatively. But his hand is in my hair now and he's not moving away, so my restraint quickly turns to fervour.

Wow, kissing Seth is definitely a sensory experience. I hear a baby crying in the distance, smell the rich scent of frying garlic wafting down from above, feel his soft lips moving gently against mine and taste the sharpness of lime. Then, it's over, and he's standing astride his bike gazing down at me. I blink, feeling dizzy. Did that actually happen? Maybe I dreamed it. I tentatively touch my bottom lip with the tip of my tongue, detecting a faint trace of lime. My heart is racing unnaturally.

'I think this street leads back to the river,' Seth remarks, as if nothing unusual has happened. 'And to your place.'

'My place?' I enquire. Surely *that's* not on the agenda...

'I'm feeling inspired all of a sudden,' he says. 'My head is full of ideas, I need to write them down, otherwise I'm going to lose them.'

'Oh.' I relax.

'For a little bit. Then we'll take the bikes back so Stefano doesn't blow a gasket.'

'OK.' I let out a breath. Not that I'm against anything else happening, I just thought we were supposed to be friends. It feels like we're quickly moving into murky waters.

When we reach the apartment, Seth hikes up the stairs with his bike over one shoulder, and then comes back for mine. 'Better not leave them outside. If they get nicked, we'll be in even more trouble than we already are.' He gives me a mischievous grin. 'Don't look so worried. It'll be fine.'

'Oh no, I'm not worried.' I shrug nonchalantly. *Liar, you hate breaking the rules.* I climb the stairs after him, my legs wobbly and my mind all over the place. I'm still astounded by his kiss; it was pretty spectacular. I wouldn't mind a repeat.

The apartment is warm and heavy with quiet after the chaos of the city streets. There's a faint smell of ripening bananas from the fruit bowl in the kitchen. I help Seth set the bikes on their stands with a clatter. Filippo must hear us because he pads mewing down the hallway.

'Seth—Filippo,' I say.

Seth bends down and picks him up before I can warn him he's not that friendly. But Filippo instantly snuggles into his chest. He does have a way with cats, I think, remembering him holding Persephone. Seth rubs his cheek on Filippo's fur. 'He's all warm.'

'Yeah, the lounge is like a glasshouse at this time of day. He's probably been sunbathing in the chair. I'll open the windows to cool it down. Do you want something to eat?' It's getting on for one o'clock, and I've well and truly digested the ice cream. My stomach is telling me I need food.

'Sure. Is there any paper and a pen?'

'Yes, in the kitchen. Go through to the lounge. I'll be in shortly.'

Seth wanders off, still holding Filippo.

When I come in with a tray of antipasti and glasses of apple juice, plus the paper and a pen, Seth's opened out the bifold windows and set himself up on the shady window seat, long legs stretched out. He's stroking Filippo, who's curled up on his lap half-asleep. A light breeze freshened by the river and peppered with outside scents and sounds floats in.

'You're a cat charmer, he's never that comfortable with me,' I murmur.

'He says all you feed him is fish.'

I jerk the tray in surprise and apple juice sloshes in the glasses. That's weird. How would Seth know that's all Filippo eats? 'Don't tell me you can talk to animals like Dr Doolittle,' I say nervously.

'No, I can smell it on him. He must've eaten some.'

'Oh.' I relax. Silly Jenna, just because you think Seth's the bee's knees, don't go giving him higher powers as well!

'Is there room up there for me?'

'Yes.' He hands me Filippo, and I deposit him on an armchair. Sorry, buddy, my turn. Seth shifts over, so I hop up and sit leaning against the opposite wall with my shorter legs stretched out beside his. The tray of snacks and drinks rests on our laps. It's a good arrangement. Seth writes while I steadily munch on bread and pesto, cheese, grapes and olives. 'Do you want anything? I'm hogging this.'

'Maybe some olives.' He takes a couple from the pot and continues writing, his hand dropping to rest lightly on my bare ankle above my sandshoe. A shiver goes through me. Seth seems oblivious though. I try to ignore it, but I can't help flinching a little, because every now and again he presses down slightly on my skin with his fingers which sends tingles up my calf. Eventually, he notices. 'Sorry. I can stop if it's annoying. It just helps me focus. You're a grounding presence.'

'It's fine,' I say. 'I'm glad you're being... creative.' Even if he was sticking needles in me, I think I'd endure it (thank God I shaved my legs this morning!). To pass the time, I take out my phone to see if I've got any messages. Oh yes, one sent an hour ago from Violet: *What are you doing?*

Typical Violet. There's no chatty preamble like, 'Hi, just checking in, how's Florence?' but a random question as if I'm in London. I sneak a peek at Seth, he's in a world of his own. Surely it's OK if I tell my friend he's here with me? I can't resist, I know she's going to freak out. Feeling incredibly naughty, I type:

Me
Just with Seth. We've been on a bike tour.

I watch the screen, waiting for it.

Violet
Seth Carver?

Me
Yes.

Violet
Very funny.

Me
He's in Florence. We're hanging out.

There's a ten-second interval... Then my screen explodes.

Violet
OMG
Seriously?

WTF
No way!

Yikes, luckily, I have my phone on silent mode. I angle it towards me, so Seth can't see the commotion.

Me
Calm down V.

Violet
This has to be a joke!

Me
No joke.

Violet
I need proof. Send a photo.

Shit. I'm not sure I want to do that. I discreetly click my camera open and discover Seth is framed perfectly. My heart jolts seeing him through the lens. His jet-black hair is slightly mussed, and he's chewing thoughtfully on an olive. His dark eyes are narrowed with studied intensity as he writes.

Wow, he's in the flow, I think. The sleeve of his t-shirt has ruched up his arm so his snaking word tattoo is on full display. Despite his father's plea not to get a tan, his skin seems less pale, more of a healthy cream. He's so beautiful my chest squeezes. I can hardly believe I'm sitting here with him.

What did I do to deserve the undivided attention of this man-god? What's so special about me?

I might wake up any minute and find myself on Violet's couch, and discover this was all a dream, based on wishful thinking, and nothing more. Maybe I need proof just as much as she does, so I can look back when I'm old and say, 'See it did happen. I was in Florence with Seth Carver and this was the day he kissed me and wrote a hit single.'

My thumb hovers over the white button, and I almost take the shot, but something stops me. Sending Violet a photo of him isn't exactly posting it on social media, but it still feels like an invasion of privacy. I tilt the camera down from his face and take a photo of his slender hand resting on my leg instead. It's less intrusive and also shows I'm not making it up. Though, I guess it could be anyone's.

I consider adding text saying "Seth's hand" and an arrow pointing to it, but I figure she'll believe me since I'm not in the habit of telling lies.

Me
Here you go. You can't tell anyone.
I mean it Violet, NO ONE!

Violet
OMG he's actually touching you!!!

Are you together?

Me
I can't say anything else. I have to go.

I can feel Seth's eyes on me, and I quickly put my phone aside. 'You've been doing a lot of typing over there,' he says, sounding curious.

'Yes, just a friend,' I say, trying not to feel guilty. 'I haven't spoken to her since I left. She was wondering how I was getting on. Have you finished? We need to take the bikes back soon.'

'Nearly. I want your opinion when it's done.'

'Oh.' I let out a breath. 'Are you sure? I'm not really the target audience remember.'

'I trust your judgement.'

'I don't know…' What if I say the wrong thing and Seth bins what could've been a massive hit? I'll go down in history as the girl who stymied Sublime Misery.

Seth smiles reassuringly. 'Don't overthink it, Jenna. Just say how you feel. There's no right or wrong answer.'

Sure, no pressure.

An image of myself, wrapped in a towel, furtively pulling his journal from under his pillow flashes into my mind. I can't help giggling.

'What?'

'I was remembering being in your studio and feeling shit-scared you were going to catch me.'

He grips my ankle softly. 'I wouldn't have been angry.'

'No?'

'Maybe surprised, but not angry. I wanted to see you again.'

'You did?' That's the first time he's actually said that. So it wasn't just me.

'I thought we had a connection. At dinner. Didn't you feel it?'

'Yes, I… I felt something. I wanted to see you again too. I thought you might come up to the house. Why didn't you?' This comes out sounding a bit petulant, but I still remember the frustration of waiting.

'I, ah… Things were complicated at that particular point in time.' He averts his eyes and seems flustered. Oh. Right. Of course, he would have someone. He's freaking gorgeous. 'A girlfriend,' I say glumly.

'I wouldn't call her that.'

'What would you call her?'

'I'm not sure.'

'I need to know if you're involved with someone. You can't kiss me in an alleyway and then drop the "oh, by the way, I've got a girlfriend" bomb, that's shitty,' I say more staunchly than I feel. My stomach is roiling, and I think I might be sick. That'll teach me for hoovering up the antipasti.

Seth removes his hand from my leg and rubs the back of his neck with a pained look on his face. 'That's fair. But I wouldn't be here with you now if I had a girlfriend. Whatever it was it's over. It was never really on in my opinion, but she had other ideas.'

I feel slightly less queasy hearing this. She's probably some Goth floozy trying to get her claws into him.

'It's my fault. I shouldn't have assumed… that this was anything… It's just business.'

Seth shrugs, but I need to know what's going on.

'Well, isn't it?'

His mouth quirks at my insistence.

'I do need to write these songs, but surely, you know it's more than that? I don't go around kissing people randomly.' I hold my breath staring at him. 'I… I couldn't help it,' he continues, avoiding my eyes and gazing down at the pad. 'I know I made it sound like my coming here was all about the band, but it's not. There's something else going on…'

He starts doodling on the pad studiously as if he knows he's just revealed too much, and he has. Seth Carver has pretty much admitted he's into me! The earth tilts on its axis. I feel I should respond with something meaningful, but I'm a little shell-shocked.

'Oh,' I say faintly. 'But what about all that stuff about the contract and the NDA…?'

He gives me a sheepish grin. 'I had to say something to

make it sound official, so you didn't think I was a psycho for wanting to hang out with you. I was worried you might go back to your apartment, think about it, and get scared off.'

'I see.' *I knew it!* I just didn't want to let myself believe it in case my judgement was warped. This is a good lesson to learn. I need to trust my instincts more and not think I'm a thicko numbskull when it comes to men.

CHAPTER SEVENTEEN

After Seth's clarification that there are romantic feelings on his side, I feel a lot better. So much better, that I want to shout it to the world, but I know I can't tell anyone. I sit there and just repeat in my head, *'He feels the same, oh my God!'* Then I clutch myself inwardly in glee.

Everything now takes on a new meaning—'Let's take the bikes back and grab an aperitivo'—I translate as: 'I want to snog you over an Aperol Spritz'.

'That sounds great,' I say breathlessly. 'Just give me ten minutes to get changed.'

'OK. I'll write some more.'

I skip off to the bedroom and rummage wildly through my clothes, flinging everything out of my suitcase and onto the bed. I'm desperate to nail the "casually sexy but haven't made any effort" look. I wish I had some clear instructions on how exactly to pull that off.

I decide on the short black leather skirt of Antonella's that I wore last night, red lacy underwear, a red crop top and strappy low-heeled sandals. I iron the frizz out of my hair, do my eye makeup and add a generous application of Firebrand

Red lipstick since Seth said he liked it.

When I walk back into the room, he runs his eyes over me slowly, 'You look nice.'

Jenna's translation, based on the new information about Seth's feelings—*you look fucking hot*. I smile at him, 'So do you.'

'I haven't done anything.' He stretches and rakes a hand through his hair so it sticks up in soft sexy spikes. Desire blossoms in my midriff and spirals down to my groin. I feel like pulling him into the bedroom right now, stuff the aperitivo. *Cool your jets.*

'Trust me, you're good,' I tell him, swallowing. 'I'll just sort out the cat, then we can go.'

'OK.'

I feed Filippo, donning rubber gloves so I don't get stinky fish all over my hands. That would definitely not be passion-inducing.

When we get outside, I realise the tight skirt I'm wearing, whilst fine for walking around and sitting in a restaurant, isn't practical for riding a bike. But I don't want to wear shorts—so I hitch it up and hope for the best. I follow Seth back along the road to the Ponte Vecchio, but I notice a few guys gawking at the indecent amount of leg I'm showing. I try to ignore them, but as we approach the bridge, a group of men hanging out on the corner stare openly. Then one of them wolf-whistles. Shit. Seth twists his head and calls back.

'What are you doing? We seem to be attracting a lot of male attention.'

'Er, nothing!' I try to yank my skirt down with one hand, hoping to God I haven't been flashing my red lacy knickers while attempting to steer the bike with the other.

'Do you want to go in front?'

'No! It's fine. Just keep riding.' I'm not sure what's worse, flashing strangers or having Seth stare at my ass.

The closer we get to the Tourist Point, the more nervous I become. We're so late, the tour finished hours ago. Stefano is going to be livid. To my relief, Seth says he'll deal with it and goes into the shop while I hang out by the bikes, trying not to make eye contact with any men passing by. I listen for yelling, but nothing happens. Huh, maybe Stefano went home or is scouring the streets looking for us with the police in tow.

When Seth comes strolling out of the shop with Stefano behind him, I cringe and ready myself for an ear bashing. But Stefano checks both bikes, nods at Seth, blatantly ignores me, and wheels them inside.

My mouth drops open. 'Is that it? No third degree?'

Seth shrugs. 'He started going off as soon as he saw me, but I said I'd pay him for the extra hours. He also wanted a fifty euro tip for the stress and angst we caused. So, I gave it to him.'

'Fifty euros!' I say shocked.

'It was worth it. I got to write a song and spend time with

you, so I had a pretty good afternoon.'

'But... He's ripping you off!'

Seth laces his fingers through mine. 'Come on, let's find somewhere to eat. I'm starving. What about pizza?' He gently guides me away as if he can sense I'm in combat mode. I take a deep breath as his touch calms me down.

'OK, pizza sounds good.'

If someone told me a week ago that I'd be strolling around Florence holding hands with Seth Carver, I wouldn't have believed them. I have to keep squeezing his hand to make sure it's really happening. He probably thinks I'm crazy, but he squeezes mine back anyway. We veer off down a narrow street, away from the hustle of tourists around the Duomo, and not long after, we come across a sidewalk restaurant. A suit of armour stands erect by the entrance, holding a shield and a sword. It guards a chalkboard menu that's almost as tall as I am.

'We're good for pizza here,' remarks Seth after giving it a cursory glance. 'This OK?'

'Fine by me.' I'm happy not to walk too far, it's humid and my sweaty thighs are starting to chafe. An amiable waiter comes out to seat us and takes our drinks order. It's still early by Italian standards, so we have the outside area under the umbrella to ourselves apart from a middle-aged couple who're eating bruschetta and drinking wine. They don't look Italian.

'This is on me, by the way, since you paid for the bike tour,' Seth says.

'What? No, you just handed over fifty euros to Stefano,' I reply with a frown.

'I'm sure I can manage another twenty for pizza and drinks. It's fine,' Seth says, putting his sunglasses on top of his head. A trio of young tanned Italian women laden with designer shopping bags happen to walk past. They all do a double take when they catch sight of him. I sigh to myself. Seth has the kind of good looks and presence that don't blend into a crowd. I'm going to have to get used to it.

I ignore them and say 'OK, well, I'll buy us gelato afterwards then.'

'Deal. You're quite into gelato, aren't you? Have you tried zuppa inglese?'

'No, only the chocolate chip one, sesame, blueberry, caramel cookie, raspberry and pistachio,' I say checking them off on my fingers.

Seth stares at me. 'You got all those in one cup?'

'Yeah. Most of it is still in the freezer. My eyes were bigger than my stomach.'

'Perhaps we should just go back to yours, since you bought the whole shop.'

I poke my tongue out at him. A hot dart of excitement shoots through me—he wants to hang out after. A pleasant vision of me licking gelato off Seth's naked chest forms in my mind. Hmm, maybe not the blueberry. The sesame might be safer. Seth is saying something, so I drag my attention back to him.

'Sorry?'

'I said that our biking really inspired me. Maybe we could try another activity...'

'Oh, sure, like what?'

'Perhaps a cooking class? Could be fun.'

'I'm up for that. I like cooking.'

'Yeah, I enjoyed your lamb rissoles.' He presses his knee against mine under the table, a private reminder.

'Though you didn't eat all your peas,' I admonish. 'What was that? A secret three-pea code?'

Seth looks embarrassed and flips his sunglasses down over his eyes. 'It was nothing.'

'Come on, what did it mean? I was trying to figure it out, but I didn't get anywhere.'

He purses his lips, and I get a sense of what he must've been like as a kid; offbeat, stubborn, hard to understand, but wanting to be understood all the same.

'That's OK. You don't have to tell me,' I say softly.

'I can't talk about it here,' he replies, 'But I'll explain... at some point.' I can see the faint glimmer of his eyes watching me from behind his sunglasses and I flush. I'm even more intrigued now, is it some kind of kinky sexual thing... involving vegetables?

'Allora,' interrupts the waiter, setting down a basket of breadsticks, an Aperol Spritz for me and a Stella Artois for Seth. He takes out a notepad from his apron and a pencil from behind his ear. 'Do you know what you want?'

'Uh…' I haven't even looked at the menu, I'm all hot and bothered after our conversation. 'Could I have a big glass of ice water, please? I'm not sure what pizza to get. Seth, you choose.'

'Hmm, I think the large Inferno pizza to share.'

The waiter raises his eyebrows. 'Just to warn you, it's spicy.'

Seth winks at me. 'We like it hot.' Oh, lordy.

While we wait for the pizza, Seth challenges me to a mini sword fight with a breadstick. The first to break the other person's wins. He's quick with his reflexes, but I'm quicker. I whack his stick with gusto, breaking off the top half, which then flies into the street. 'Yesss, score!' I cry, earning disapproving looks from the middle-aged couple. I don't care. We're having fun.

'Remind me not to get into a battle with you with a real sword,' says Seth, nibbling on what's left of his breadstick.

'I'm a merciful opponent. I wouldn't chop off your head or anything,' I reply. 'I'd just leave my mark so you know not to mess with me in the future.'

'What would that involve?'

'Maybe cutting your shirt off,' I say, warming to the

subject. 'And your trousers.'

Seth's lips twitch. 'I'd be impressed if your superior swordsmanship could manage that. What would you do with me next?'

I can think of quite a few things, but I'm saved from having to answer by the arrival of our sausage pizza, swathed in mounds of gooey mozzarella and melted cheese. Oh good, I'm so hungry I could eat the entire thing. I take a large bite and instantly regret it. My mouth explodes into a fiery hell. 'Oh my God,' I gasp. I like spicy food, but this is unbelievably hot, like it's been doused in ghost chillis. Hunger wins out over pain and I manage to finish my slice, though tears are spouting from my eyes.

'Next time I'm choosing the pizza!' I chug down a few gulps of iced water, which eases the burning a little, even though my tongue still feels like it's been dipped in molten lava.

'It's not that bad,' Seth mumbles, chewing on his second slice, but for once he's sweating and he keeps swiping his face with a napkin. He reaches over and downs the last of my water.

'Hey!'

'I'll get some more.' He goes over to the stand near the entranceway that has extra cutlery, napkins and condiments, and brings back an entire jug of ice water and a spare glass. He takes a bite from his third slice and puffs out his cheeks:

'Fuuuuck, that's hot!' I start laughing but then wince as my lips smart from the chilli. I pull some cheese off the top and avoid the sausage. Turns out, that's just as bad, and I'm inflicted with more pain.

'Maybe we should feed the rest to a passing dog,' I say.

'I think it might kill it.'

'Rooo-rooo-rooo.' I do an imitation of a dog howling on its last legs with my head on the side and tongue hanging out but then start coughing. Seth pats my hand. 'We ate half of it at least. Shall I order something else?'

'I think my tastebuds have been seared off. But go ahead if you're still hungry.'

'I'm done. Maybe… gelato at yours to recover?' He says it casually, but there's definitely an underlying meaning. My face goes an even deeper shade of pink. I pour myself another glass of water, trying not to react, but my hand shakes. 'Sure,' I say, equally as casual. 'You can have the blueberry.'

He goes inside to pay the bill, and I sip water to cool the sudden heat that has nothing to do with the scorching pizza. My mind is racing. The bedroom is a mess. There are clothes all over the bed and the floor. I'm going to have to do a whip round and make it presentable. Also, will we be going all the way? I don't have condoms, does he? Should I suggest stopping by a chemist on the way back? Or will that look too obvious? Damn, why didn't I stock up! Should I even be having sex with him? Do we need to hang out more first? I'm not sure what to do.

'Everything OK? You're miles away.' Seth is looking down at me enquiringly.

'Yes, fine.' *Just the usual condom conundrum.*

Seth holds out his hand and pulls me up towards him, so I'm face to chest. He bends down and kisses me.

'Mmm, you taste like chilli and sunshine,' he says, and I melt into him like mozzarella, wanting more. Suddenly, there are no pressing questions that need to be answered. I trust him, I want to be with him. We can figure things out as we go.

CHAPTER EIGHTEEN

It's dusk, and the street lights are winking on as we stroll back to the apartment hand in hand and, strangely for us, in complete silence. I'm not sure what's going through Seth's mind, but I'm trying not to imagine how this evening is going to pan out. He keeps squeezing my hand as if to reassure me and say, 'Don't overthink it'.

Crossing Ponte Vecchio with its shuttered shop fronts, he leads me through a gaggle of tourists, turning back and flashing a quick smile; ignoring all the women gawking at him. My heart flutters. He makes me feel like I'm the only girl in the world, which is something I'm not used to. For the five years I was with Gabe, he never made me feel this way. The loss was more a readjustment of routine rather than a healing of the heart.

We turn into Via de' Bardi and are almost at the apartment door when Seth stops in his tracks. 'Do you hear that?'

'No, what?'

'Music.' He swivels his head like a satellite dish trying to pick up where the sound is coming from. He heads off down a side street, which branches off into another narrower alleyway. I trail after him. Seth pauses outside a carved wooden door, listening. 'It's in there.' I'm starting to hear it now. A dull thumping. 'It's probably just someone having a party. Let's go and have some *gelato*,' I say meaningfully, attempting to get him back on track.

The door opens and a suave businessman with slicked back hair, wearing a designer suit slips out, walks off. The music briefly intensifies in his wake, a steady pulsing bass overlaid with a mournful synth that makes me feel nostalgic and I don't even know what for. It obviously appeals to Seth though because he edges closer to the door.

'It's a nightclub. Let's go in,' he says determinedly.

'I'm not dressed for night-clubbing.'

'You look great. We'll just stay for a bit, have one drink. Listen to the music.'

I'm not really a nightclub kind of person, but Seth looks so animated, I don't have the heart to say no.

'OK, just for a bit,' I say, but Seth's already opened the door and gone in. I follow behind and find myself in a dimly lit foyer with a black-and-white tiled floor. There are purple crushed velvet curtains draped around the walls, a fake candelabra floor lamp and an archway covered by a black curtain, behind which I assume is the nightclub. The eerie-sounding music is coming from there anyway. It's sort of weird, almost spooky. But as Seth said, it's just for one drink.

We're about to go through the curtain when a bouncer

materialises, holding out his arm to stop us. I'm guessing he's a bouncer, he has that look about him. Thickset, bald and wearing an earpiece. Either that or he works for the mafia. He looks me over and says something in Italian to Seth.

'Si,' Seth says and rattles off a reply gesturing at me. His Italian is pretty good, I think impressed. Better than mine anyway.

The bouncer's forehead corrugates, and he shakes his head.

'What's the problem?' I ask Seth.

'He doesn't think you're over twenty-one.'

'What?' I snort. 'Tell him I'm twenty-six.'

'I did, he doesn't believe me. Have you got any ID?'

I rummage in my purse and produce a dog-eared library card which has my photo and date of birth on it. It looks fake, but it's the best I can do. The bouncer peers at it, looks at me, scrutinises it again and says 'OK' and hands it back.

Seth's face relaxes. 'Good job, Jenna.'

'I didn't think they'd be this strict at a nightclub,' I mutter, stuffing it in my purse. 'And how do you know my age anyway?'

'I asked India.'

'Oh.'

The bouncer says, 'Un momento', and reaches into a bum bag he has slung around his hips. He slips Seth something that looks suspiciously like condoms, winks and smiles lasciviously at us. 'Have fun,' he says in heavily accented English.

Seth quirks an eyebrow at me, but then quickly pockets them and ducks through the curtain. I follow, my face flaming. What is this place? I'm starting to get suspicious.

On the other side of the curtain is another dimly lit room, with more velvet curtains and fake candelabras. A blue-lit bar runs down the left-hand side. The room is full of people dancing. The music is even louder here. It's like an entity, the driving bass reverberates through the walls, the floor, I even feel it in my groin, like someone's tickling me with a feather duster.

Seth makes a beeline for the bar, and I notice, as my eyes adjust to the darkness, that there are a heck of a lot of scantily clad women. Some of them look like they're only wearing lingerie. Come to think of it, the men aren't wearing much either. Most of them are shirtless. My eyes widen as a man unhooks a women's bra, and puts it on his head like a hat. She laughs, then twirls and shakes her boobs at him. Then leads him off to one of the alcoves placed around the wall, which all have dark curtains. I gulp. Fuck—my suspicions are starting to be confirmed. I barrel after Seth trying not to see anything I shouldn't. 'Seth!' I say loudly when I reach the bar. 'We have to leave!'

'Huh?' he says distractedly, looking around for the barman. 'We just got here. What shall we get, cocktails?'

I nod for the sake of it and sit next to him on a bar stool. I beckon him to lean in so he can hear me over the music and put my mouth to his ear. 'This. Is. A. Sex. Club.'

He draws back and looks at me, then leans in so I can hear. 'I don't think so,' he replies.

'Then why did the bouncer give you condoms?'

Seth shrugs. 'I don't know. Compliments of the club, perhaps?'

Just as I open my mouth to tell him about the topless woman and the alcoves, he glances over my shoulder and makes a choking sound.

'What?' I turn my head so I can see what he's looking at, but he places his hand on the side of my cheek.

'Don't look!' he says, staring wide-eyed at whatever's going on.

'Why not? You are.'

'You're my muse. I need your mind pure.'

'A bit late for that,' I scoff. 'If you wanted me to think pure thoughts, you shouldn't have brought me to a sex club.'

'I'm still not convinced it's a...' but a breathy moan sounds from behind me and Seth says quickly, 'Maybe we should move barstools.'

'I'm quite happy where we are, thanks,' I say. Well, he's the one who wanted to come in here, besides, I've never seen him look so unnerved before. It's kind of funny. A barman takes Seth's order, and starts pouring out a couple of shots.

I'm not exactly sure what changed his mind, but he seems to have decided to make it a really quick drink.

Perhaps it's whatever is happening behind me, as it appears to be racking up a notch. I can hear a guy saying something in Italian. By the way the woman groans, it must be something sexual. Seth's eyebrows are nearly touching his spiky fringe which has flopped down over his forehead. The look on his face is priceless.

'What did he say?' I ask curiously.

'I can't tell you. It's filthy.' Is Seth Carver actually blushing?

'Oh, go on.'

He sighs. 'I want to make you come like a rhinoceros.'

I let out a large snort, possibly a little like said rhinoceros. 'How romantic!'

'Yeah, not a lot of thought went into it.'

'What would you do?' I ask curiously.

He looks at me blankly.

'To get someone in the mood, I mean.'

'Not say *that*.'

'Si, oh, si amore!' cries a woman behind me.

Seth silently takes my hand.

'Si, si, si… siiiiii!'

Seth grips my hand tighter with each "si" until it dies down.

I can't help laughing at his expression, he looks like a

startled rabbit. 'You were saying?'

'Oh, yes, well.' He coughs. 'For a start, I wouldn't take her to a sex club.' Whatever just happened behind me seems to have finally convinced him it is one.

'No?'

'Definitely not. There would be good red wine, music playing...'

'One of your own songs?'

'I'm not that egotistical. But something mood-inducing.' He trails his fingers down the side of my face and leans closer. 'Maybe I'd whisper something like... "You're hotter than chilli pizza". Then kiss her lips gently and see how receptive she was to that. Then take it from there.' He's looking at my mouth intently as he says this, and I swallow hard, remembering the chilli-infused kiss from dinner.

'It's not bad,' I reply. 'It may need work. No girl really wants to be compared to chilli pizza.'

'Hmm, true. What about... "I want to get naked with you and roll around on my sheepskin rug",' he murmurs in my ear. I gulp as he kisses the spot between my jaw and my neck.

'That would probably do it,' I say weakly. Oh God.

Seth seems to be teasing me about the rug. But I'm getting extremely agitated because I've seen his sheepskin rug, and I now have a vivid picture of us rolling around on it.

Him whispering in my ear about getting naked and the sexy time happening around us is turning me on considerably.

Then the music changes and the reverberations get even more intense, going straight up the bar stool to my groin. I shift my butt cheeks trying to stop the vibration, but it's pleasurable whichever way I sit, and I start seeing stars, *Oh God, please no, don't let me come. Not in front of Seth Carver.*

'Jenna...' Seth looks deep into my eyes, and it tips me over the edge. I manage to keep my expression neutral, but I tense and shudder a little from the sudden jolt of pleasure, and he notices.

'Did you just...?'

'No!' I look away, my face flaming. *Shit, how bloody embarrassing.*

'Wow. You did.' He sounds awestruck.

'Let's get out of here.' I finish what's left of my shot, hop down off the vibrating bar stool and push my way through the writhing semi-naked bodies. How absolutely mortifying. I am never going to be able to hang out with Seth again. Now he knows I find him so attractive, that he can make me orgasm simply by looking at me.

But he grabs my shoulder before I can reach the door and turns me to face him. We stare at each other like a couple of statues in the midst of a thronging piazza.

'Dance?' he mouths.

'Um...' It's a better alternative than going out onto the street and having to make small talk after what just happened. But it's Dirty Dancing on steroids around us. Are we going to do that?

'OK,' I mouth back uncertainly.

He hooks my arms around his neck and his hands circle my waist. 'Just relax, we'll do our own thing,' he says in my ear and, bizarrely, we sway to the music like we're at a school prom while everyone gyrates around us. To be honest, the way Seth makes me feel, I'm kind of glad that I already came, otherwise I might be dragging him to an alcove and humping him.

CHAPTER NINETEEN

After leaving the club, Seth walks me back to the apartment. There's an awkward silence, mostly on my part. I'm still thoroughly embarrassed. At the entranceway, he looks as if he wants to say something, but I avoid his eyes, so he kisses my hand, says, 'Goodnight' and melts away into the darkness.

I pelt up the stairs and don't even bother turning on the lights when I get inside, seeking the solace of my bedroom. I shove all my clothes off the bed and dive under the duvet hoping to fall into dreamless oblivion.

An hour later, I'm still lying there, catatonic with shame. I keep replaying the scene from the club in my mind (especially Seth's surprised face when he realised what had happened). Each time it brings on a fresh bout of despair. It was nice of him to ask me to dance as a distraction, but now I'm reliving the whole thing and it's excruciating. I'm going to have to try and forget about it somehow.

My phone buzzes from my handbag, and groggily, I get out of bed to retrieve it. I'm expecting it to be Violet, but my heart jolts when I see who it's from.

Seth
Don't be embarrassed.

Erk, sometimes he's too good at sensing how I feel. I crawl
back under the duvet with my phone, unsure what to say. Oh,
well, there's no point lying.

Me
I really am though.

After a short wait I get:

Seth
I came back here and couldn't stop fantasizing about you.
So I had a wank in the shower.

I suck in my breath and blink rapidly.

Me
Seriously? Are you joking?

Seth
Nope, 100% truth.
Just wanted to share something embarrassing to make you
feel better. Do you feel better?

Strangely enough, I do.

Me
LOL yes!

Seth
Good. And sorry about dragging you to that club, not one of my finest moments.

Me
That's OK x

Seth
If you're still up for it, I booked us into the cooking class for tomorrow at 10. Meet me at Ponte alla Carraia on your side of the river at 9.45?

Me
Yes, I'm still keen.
OK, see u then x

Seth
Sweet dreams xxx

Thank God, everything is still OK. I sit up and turn on the bedside light. But... OMG. I look at Seth's message and laugh. Holy hell, I can't believe he sent that! Yet, it was exactly the right thing to say. Otherwise, I would've been on the backfoot, and knowing me, I would've let it fester until it ruined things. Seth not only brought it up, he chose to embarrass himself so things were equal between us. It's so freaking lovely, and so warped at the same time, that it brings tears to my eyes. I didn't think I could like him more, but I do. I like him fifty times more. And the fact that he was fantasizing about me while jerking off in the shower... Well, that is pretty hot...

All things considered, I have a decent night's sleep, only waking briefly in the early hours when Filippo decides to jump on the bed. He pads around looking for a comfy spot, but soon settles down and his purring sends me drifting off again. The next morning, I wake and immediately get excited about the cooking class, and even more about seeing Seth.

I feel so much better having cleared the air and knowing he's still into me. It's like we have a secret now. Though, somehow, I think Seth has a lot of those, and if I want to really know him, I'm going to have to unlock quite a few doors.

It's only a ten-minute walk to the bridge where I'm meeting him, so I don't have to rush. There's hardly anyone around. I stroll along in the sunshine beside the river enjoying the beautiful still morning. The deep blue cloudless sky promises another hot day and the Arno is like glass with the buildings on the opposite bank and the arches of the bridge mirrored in the water. I lean over the edge of the wall and get a perfect shot. One for Instagram later, I think, and I can take some of whatever we're cooking.

As I approach the bridge, I spot Seth propped against the low wall, arms crossed and face tilted up to the sun with his eyes closed. He's dressed in black as per usual, and looks so gorgeous that my gut hops nervously. Is this going to be weird?

'Hey,' I say.

He opens his eyes, smiles at me and says 'Morning, beautiful.'

'Hah,' I reply to brush off the compliment as my insides do a slow somersault. He gives me a once-over and I admit I did dress up a bit in an attempt to look casually stylish without trying. I put on the cream shorts I had on yesterday and a blue-and-white striped shirt with the sleeves rolled up. My hair is in its usual daytime ponytail, but I've added some gold ear studs.

'I like these.' He peers at my earlobes. 'What are they?'

I sidle closer so he can get a better look. 'Seahorses.'

'Cute.'

By this time, I'm inches away, so it feels natural that he draws me in for a hug. All my nervousness disappears as I hook my arms around his neck. Now I see why he wanted to meet earlier.

'Mmm, you smell nice,' I remark, snuggling into him,

trying to get as close as possible. 'Like peaches.' The ends of his hair feel slightly damp against my cheek.

'Yeah, I had another long shower this morning, used all the shower gel.'

'Oh, er, great,' I mumble, blushing.

There's a tense silence, and then he laughs and pokes me gently in the ribs. 'I'm joking,' he says, and I giggle in relief.

'Maybe we shouldn't talk about showers.'

'Or we could just have one… together.'

I shiver. 'Possibly.'

I'm trying to play a little hard to get but truthfully, I'm up for anything he suggests, and he probably knows it. Seth kisses down the side of my cheek, and when he heads towards my mouth, I don't resist. Engaged in a liplock with Seth on the bank of the Arno, with a beautiful view and his arms around me, I'm in heaven. Reluctantly, I break away, worried we're going to be late. 'Shouldn't we get going?'

'Or… We could just stay here and snog,' he murmurs, pulling me back in for another kiss, and I don't complain. Now we've started, it's kind of difficult to stop. Also, he's a great kisser. But I do want to do the class… I break away again feeling heady and breathless.

'But you booked it specially.'

'True.' Seth sighs, releasing me. 'OK, let's go and maka da pasta.'

Why do I get the feeling he's not going to be concentrating

much on cooking?

Not long after, I'm wearing a black apron and busy chopping tomatoes on a trestle table in an industrial-style kitchen. Seth is opposite me, on his own station. There are six other people positioned down the length of the table doing the same. The introductions were brief, but I was amused that there are two Donna's, a Diane, a Deborah and a Dana, all related and all from Florida. There's also Danita, but she's unrelated.

Over the next hour, we'll be creating handmade ravioli and tortelli with different sauces and accompaniments. Since Seth booked the VIP option, we also get two free bottles of wine and some complimentary Italian chocolate. I smile at him as I work, and he grins back. He's chopping haphazardly but with enthusiasm, and he's already got a fan in the female cooking instructor, Sofia. She's a mother-earth type with large breasts, generous hips, dyed blonde hair twisted up in a chignon, and trendy tortoiseshell cat-eye glasses. Every so often, she sashays over to give him special attention and chatters away in Italian, delighted he can understand it.

'She says I remind her of her son,' Seth mutters to me when she's out of earshot after the fifth time she's come over. Hmm, the way she's eyeing him isn't exactly motherly, it's more cougarly as far as I'm concerned, but I'm not too bothered. Not after the Arno kissing session, which I've tucked away in a special corner of my mind to daydream about later.

When we're all crushing garlic, she comes over once again and says something to Seth, glancing at me. He shakes his head and replies briefly. She raises her eyebrows, scrutinises me intently and purses her lips. 'What was that about?' I enquire when she's taken off again.

'She asked if you were my sister.'

'Oh. Did you set her straight?'

'Yeah, I said you were my girlfriend.'

I press down hard on my large bulb and bits of crushed garlic squirt out everywhere.

'I hope that was OK?' he enquires when I don't say anything.

It's difficult for me to speak, so I just nod and blush madly, infused in happiness and garlic juice. Seth Carver's girlfriend!

He keeps peeking glances at me, to make sure I really am OK, but by the way I'm now tearing into a bunch of spinach with wild abandon and tossing it joyously into a bowl, I think it's pretty safe to say I'm more than alright with it. Phwoar, I'm so bloody lucky! I want to fling myself on him and hug him, then rip off his clothes. But I manage to control myself and focus my energy on ripping open a packet of ricotta instead.

After we've prepared the fillings, we get to pair up. There are only four pasta makers and, since we're beginners, it's easier to feed the dough through the machine if you have help. I thought we might have to make the dough, but Sofia brings out some already prepared, so all we have to do is roll it through five times on the widest setting, folding it up each time like a letter, and then two times on the narrower setting.

Still trying to adjust to the idea of being Seth's girlfriend, I keep spacing out and forget to count. Seth seems to be in a similar mood, folding up the dough and passing it back to me automatically. The pasta keeps getting thinner and and longer each time I roll it through.

'What are we up to?' I ask him.

He shrugs, and passes it to me.

I roll it through again. Now it's practically transparent. A big hole appears. Yikes, I don't think it's meant to look like that.

'Oh, no, no!' exclaims Sofia bustling over, 'Troppo! Cinque e due, due e cinque.'

'Sorry,' I say, feeling bad. Looking around, I see that everyone else has begun making their ravioli. 'We'll have to start again.' I attempt to gather up the dough to squash it together, but it breaks and half of it flops onto the floor. This is not going well. 'Uh, is there spare dough?'

'No,' says Sofia folding her arms.

I widen my eyes at Seth to help and he launches into an impassioned spiel. I have no idea what he's saying but Sofia replies and nods, looking mollified. 'That way,' she says, more gently and points to the back of the room.

Seth grabs my hand. 'Come on.'

'Where are we going?'

'To the storeroom to get flour and eggs. I pleaded with her to make us a small amount of dough and said we'd forgo the wine and chocolate for the hassle. She agreed.'

'Oh no, I was looking forward to the wine and chocolate!'

'There's a shop near the hotel that sells both, we can get supplies on the way back. If you want to come back to mine, that is. I thought you could listen to some of our songs and check out what I've written so far.'

Mr Smooth. 'You've thought of everything,' I say, impressed at his diplomacy skills.

'Easy if you know what you want,' he replies, glancing at me with twinkling eyes. I don't ask what it is that he wants. Since I'm now his *girlfriend*, I can pretty much guess—whoop!

The storeroom is a largish cupboard that's packed to the gunnels with canisters, sacks and crates of vegetables and herbs. It smells like a whole food store. 'Did she say exactly where the flour and eggs were?'

'No, we'll just have to check things. Those shelves look promising.' Seth points to the shelves higher up, which are lined with rows of small brown paper bags 'Eggs, perhaps? I'll scout around for the flour.'

'OK.' I spot a low step ladder in the corner, which I drag over. I climb up, sit on the top step and peer into one of the bags. But it's not eggs, it looks like pearl barley. Another one has brown rice. Oooh. On the shelf below, I've spied a pot of raw liquid honey. I can't resist lifting the lid, swiping my fingers over the wooden dipper and sucking them. Yum, delicious. I have some more. I've got a terrible sweet tooth at the best of times. 'Found the eggs yet?'

I turn around with sticky lips to find Seth looking at me, amused. I feel like Winnie the Pooh caught red-handed, with a paw in the honey jar. Since I'm sitting on the ladder, I'm practically face-to-face with him. 'Ah no, not yet. But the honey is delicious. Try some.' I hold out my hand to him, and he sucks it off each finger, slowly, staring directly into my eyes. Oh no, it's extremely hot when he does that. Sex-club hot. I shift slightly, feeling a twinge between my legs. 'Maybe I should get down now,' I say nervously, not wanting a repeat of last night, but Seth has other ideas.

'You have honey on your cheek,' he says, licking it off. 'And here.' He licks an outline around my lips with the tip of his tongue and then gently teases his way inside. I groan at the sexy sweetness of him invading my mouth and slide my sticky fingers down the back of his t-shirt, feeling his smooth silky skin, pulling him closer. His hand gently caresses the side of my thigh, then disappears up inside my shorts, tracing the outline of my g-string knickers. We're so engrossed in each other, that we don't hear the door open.

CHAPTER TWENTY

Sofia clears her throat loudly, and we jerk apart like guilty teenagers. She raises her eyebrows and points to a crate on the floor inside the door. 'Allora—Eggs. Flour.'

Oops, awkward.

After collecting the items herself, she heads back to the kitchen. Blushing, I glance at Seth, but he doesn't seem too contrite. He wrinkles his nose at me, 'I guess playtime's over.'

I descend from the ladder, wiping honey residue off my mouth with the hem of my apron. My ponytail is lopsided and falling out of its hairband, so I retie it as I follow Seth out of the storeroom. We weren't doing anything too terrible, I think, it was just a bit of snogging. Not like we were having sex on a flour sack.

Sofia doesn't say anything, but I get the feeling she's keeping a sharp eye on us. Luckily, she's soon too busy making our dough and sorting out two of the D-named women who're making gigantic ravioli. She tasks us with stirring the sauces that are bubbling on the stove, while fielding multiple calls from "Mama" on her cellphone.

'What's she saying?' I ask Seth after the fifth call. He's got hearing like a bat, so I'm sure he's picking up every word.

'Basically it's along the lines of, "No Mama! I don't want to hear about Uncle Mario's bad hip! I'm teaching! Stop ringing me!"'

I giggle. 'Poor Uncle Mario.'

'Yeah.'

'How come you know Italian so well?'

'I had a gap year in Rome. We've some family friends who work for the UN, so I stayed with them and basically mooched around writing poetry and listening in on locals' conversations at cafes. I learned quite a bit through language books too. I also did some woofing in Sorrento, so I got to practise.'

'Woofing?'

'Yeah, working on an organic farm, picking olives.'

'You? Picking olives?' I screw up my face trying to imagine it. Nope, I'm at a loss there.

Seth chuckles at my expression. 'It's all true. Well, maybe it was more flirting than picking. The owner's daughter was rather pretty. Her father wasn't too impressed and I got kicked out early.'

'Oh.' I know he has a past, but I don't really want to hear about it. Just like he probably wouldn't want me going on about my sex life with Gabe. I stir my tomato sauce vigorously, trying not to mind.

'She wasn't as pretty as you though,' Seth adds, sneaking

a look at me. Charmer. But it works. I blush, and he places a sneaky kiss on my lips when Sofia's back is turned. He's so naughty, I can imagine exactly what he was like in the olive grove.

Just when I think my arm is going to fall off from stirring, Sofia brings out some bottles of local white wine and some Pecorino cheese as an aperitivo. Before long, we're all feeling the effects of the wine, the heat and the aromas pouring from the stove. One of the D-named women even gives us a quick Irish riverdance on the terracotta kitchen floor, and we all applaud. Then Sofia, unprompted, breaks into the chorus of *Time to Say Goodbye* by Andrea Bocelli (the Italian version). She's not half bad, and we all clap and cheer.

I nudge Seth to get him to sing something, but he refuses outright. I don't think he's drunk enough wine.

The amount of pasta we end up making is half the size of everyone else's so when we leave I'm still hungry. But Sofia gives us our wine and complimentary chocolate anyway, and a kiss on each cheek, pronouncing we are a "coppia dolce", which Seth tells me means "sweet couple".

The class was fun but chaotic, so it's a relief to arrive back at Seth's hotel and walk into the cool, calm foyer. As we pass the front desk, Giacomo looks up and says, 'Mr. Carver, you have an urgent message' and proffers a bit of paper at him. Since Seth has his hands full from carrying two bottles of red wine, he says to me, 'Can you put it in my back pocket? It's probably Dad freaking out that I'm not writing or something. Though, I'm not sure why he doesn't message me on my mobile.'

I fold over the bit of paper, not looking at it, and stuff it into his pocket. '*Are* you still writing?' I ask curiously.

'Yeah, so much. I can't stop.' He smiles at me. 'Are you hungry? I feel like I need a second helping of pasta.'

'Yes, starving.'

We head straight to the garden bar, where the hotel staff are happy to seat us, take our orders for more ravioli and a green salad. Seth also orders me a large plate of fries with tomato ketchup, which isn't on the menu. The waiter says, 'Of course, Sir,' as if it's no trouble at all. This hotel is great.

'That was heaven!' I say when I can't fit in another mouthful. I lean back in the chair, patting my full belly, resisting the urge to do a loud belch. Not a good look. Seth is ploughing his way through my leftover fries, so I check the photo I took of the hotel's ravioli. It looks way better than what we made. I'm about to go on Instagram to upload it with a suitable caption, when I get a message.

Violet
Hi, can you call me asap?

Me
Not really, I'm at lunch. Can it wait?

Violet
No.

Me
OK, give me a minute.

I sigh. 'Hey, sorry, I have to call a friend. I'll go outside,' I say to Seth.

'No problem. Shall I meet you up in the room?'

'No, no, I won't be a moment.' I get up and kiss him on the cheek.

'OK, meanwhile, I'll check my *urgent* message.' He rolls his eyes and chews unconcerned on a fry.

I go out to the small garden area by the pool, where we paddled our feet the other night, and stand under a shady tree. Violet picks up on the second ring. 'What's up?' I ask, somewhat impatiently, eager to get back to Seth.

Violet doesn't mince words. 'It's Gabe. He's trying to get hold of you.'

'Gabe?' I say surprised. 'What does he want? And why is he contacting you?'

'He didn't have your number, but you'd given him mine for some reason.'

'Yeah, I gave him your number when I moved out in case he found any more of my stuff at our flat,' I tell her. I don't mention that I changed my SIM card so he'd stop texting me.

'Oh, well anyway, he rang last night trying to track you down. He said he's leaving his job and he's been tasked with finding a replacement so if you apply it's pretty much yours if you want it.'

My ears prick up at that. Gabe's role was more senior than mine and he was on a much higher salary. Then again, if it means having to interact with him to get it, I'm not sure I want it.

'What else did he say?' In my experience, if something sounds too good to be true, it usually is.

'He said he felt bad that he made you leave in the first place, and that he was just upset he got dumped. I think he'd been out for a few drinks, so I ended up hearing his tale of woe; how he hasn't been able to find anyone else, how he still has feelings for you, how he's been making major life changes, yada yada yada. He wanted to know where you were and, well, after he'd spilled his guts, I couldn't exactly lie. I said you were house sitting in Florence for a few weeks.'

I listen without reacting. Apart from the job news I'm not sure I why I need to hear the rest of it.

'That's OK,' I reply. 'I can't meet up with him if I'm not in London. Even if I was there, I wouldn't want to, we're over.'

'It kind of gets worse,' says Violet tentatively. 'Don't freak out.'

'What?'

'I may have mentioned you were hanging out with Seth Carver. After that, Gabe was pretty determined to talk to you face-to-face. He was quite insistent, asking me for your phone number and the address. I gave him your number, but said I didn't know where you were staying...'

'What are you getting at, Violet?'

'He's coming to Florence. To win you back.'

Shit!

'Violet, I told you not to tell anyone! You should've just hung up on him!'

'But he seems like a nice guy, and he obviously still cares about you. He was going on about wooing you under the Tuscan sun... Maybe you should meet up with him.'

Arrggh, maybe she should stop interfering in my love life!

'Gabe can come to Florence if he wants, but I'm under no obligation to see him. I have my own life to live. I'm moving on and so should he. There's going to be no wooing. Besides, I'm with Seth. It's official.'

I hear Violet gasp in shock.

'*What?*'

'We're a proper couple,' I state smugly (even though it's been barely two hours since that was established).

'Surely that's not going to work? You're so different from him.'

'It's working fine so far.' I think about Seth kissing me in the storeroom and smile to myself.

But Violet doesn't offer her congratulations.

'At least talk to Gabe. Don't burn your bridges if it means getting his job. You'd be stupid not to.'

I make a non-committal grunting sound. 'Perhaps.'

In actual fact, I'm thinking I'll just ignore Gabe when he calls or messages. Florence is a largish city. What are the chances of bumping into him? Thank God, I didn't tell her the address or he could have staked out the apartment.

After saying bye to Violet and reassuring her that it's fine she told Gabe where I was and I'm not annoyed, I head back inside. Truthfully, I'm mightily pissed off that she's been a blabbermouth, and I now have to deal with this.

I'm also disconcerted about Gabe.

It's been over between us for a year so I'm perplexed as to why he's insisting on reopening old wounds. He's just going to get hurt. But I try to push it out of my mind for the time being. Hopefully, Seth has finished eating, so we can go up to the room. I fancy a bit of chocolate, snuggling on the bed and whatever else that might lead to. But as I approach the table, I see there's a slim girl with short blonde hair sitting in my seat, talking intently to Seth. Judging by the sulky look on his face, he doesn't appear too happy about it. Oh no, is she a fan? I'm going to have to rescue him.

I don't get a chance to say anything though. When she sees me, she stands up, cool as a cucumber, and stretches out her hand. 'Hi Jenna, nice to meet you. I'm Calypso—Seth's muse.'

CHAPTER TWENTY-ONE

I stare at the girl stunned. *His muse?* Her hand is still outstretched towards me, so I shake it on autopilot. She's taller than me, thin, dressed in white jeans and a white cotton blouse. Pretty in an angular way. Her accent sounds posh.

What the fuck?

'Uh, I should go.' When faced with an uncomfortable situation, my first instinct is always flight rather than fight.

'Oh no, don't leave. Seth told me about how he met you doing the house sit,' she says smoothly.

Calypso seems sincere about wanting me to stay, but since she's taken my seat, where am I supposed to sit? I look around for another chair and catch Seth's eye. 'Sit here,' he says and pulls me down onto his lap. He slips an arm around my waist. It makes me feel slightly better after the mini-shock I've just had about Calypso. I stare at her and she stares back, resting her elbows on the table. Her white-on-white outfit, urchin haircut and small frame make her seem fragile. However, the persona I'm picking up is anything but. She narrows her large blue eyes at Seth.

'So you really *are* together,' she murmurs.

'Yup,' says Seth firmly. 'And you can report to Dad that everything's going fine writing-wise.'

'I might need to see evidence of that. The writing I mean, not you two being together—eww.' Calypso wrinkles her nose and lets out a short neigh of laughter at her own joke. Which I don't find funny in the slightest. It's a bit insulting, why is it *eww*?

'What's going on?' I ask Seth, tilting my head slightly towards him. I can tell he's tense, his legs feel like blocks of wood.

'Dad sent her over to check up on me to make sure I'm writing,' he says brusquely.

'Oh, I see,' I say, not really seeing at all. Is she the 'whatever it was it's over' girl he mentioned on the window seat?

'Calypso's a family friend,' says Seth in answer to my unspoken question. 'Her Dad and my Dad are mates.'

'I've got a flat in West Hampstead with two other girls,' Calypso explains as if I need to know the exact details of her living arrangements. 'I'm also the unofficial band photographer. If you've been onto the website, all the profile photos were taken by me,' she says in a proud tone.

'Right,' I say. 'I'm sure they're good, but I haven't seen them.' I feel a bit bitchy saying that even though it's true. Now that we're together, I don't exactly want to see Seth looking like a Goth god, it makes his fame all too real. I'd rather have my own down-to-earth image of him.

'Oh.' Calypso bites her lip and gazes at Seth. 'I know it looks like I'm spying on you, but honestly, it's not like that,' she says ingratiatingly.

'How is it then?' he asks.

'I ran into India in the Village and we got chatting. I told her I was stopping off in Florence for a few days before heading to Rome to meet with some friends. She must've mentioned it to your Dad because he rang and asked me to check in and see how you were getting on. I messaged you this morning but you didn't reply. So I rang and left a message with the hotel directly. I was in the area, so I thought I'd drop by on the off chance you were here having lunch.'

I can't tell if she's keen on Seth or not, her face doesn't show a flicker of emotion. Either she isn't or she's good at hiding her feelings. But I still don't trust that she's not after him in some way. There's definitely history between them, judging by her muse comment, and she's obviously the Calypso from Instagram.

'Where are you staying?' I ask. *Please, God, don't let it be here!*

'A cheap Airbnb, near Santa Croce—not all of us have fathers willing to pay for five-star hotels,' she says pointedly, looking at Seth.

'I'm sure Jack would if you asked him,' he says tersely.

Hearing his tone, I relax a little. It's totally different to the light teasing manner he uses with me. I'm picking up distinct vibes that he's intensely irked by her. But she appears oblivious to it.

'Since I'm here for a few days, perhaps we can all hang out? Or we could go shopping, Jenna, if Seth's busy?'

'Mmm, perhaps,' I say non-committedly. I don't really want to hang out with her or go shopping. Besides, if Gabe turns up, I'd rather not be on the streets and increase the chance of bumping into him. Also, what about me and Seth spending time together?

The thought must be on his mind as well as he says, 'I'm not sure that's going to be possible, I've got a tight deadline, and I need Jenna's help.' Whoop, yes, go Seth! Calypso doesn't react, but I can sense she isn't pleased.

'Well, maybe just show me what you've been working on, so I can tell your Dad I've seen it with my own eyes, and I'll get out of your hair,' she says breezily.

I don't think Seth is going to agree. But maybe he thinks it's the best way to get rid of her. He sighs. 'Fine, let's go to my room. Then, I need to do a writing session.'

'Should I come too?' I whisper to him.

He kisses my cheek, and says, 'Of course, you're part of the writing session.'

Whether or not he has a writing session in mind is a different story, but I'm happy to tag along, so he's not left alone with Calypso. I'm surprised that he trusts her enough to give her his stuff to read—it's making me suspicious that she's more than a *family friend*. Otherwise, why would he let her see his songs? I haven't even seen them yet!

We all traipse along to the lift and head up to room 312. Seth swipes the door card and lets us both in. We enter into a lounge area, featuring a beige couch with dark brown swirls, an armchair in matching fabric and a slim-legged writing desk. He goes over to the desk, takes his black journal from one of the drawers and gives it to Calypso. It's the same one I saw under his pillow in the studio.

Seth sprawls on the couch, and I perch on the edge next to him. It feels like we're under surveillance. Calypso walks around flicking through pages. I stare down at the red and gold carpet, wondering where the bedroom is. There's an adjoining archway to the left, so I assume it's through there.

There's a loud noise as she snaps the journal shut and stares at Seth. 'Well, these are different from your usual,' she says.

'So?' he says defensively.

Calypso looks at him like he's thick.

'Seth, these lyrics are positively cheerful. I don't think your Dad is going to be pleased.'

He glances at me. What on earth has he been writing? Oh no, don't tell me I've inspired him to write happy clappy songs!

'I'm just writing what I feel. I'm not going to censor myself to please people.'

'Well, the *people* that like Sublime Misery like it because of a certain angsty vibe. These aren't angsty in the slightest.'

Seth shrugs. 'Maybe the fans need cheering up.'

I'm itching to read what he's written. If Calypso left, I could actually look at them myself. After all, *I'm* his muse. I slide my hand into Seth's and squeeze it purposefully. He squeezes it back.

'Anyway, you've seen them now, so it's time to go,' he says, taking my hint. 'We've got stuff to do.'

Calypso rolls her eyes. 'Fine.' She places the journal on the desk and flounces towards the door but before going through it, tosses back 'I'll be in touch,' over her shoulder. It sounds like a warning. She doesn't bother saying goodbye.

I let out my breath when she's gone. 'Wow, that was unexpected.'

Seth rests his head on the back of the couch and shuts his eyes. He looks tired. 'Sorry about that. I had no idea she was coming to Florence.' He opens one eye a crack. 'Do you hate me?'

'Hate you? No! And you have nothing to be sorry about,' I say, not wanting to pry into their relationship but feeling put out she's turned up all the same.

Seth rubs the back of my hand with his thumb.

'If there's anything you want to know about Calypso, please ask me. I don't want any confusion between us or for you to have the wrong idea about her.'

Is there anything I want to know? I flatten my tongue against the roof of my mouth. Just one burning question. I make myself say it: 'Have you slept with her?'

Seth tilts his chin down slightly, and I get a sinking feeling.

'No, but a couple of weeks ago we did kiss and fool around a bit,' he says. 'I was feeling lonely and depressed because I couldn't write, so I invited her over. We had a few drinks and one thing led to another. Perhaps I thought it would help, I don't know.'

Pain burns my heart, and I can't speak. Seth tightens his grip on my hand as if he knows I want to snatch it away.

He continues, speaking more rapidly. 'Anyway, she wanted to take things further, but I wasn't feeling it and asked her to go. I rang her afterwards and said I was sorry and that it had been a mistake, but she was pissed at me. It's taken a bit of grovelling to get things back on track with her. I thought everything was OK and we were friends again. The fact that she's leapt at the chance to check up on me suggests she might think there's still a chance of something more. I shouldn't have done anything with her, I'm an idiot.'

I try not to show him I'm upset, but it's gut-wrenching to hear my suspicions about Calypso confirmed. Seth is watching my face with a worried expression. I blink hard, determined not to get all weepy in front of him.

'I don't feel anything for Calypso, Jenna,' he says gently.

'You must do, you have history with her. You hardly know me.'

'It's different with you. We have a connection. I knew it as soon as I saw you. I got goosebumps.'

I let out a breath, remembering when I first laid eyes on him in the kitchen. 'Yeah, me too.'

Seth kisses my hand. 'What we have is special. Calypso doesn't even come close to you. I wouldn't have told Sofia you were my girlfriend otherwise.'

The fact that he's being so open about Calypso is helping his cause. If he'd been secretive and unwilling to talk about it, then I wouldn't believe him. And I'd already picked up on the fact he wasn't interested in her anyway.

'So are we going to all *hang out* as she suggested?' I ask.

'That's up to you. If you don't feel comfortable, then, no, we won't.'

I take a deep breath and get over myself. *He didn't sleep with her.* 'Well, she's only here for a couple of days. I don't want to go shopping but having dinner or something should be OK.'

Seth looks relieved. 'Thank you.'

'For what?'

'For trusting me. For accepting the situation.'

I hitch a shoulder in acknowledgement. 'Thank you for being honest with me. Although, I'm a bit worried about what you've been writing. Maybe I should make things difficult for you so you can write an angsty song.'

Seth laughs. 'Yeah, maybe.'

'If they're too happy, you'll have to stop wearing black and bleach your hair blond,' I tease him.

'Let's not go that far,' he says dryly. 'Maybe they're slightly less depressing than usual, but they're still on brand.'

'As your current muse, I think I need to listen to a few of your songs. It's getting a bit ridiculous that I haven't.'

'We can easily rectify that.' He gets up and tugs me into the bedroom where there's a massive king-sized bed with a crisp white duvet, plump white pillows and a dark-green satin throw. A medieval painting of the Arno with its bridges and people rowing old-fashioned wooden boats graces the entire wall above the bed. 'Lie down, I'll get my earbuds.' He rummages in a bag next to the bed. Too late I realise that I'm going to be listening to his music right in front of him. What if it's bad or I don't like it? I lie on the bed as stiff as a corpse, and he laughs when he sees me.

'There's no pressure, remember? You don't have to give me an in-depth account of what you think of it.'

'Thank God.'

'Anyway, I'll know by your face, you're pretty easy to read.'

'Shit. Here I was thinking I was unreadable.'

Seth laughs and gives me his earbuds, then scrolls and taps his phone.

'Start with *Season of Death*, it's the least depressing.'

I gulp. 'Great.'

He sits on the bed, watching me intently.

'Um, could you maybe do something else?'

'Sure, sorry.' He leaps up and heads back into the lounge area. 'I'll just be in here.'

'OK.'

I close my eyes and let the atmospheric electronica flow over me. When Seth's smooth, rich vocal begins it gives me the shivers. No wonder the Goth groupies are going mental over him. I take out one earbud—'Oh my God, your voice is divine,' I call out.

He calls back 'thanks!' I put the earbud back in and keep listening. The song doesn't make me feel down at all, but erk, the lyrics aren't too flattering—is it about Calypso?

Winter rain falls over me
You're the harbinger
The soul flayer of decay.
White silence reigns over me
You're corrosion, dissolution
The poison washing life away…

There's the sound of rain falling in the background of the track. I start nodding off.

Something pokes my shoulder, and I jerk awake. Seth is

peering down at me with an amused look on his face. 'Is it that boring?'

'No, it's great, I love it. It's just… really relaxing. Your voice is hypnotic.'

Seth lies down next to me and pulls up the satin throw over us. 'Shall we have a nap?'

I yawn. 'That sounds fantastic. I'll keep listening though.'

I drift off with his voice in my ears and my head on his shoulder.

When I wake up the light in the room is muted, I don't have the earbuds in and Seth is lying next to me listening to something.

'What time is it?' I ask groggily.

'Oh hey, you're awake.' He checks his phone. 'Getting on for six. You were out to it, I didn't want to wake you.'

I rub my eyes. 'I have to feed Filippo. I should go.'

'Do you want to come back here? Or I could meet you, and we could get some dinner?'

'Honestly, I think I might just have a bath and go to bed,' I say. I need time to think about everything he's said about Calypso, and to get my head around what to do about Gabe. In typical Jenna fashion, I'm still hoping I can avoid him.

'OK.' Seth looks disappointed. 'I'm sorry our romantic afternoon got ruined. I had good intentions. Even got some wine and chocolate to set the mood.'

'I know. Come here.'

He rolls over towards me and we have a full-length hug. I wrap my arms around him, burying my face in his neck, and he runs a hand lightly up and down my back. 'Shall we try again tomorrow?'

He smells so good and his body pressing against mine feels extremely nice. I'm tempted to say that the cat won't starve, and why don't we make it now? But I keep picturing Filippo meowing pitifully, and I know I'll feel bad if I skip my house sitting duties.

Seth nuzzles my hair and his hand moves down over the curve of my hip, and murmurs exactly what I'm thinking 'Or we could make it now.' He kisses me with single-minded intent and I don't protest. Our tongues entwine and heat sears through me. I know if I let it continue, very soon there's going to be nakedness, and I'll still have to go and feed the cat. With a force of will I don't even realise I possess, I pull away breathing heavily. 'I can't believe I'm saying this, but it's going to have to be tomorrow.'

Seth puffs out his cheeks. 'Wow, you chose Filippo, I'm jealous.'

'It's not even a competition. I'd much rather stay here.'

'Hmm. I'd much rather you stay here too.' He leans towards me, and I put my hand on his chest.

'Don't kiss me again or I'll never leave. You're way too gorgeous.'

Seth grins, his eyes sparkling with amusement. 'Am I?'

'You know you are.'

He sighs and lies back, stretching his arms above his head. He tilts his hips a little, and I can't help noticing that he has a distinct bulge happening. 'Well, you know where I am if you want me.' I swallow. Damn, seeing that he's turned on is so freaking sexy. It's making it really difficult to leave. With a superhuman effort, I get off the bed and shake loose my ponytail, which is completely smooshed to one side. I can feel him watching me, willing me to stay.

'So I'll talk to you later?' I ask.

'Yup, if you don't hear from me for a while, I may be in the shower,' he replies huskily.

Oh lordy. Just start walking Jenna.

'OK... Well... Enjoy that,' I say, heading towards the door, still not looking at him. Seth chuckles.

CHAPTER TWENTY-TWO

I'm half-way down the corridor, heading towards the lift, when I get an attack of the guilts. Seth has been so open about Calypso, and I haven't exactly been forthcoming about Gabe. It's not like he's actually turned up in person, but there's a good chance he will. Gabe is like a dog with a bone when he gets an idea in his head. He'll track me down one way or another. I turn around, walk back to the room and knock. Seth opens it after a beat and looks surprised to see me.

'Hello, did you forget something?'

'There's something you need to know. I should've told you before.'

'OK, sounds serious, come in.'

I sit on the arm of the couch while Seth leans against the desk with his arms folded, looking apprehensive.

'It's nothing bad,' I reassure him. 'Well, it could potentially be annoying, but since we're being open and honest with each other... The phone call I made at lunch was to Violet. She wanted to warn me my ex is on his way to Florence.'

'The ex who made you quit your job?'

'Yes, that ex. Gabe. She let it slip that I was here and now apparently he's coming over.'

'Oh. Why?'

'Because he's leaving his job. And he's giving it to me if I want it. Essentially, he's going to try and use the job as leverage to win me back.'

'Interesting. So have you spoken to him?'

'No, he hasn't called or messaged. I've just got a bad feeling he'll show up when I least expect it.'

'Do you want him back?' Seth asks evenly.

'Definitely not.'

He gives me a wry grin. 'Aren't we popular? We've both got people we don't want following us to Florence.'

'Hmm, I just wish they'd go away and leave us in peace. Now I feel all jumpy that he's going to be waiting for me at the apartment. Not that he knows the address but still...'

Seth suddenly levers himself off the desk and disappears into the bedroom. He comes out a few moments later with a purple toothbrush sticking out of his front pocket, and collects his phone, room key and wallet from the desk.

'What are you doing?'

'Coming with you. Just in case he's there.'

I stare at the toothbrush then give him a querying look, and he grins. 'That's just in case I stay over.'

'Ah.'

We catch a taxi back to the apartment. I get nervous as we approach, half expecting Gabe to be sitting in the entranceway with a takeaway pizza. But it's empty, which is a relief. As we go up, we do happen to bump into Antonella who's coming down the stairs though. She's in a short black tank dress and denim jacket, and looks like she's on her way out to dinner.

'Hi, stranger!' she exclaims upon seeing me. 'I was going to text you to see if you were still alive.'

'Hi, sorry. I've been a bit busy the last couple of days.'

'No problem,' she says, gazing past me. I note a faint stain of red appear high on her cheekbones underneath her carefully applied blusher. The Seth effect at work again.

'Uh, this is Antonella, my neighbour,' I offer lamely. Should I introduce him as my boyfriend? I have no clue. But he saves me from having to explain anything.

'Nice to meet you, I'm Seth,' he says from behind me.

'Hi, nice to meet you too. I'm just going out, but we'll have to do a catch up soon, Jenna,' says Antonella continuing down the stairs. She stops on the stair below us. 'Oh, by the way, there was a guy buzzing all the apartments asking if you were staying here. It was kind of weird, so I said you weren't. I hope that was OK?'

I could hug her. 'It's absolutely perfect. Long story, but I'll explain when I see you next.'

My stomach lurches. I had a feeling Gabe would find out

somehow. I cross my fingers that Antonella has put him off the trail.

'OK, bye then. Bye, *Seth*,' she says meaningfully. I happen to glance down the stairs when we get to the top and catch her checking him out. She's sees me looking, fans herself with her hand and mouths 'FUCK!'

I giggle to myself.

As soon as I open the door to the apartment, Filippo comes scampering down the hallway meowing. 'Oh yes, you poor starving thing. I'll get you your dinner. Come through to the kitchen,' I say to Seth. 'I'll sort out something for us as well.'

Seth sits at the counter, watching as I chop fish wearing the rubber gloves. 'So Gabe's been here then.'

'Looks that way. Hopefully, he gives up and goes back to London.' I dump the fish in the cat bowl and put it on the floor for Filippo who chows down with gusto. Not much wrong with his appetite even if he is a senior citizen. I fill up his water dish as well.

'What should we do for dinner? I can cook some pasta…' I catch Seth's eye and feel like giggling remembering our half-assed attempt at pasta making this morning. Low blood sugar and this very strange day is starting to make me feel hysterical. I check the cupboards, 'Or I can whip up a cheese omelette and a salad?' I really need to do a shop soon, I'm running out of food.

'A cheese omelette sounds great.'

'Thanks for seeing me back. If you did want to take off after dinner, I'll understand.' I'm hoping he'll stay, but I don't want to appear helpless and needy.

Seth shakes his head. 'No, I think I'll stick around. Especially since your ex seems to be stalking you.'

I roll my eyes. 'I don't know why he doesn't message.'

'Probably thinks you'll ignore it.'

I get the eggs out of the fridge and start cracking them into a bowl. 'Well, yes, that was the plan.'

'Maybe you should be proactive. Agree to meet him, so he can get whatever it is he wants to say off his chest. And if the job thing is real and you want it, I'm sure I can have a part-time muse when we get home.'

He says it lightly, but I give a little start at hearing the words: *when we get home.* Up until now, I don't think I've comprehended that Seth considers me his girlfriend. On one level, I get it, but for some reason, I haven't let myself fully believe it. However, it's starting to filter through. He wants to see me all the time, go out on dates, have sex... I lean against the counter, suddenly lightheaded as realisation washes over me.

'Are you OK?'

'Yes, I... Do you mind beating the eggs? I have to use the bathroom.'

He looks at me strangely, 'Are you sure you're OK? Your face is really red.' He comes around the counter, and I thrust the whisk at him. 'Please, beat the eggs!'

'What did I say? I said something, didn't I?'

'I … just … everything's happening at once!' Oh no, I can feel tears threatening. A couple overflow and run down my cheeks.

Seth takes the whisk out of my hand as if he's worried I'm going to hit him with it. 'I know, it's all a bit fast and furious right now but sometimes life works like that,' he says. 'Everything's OK. Go into the lounge and chill with Filippo and I'll make dinner.'

I sniff looking at him. 'Really?'

'Sure. I can cook. Probably not as well as you, and there may be burnt bits, but it will be edible, I promise.'

He kisses my wet cheek and hugs me. 'Don't freak, it'll all be fine.' I get the sense he's not talking about the omelette.

'It's just… I like them so much,' I gulp against his chest.

'I like them too. A lot. They make me feel all gooey every time I'm around them.'

I start crying harder hearing that. 'Me too. It's the mozzarella. I adore the mozzarella.'

I have no idea what I'm saying, but Seth hugs me tighter and I'm cocooned in his arms. 'Definitely, it's just a big old goo fest,' he murmurs, against my hair. 'Uh, I don't suppose you have any mozzarella?'

I try to think. 'No. Just Parmesan.' He laughs, and I feel the tension leave my body. Phew, that was a very weird conversation, but I think we're both on the same page.

'Well, I better start cooking this perfect omelette then.'

'No pressure,' I say sniffling. 'I'll still eat it even if it's got burnt bits.'

At the doorway, I can't help pausing to snatch another glimpse of him. He glances round and gives me a devastatingly gorgeous smile, which launches my heart into free fall. Yikes, I really hope we're on the same page because I don't have a safety chute.

While Seth bustles around in the kitchen cooking dinner, I go into the lounge and sit on the window seat in *our spot*, as I'm beginning to think of it. Filippo follows and hops up next to me, purring. He seems much more amiable when Seth's around. Or maybe he's just realising he won't get fed if I'm not here. I pull my phone out of my pocket to check Instagram. Wow, it's steadily going off from the Arno photo I posted this morning and the arty pasta shot I took at lunch. Between them, I've got over two hundred likes, plenty of "amazing" comments and lots of new followers. Idly, I wonder what sort of reaction I'd get if I posted a selfie of me and Seth canoodling on the window seat. My account would explode. But I know it's never going to happen, and that's OK. I get that he wants his privacy.

I check if I've got any further messages, dreading to see one from Gabe, but there's still nothing. Where is he? If he's planning a surprise ambush, it's taking a while. Seth's right, it would be good to deal with him in an upfront manner, so I can make a decision about the job, if indeed that's on the cards. Maybe I can negotiate a contract so that I can still do freelancing on the side. That way, I can have the security the job offers, but also not be wholly dependent on it like I was before. Although, I don't want to be working all the time if I'm with Seth. But if he's recording an album, I might not see him much. Or perhaps he'll want me to be there if he is? That would be kind of fun. I could be the cool hipster girlfriend, wearing a hoodie with my hair in plaits, drinking coffee and listening to a playback, while he's on the other side of the glass in the recording booth. But, honestly, I don't know how it works or anything about the process, or if the other band members would even want me there. The last thing I want to do is give off a Yoko Ono type of vibe.

Just as I'm about to start gnawing on my arm, Seth comes into the lounge, carrying two dinner plates. 'I hope you're hungry,' he says, handing me one and a fork.

'I'm starving.' My eyebrows raise. The omelette he's made is gigantic. It covers the entire plate. There's no salad. 'Uh, thanks. I think that will be more than satisfying.'

He settles down opposite me, holding his own massive cheesy egg creation.

'How many eggs did you use?'

'Twelve,' he says, cutting into it with the side of his fork.

I choke on a mouthful. 'The entire pack!'

'I don't do things by halves.'

'No kidding!'

Strangely enough, I manage to wolf down the whole thing without too much trouble and lean back feeling sated. 'Thanks, that was great. It really hit the spot.'

Seth looks smug. 'I knew you needed the protein. I told you, I can read you like a book.'

'I can read you too, smarty pants.'

'Oh really? What am I thinking right now?' He stares into my eyes intently, and I get a strange little tingling jolt. Sometimes when he looks at me like that, it's like my circuits overload.

'You're wondering if I still have the gelato in the fridge,' I say, taking a stab in the dark.

'Hmm, that was a passing thought when I was cooking, and I checked, you do. But my current thought is trying to figure out if you're prettier with your hair up or down.' His eyes rove over my face and I immediately feel hot and flustered. I reach up a hand and touch my hair in case it's frizzed out like a puffball.

'But sadly,' Seth continues, 'it's one of those mysteries that are unsolvable. You're stunning both ways.'

I let out a slow breath. Coming from him, that's the compliment of the century. If he's trying to get me to sleep with him, it's a done deal. He really doesn't have to try that hard. But perhaps this is his way of wooing me. If so, it's working. I hope he's brought those condoms along with him. 'So what am I thinking now then?' I ask.

'You're wondering if I still have those condoms from last night in my pocket.'

I look at him in shock. 'Wow, you're good!'

He raises an eyebrow, the one with the piercing. 'I told you. Let's see.' He takes his toothbrush out of his front pocket and digs around. 'No, not in there.' He reaches into one of his back pockets and produces two condoms, then a third from the other. 'Huh, looks like I did.'

'You're the master of foresight,' I say weakly. I feel like a fish being reeled in by his considerable charms. I can't resist him emotionally or physically. The attraction is too powerful. I want him so badly, I'm starting to ache all over.

We stare at each other and the sexual tension amplifies, until finally, he gets up and holds out his hand. 'I think we should go to bed, otherwise I'm going to ravish you right here and now.'

Somehow, I knew he was going to say that.

CHAPTER TWENTY-THREE

After a passionate snog in the hallway that makes my knees buckle, Seth says he'll just have a quick shower. 'There are towels and toothpaste in there,' I say, straightening my shirt and composing myself. 'I'd offer to lend you a clean t-shirt, but I don't think any of mine will fit you.'

'That's OK. I don't usually wear anything to bed,' he replies. Leaving me with that tantalising thought, he saunters into the bathroom. Moments later, the shower turns on, and barely two minutes later it turns off again, which makes me giggle. Quickest. Shower. Ever.

Seth comes out of the bathroom clutching his clothes against his chest and a blue-and-white striped towel slung around his hips. He looks surprised to see that I'm in the same position he left me. 'You were hardly in there long enough to get wet,' I tell him by way of explanation. I avert my eyes, trying not to stare at what I can see of his bare chest. But a quick glance has shown me there's at least one barbell nipple piercing and another word tattoo snaking its way down his lower torso.

'Yeah, I hurried. See you soon,' he says and heads into the

bedroom.

I take a bit longer than two minutes in the shower. Whether I'm stalling or trying to mentally prepare myself, I'm not sure. My brain is all over the place. I can't stop thinking about his nipple piercing. Trust Seth to have something sexy like that. There must be one on the other side too. Are there any more? I've never particularly been into guys with piercings and tattoos but, for some reason, the combination of his excites me. Then again, everything about him excites me. He's like a new world waiting to be discovered, and I don't have a map or a guide book.

It seems redundant to put on makeup, so I attempt to brush out my hair instead, which is now definitely frizzing after the shower. I moisturise my face and slap a bit on my legs for good measure. Wrapping myself in a towel, I peek hesitantly round the door into the bedroom. Seth's lying on his side under the duvet facing me, cheek propped in the palm of his hand. He's switched on one of the bedside lamps, which has bathed the room in soft light. His naked chest is now on full display. I catch my breath. In repose he looks like a painting; pale lean muscle, black hair standing on end, like he's casually raked his fingers through it. His torso tattoo is dark against his skin, snaking down the side of his hip, across his stomach and disappearing out of sight underneath the duvet. And yup, he has two nipple piercings.

He looks up from his phone as I come into the room. His

black eyes flick over my towel. I adjust it tighter, heart pounding. Part of me wants to run away, the other is drawn like a magnet, wanting him desperately.

He pats the bed, and says softly 'Are you getting in?'

I nod and approach the side, still wearing the towel to protect my modesty.

He looks amused. 'Is that coming in too?'

'Just give me a minute,' I say, working out my plan of action. I hop into bed and pull the duvet up to my chin, then undo the towel and wriggle out of it. Now I'm naked but fully covered, and he can't see anything. I kick the towel out of the bed, so it lands with a plop on the floor.

Seth slides closer and peers at me. 'You're funny.'

'I know, I'm a laugh a minute.'

'Don't you want me to touch you?'

I close my eyes briefly. 'Yes, but…'

'But what?'

'Your hardware is intimidating,' I say nodding at his nipple piercings.

'Ah,' he says, 'Understandable. We'll start slow. I'll talk you through the basics.'

My eyes widen. What the hell are we going to be doing?

'I'm joking,' Seth says hastily, seeing the look on my face. 'There will be no BDSM involved.'

'I'm not adverse to *different stuff,* I just like to know what I'm getting into,' I say, primly pulling the duvet up even higher.

'Of course,' he says soothingly as if he doesn't believe me one jot. 'They're nothing to worry about.'

I feel like I'm overreacting a bit, but my nerves are kicking in. At this rate, he'll be turning out the light and going to sleep.

'Sorry, I'm being a passion-killer.'

'It's OK. I'm nervous too.'

I don't believe it, he sounds completely composed. I roll over to face him and take his hand. It is trembling a little. That makes me feel a lot better. I stroke his cheek and peck him on the lips to show I am actually interested.

'That's a good start,' he says, smiling at me.

He's so kind and patient, and I'm a big baby.

'Can we loosen this a bit perhaps?'

He tugs down the duvet slowly from my neck so the tops of my breasts are exposed, but he doesn't touch me there, just traces circles on my upper arm and kisses me gently. I start to relax; this is nice, this is lovely.

As the kissing progresses, my hand wanders to his chest and I accidentally brush one of his nipple piercings; he tenses.

'Sorry.'

'No, it's fine, they're sensitive, but you can touch them.' He tugs and twists one to show me. 'Like this.'

Following his lead, I place my fingers on the ends of the nipple piercing and tug softly.

Seth swallows. 'Yeah, that feels pretty good,' he says. I can tell it's turning him on which makes me want to do it more. It's kind of fun. I tug and twist it slightly harder, and he groans. 'You act all innocent, but you're actually a sadist.'

I giggle. But then yelp as he reaches inside the duvet and tweaks my nipple in return. Even though the feeling is an odd mixture of pleasure and pain, I don't mind it.

'Maybe I should get nipple piercings too,' I say.

'Hmm. How do you feel about needles?' He takes hold of my nipple and squeezes gently, as if sizing it up for the procedure. But I think he's just using it as an excuse to have a proper look, since the duvet has slipped down and my boobs are now on show.

'Not pro,' I say, watching as he explores with inquisitive fingers, caressing and squeezing.

'Mmm, can't get enough of these,' he murmurs. He bends his head and starts slowly sucking on a nipple. Heat courses through me. I can't remember Gabe even really bothering with my breasts. He was very much 'let's get this over with' in bed, which was part of the reason I dumped him. Seth, on the other hand, is quite enthusiastic with his sucking, giving equal attention to both breasts, his tongue stud occasionally flicking against my nipples, which is incredibly erotic. I run my hands over his shoulders, feeling the muscles move beneath his smooth skin, and then up the back of his head. He has such touchable hair. Silky and thick. Suddenly, he comes up for air, with moist lips parted. 'Was that nice?' He sounds breathy, like he's been running.

'Extremely nice,' I tell him.

'Is it turning you on?'

'Slightly,' I say, embarrassed to admit I've got a swimming pool happening between my thighs.

'Only slightly?' He frowns. 'I might have to rectify that.' His hand trails lightly down my stomach heading south, and I gulp. I thought we were meant to be exploring him, but the tables seem to have turned, and he's intent on exploring me.

'Maybe work up to it,' I say, shifting his hand back up. I have no idea why I'm acting like a nun, it's not like I haven't had sex before. It just feels different being with Seth, like I've got more to lose because I'm so emotionally invested. If I give myself to him physically as well, then I'm leaving myself wide open to get crushed. Which makes no sense whatsoever since I'm already naked in bed with him. *What did you think you were going to do here, Jenna? Play cards?*

'This is amazing,' I say, changing the focus onto him. I trace his torso tattoo with my finger, the black letters twisting and swirling. 'How far does it go down?'

He guides my hand down across his abs and under the duvet, avoiding his crotch, over his hip bone to his opposite thigh. 'To about there,' he says, drawing a line with my finger across mid-thigh.

'Did it hurt?' I say, stroking his thigh. The flesh there feels firm to touch but slightly rough from his leg hair.

'Yeah.'

'And these?' I tentatively kiss his nipple. 'Did they hurt too?'

'Not as much.'

I trace his piercing with my tongue, then suck on it, and he stretches out sighing, 'Oh, yeah. I like that.'

I end up licking and kissing my way around his entire chest. He tastes like sweet gelato, and I can't get enough. When I've finished, he looks down at his glistening skin and laughs. 'I might need another shower.'

'You're delicious,' I say giddily, drunk from him. 'I want to eat you up.'

I'm sitting on my knees, the duvet snagged around my waist. Seth runs half-lidded eyes over my breasts. 'Sounds good.'

Feeling more confident, I lean over so my breasts swing near his mouth and he grasps one and swirls my nipple with his tongue, his other hand massaging my butt cheek. The angle is just right for him to reach under and trace my wet crease with a finger. I don't react, but he removes his mouth from my nipple.

'This OK?'

I acquiesce with a grunt of approval, and he sinks his fingers deeper, until he's stroking rhythmically. He draws me in with his other hand for an open-mouthed kiss while using two fingers to gently play with my clit. What he's doing feels so good, I can't focus on anything but the sensation. I break the kiss and breathe heavily against the side of his cheek.

'I can stop,' he says, sliding his fingers away from my clit to run them along my opening. 'If it's too much.'

'No… Keep going,' I manage, not wanting him to stop in the slightest. I move my legs apart to encourage him and he takes the hint, caressing my thighs and mound, then slips in a slim finger to explore me. 'Do you like that?' he murmurs stroking my G-Spot. I nod; partly in amazement that he knows what he's doing, but mostly because I'm so aroused I can't actually speak. He draws out his finger and slowly rubs my throbbing clit. The pleasure is overwhelming, and I clutch his shoulder, panting hard. He pumps his finger again, then lightly flicks my clit, until I'm tensed, moaning into his neck, my fingernails digging into his skin. He strokes away teasing, as if he knows one more slight touch will tip me over the edge. *Oh please, oh please*, I think as he buries two fingers inside me, then draws them out slowly and fondles my swollen clit. My orgasm builds like a tidal wave. 'Ohhhhh yes, ohhhhh fuuuuck,' I groan as a hot surge of pleasure crashes over me. I slump onto his chest, shuddering uncontrollably and he carries on stroking me, not letting up until my orgasm subsides.

Seth silently rubs my back while I lie in a post-orgasmic daze. I can't seem to move. Eventually, I heave myself off his chest, my limbs all weak and floppy. 'Mamma freaking mia,' I say shakily, and he chuckles. I swing a leg over so I'm lying on top of him, our bare chests meeting but the duvet still covering his lower half. I thrust my tongue in his mouth, and Seth moans, clutching my hips and grinding me down against his hard crotch. Instantly I'm turned on again, it's like he's flipped a switch and I'm out of control. I want more, I want him inside me.

'Where are the condoms?' I ask, looking around wildly. 'In your pocket?'

'Hang on,' he gasps, 'there's something you should know.'

CHAPTER TWENTY-FOUR

After hearing Seth say that, I freeze on top of him. Uh oh, here it is. The catch. A number of different scenarios flicker through my mind. He's got a horrible disease, he needs a penis pump, he uses a strap-on…

'Remember the triangle of peas?'

'Yeees, you were supposed to explain that,' I say. *Please don't let it be anything horrific.*

'I was hoping you'd get it after seeing these and I wouldn't have to.'

'Huh?' I sit upright and see he's pointing to his nipple piercings with both index fingers.

'So, there's another one to make up the triangle…' he prompts. My glance falls on his belly button, a cute innie with an even cuter snail trail of dark hair leading beneath the duvet. But it's metal free, so the other piercing is… My jaw drops as I realise.

'Yikes!' I wince. 'Why would you do that? I can't even imagine how much that would hurt.'

'It didn't hurt as much as you'd think it would. And as to the why…' He shrugs. 'It's the trifecta of pleasure.'

'What does that mean?'

'All three piercings tweaked at once set things up to be mind-blowing, and not just for me. I couldn't exactly tell you about that when we first met, so it was a roundabout way of saying I liked you, and this is what I'm into if you were up for it. A bit obscure, I know.'

Dammit, I knew the pea code was a secret message. But I never would've figured it meant that!

'Have you not done the, er, trifecta before?' I ask.

'No, this …' he gestures down at his bits, 'is a recent addition. So even I'm not sure what it will be like. But judging from solo practice runs… Pretty hot. Up until now I've only had two hands though.' He holds up his palms and does jazz hands, which makes me laugh.

'Yeah, you'd need to be a contortionist,' I snigger.

'Exactly.'

I feel a bit chuffed that he wants me to be the guinea pig for his pleasure fest, even though I have no idea what I'm getting myself into. Missionary position and the odd blow job are about the extent of my experience.

'Well, I'm interested in… sexual experimentation,' I say. 'And I trust you.'

Seth nods. 'I trust you too, and as I said before, we can go slow and talk about it. It's not just about me, it's about what feels good for you as well.'

We seem to have moved from a night of reckless

abandonment to Sex Communication With Your Partner 101, but I get the sentiment. He's trying to make sure I'm OK with everything. Though talking about it is one thing…

'Can I see it?'

'Sure. Probably best if you do anyway, so you don't freak.'

'I'm not easily freaked,' I say huffily, and he raises an eyebrow. OK, so he does know me a little.

'Right, let's have a look at this specimen,' I say in a confident medical professional tone. Seth's lips twitch, but he obediently lies back on the pillow and looks up at the ceiling, while I edge the duvet down to expose his hardware. This is probably not really how he imagined things going.

When I clap eyes on his tackle, I almost exclaim, 'sweet Jesus, hallelujah!', but bite my tongue. I now officially know that all of Seth is magnificent, even in a semi-erect state.

'Hmmm,' I say thoughtfully, peering at the tip which has a silver barbell vertically rammed through it. It's not as much paraphernalia as I was expecting, but surely, it still must've hurt. 'Does it have a name?'

'My penis?'

'No, silly, the piercing!'

'It's an apadravya. Supposed to hit the G-spot, as well as the A-Spot and C-Spot.'

'All those spots are good,' I agree, nodding seriously as if I know exactly what he's talking about. *There are other spots?*

Seth shifts his hips, and I note he's gone from semi-erect to fully erect in a matter of seconds. I glance up at him. He's watching me sultrily, one hand tucked behind his head.

'Your inspection of my specimen is turning me on,' he admits. He doesn't appear embarrassed in the slightest. Since he doesn't mind me looking at him, I take the chance to drink in the spectacle of Seth Carver in all his naked glory; my retinas burning from the sight. I want to give him the same groan-out-loud pleasure he gave me. I want him begging me not to stop. Just thinking about it makes me hot beyond belief.

'I could do a closer inspection with my mouth,' I say, licking my lips seductively.

Seth lets out a slow breath. 'You don't have to.'

'I want to. I *really* want to.'

'That's my shower fantasy,' he says, sliding lower so he's positioned right under me.

'Is it now?' I say, leaning forward and giving him an experimental rasp with my tongue.

Seth gasp-moans. 'Feel free to stop at any point... or before I... You know.'

'I don't have a problem with that, just lie back and relax,' I say, busily tucking my hair back behind my ears like I'm an old hand at this. I've given approximately five blow jobs in my life, all with Gabe, and I gagged each time. Hopefully this will go better, and I don't crack a tooth.

I'm just about to slide my mouth around Seth's apadravya, when there's a loud *meow* and Filippo lands on the bed on all fours, runs over and starts pawing madly at his stomach.

'Ow, fuck!'

I giggle. 'You don't mind a bit of metal piercing your willy, but you can't handle cat paws?'

'They're like tiny knives!'

I watch, fascinated as the claws rhythmically dig into his skin. 'I think Filippo might be dead set against you getting a blow job.'

'Well, he doesn't get a say in the matter.'

Seth extracts each of Filippo's claws delicately, and small beads of blood appear. 'I might need extra special medical attention after this. I'll take him out to the lounge.'

'Make sure the door's closed properly or he'll push it open again,' I advise. 'Maybe give him some milk.'

'I'll be right back. Hold that thought.'

He scoops up Filippo in his arms and gets off the bed. The cat's tail falls down between his legs, neatly hiding his erection. *The purrfect cover-up,* I think, smiling to myself. But I manage to sneak a peek at his bare arse before it disappears out the door. Damn, he has sizzling hot buns.

While he's gone, I spend a few minutes limbering up my jaw in preparation. Then decide to grab the condoms out of his jeans pocket and put them in the bedside drawer on standby. Might as well close the shutters too. Passersby don't need to hear his moans of ecstasy and it might provide sound proofing.

Thank God Antonella's out to dinner, otherwise she'd hear everything through the walls which would surely make our next meet-up a tad embarrassing. Flicking the wooden shutter from its catch, I pull it round to cover the window. I glance out idly and happen to see a guy with short sandy hair leaning against the wall by the river under a street lamp, his hands in his pockets. He's wearing jeans and a t-shirt with a knitted vest over the top. He looks like a tourist to me, but when he turns his head and stares up at the apartments, I shrink back from the window in shock. Fuck, I thought that vest thing looked familiar. It's Gabe. Staking out the apartments, trying to figure out which one I'm in. I groan at my stupidity. He's obviously checked my Instagram and seen the initial photos I took from the lounge of the Ponte Vecchio. From the angle it's not hard to figure out I'm staying here.

I take a step backwards and look around for my clothes only to realise I've left them in the bathroom. Flipping open my suitcase, I put on a random t-shirt and a pair of unsexy knickers. Then creep back over to the window and peer out cautiously from behind the edge of the shutter. Gabe is still leaning against the wall, staring up at each of the windows. I was just lucky he wasn't looking at mine when I happened to be glancing out.

Behind me, I hear Seth open the door. 'That's him sorted,

now where were we...' he says, then there's a pause. 'What are you doing?'

'Gabe's outside!' I hiss over my shoulder.

'Where?'

'By the wall.'

'Seriously?'

Seth materialises beside me and stands in the window looking out, everything on display. I'm a bit surprised he's not being more cautious. Then I see Gabe hold up an object in front of him. There's a small flash of white light.

Seth immediately jerks back from the window, flies to the bed, rips the duvet off and swathes it around himself so he resembles a large white marshmallow.

Confused, I slam the shutters over the window and stare at him. 'What just happened?!'

'Your bloody ex took a photo of me starkers!'

'Are you sure?'

'Yes! With his phone.' He groans and falls backward on the bed, his arm over his eyes. 'Oh, this is bad. So bad.'

'I'm sure he didn't get a very good shot,' I reason, trying to be practical but feeling guilty that I've got a stalkerish ex-boyfriend who I'm not dealing with. 'He wasn't that close to us and zoom never works well at night. You were probably just a blurry blob.'

Seth sits up and grimaces, rubbing his eyes. 'If it was the latest iPhone, then the zoom will work pretty well. Also, he used the flash which makes the image clearer.'

I shake my head, 'Gabe's too stingy to splash out on the latest iPhone. Last I saw, he was pretty attached to his iPhone 8.' So attached, he preferred to scroll on that rather than bother making conversation with me.

But Seth has switched to a different train of thought. He stares at me with a panicked expression. 'Oh God, if he sends it to the British tabloids, I'm screwed!'

'I'm sure it won't come to that. Anyway, it might help you get more plays on your songs,' I joke, trying to get him to see the lighter side. He isn't amused.

'You don't get it. Even if they don't use it straight away, it'll be there in their files like a fucking ticking time bomb. At the slightest sniff of fame and fortune, they'll publish it. I can see the headline now: SETH CARVER OF SUBLIME MISERY CAUGHT WITH HIS GOOLIES OUT. So humiliating. I'll be the laughing stock of London.'

I feel his pain. I know how private he is. I'd also hate to have naked photos of me floating around, not knowing where they were going to end up, and I'm not even famous.

'Shit, I'm so sorry,' I say, coming over to the bed and trying to put my arms around him, which proves difficult since he's four times his normal size wrapped up in the duvet.

Seth sighs and rubs my arm. 'It's not your fault.'

'What can we do?'

'I'll get dressed and ring Dad. I have to warn him that he

may need to do damage control or get a lawyer or something. I don't know, I've never had a naked photo splashed all over the tabloids before.' He groans. 'What if it ends up on the front page!'

He sounds like he's starting to spiral.

'Don't think about that! Look, it's getting late,' I say. 'Let's just go to bed and sleep on it, and you can ring your Dad in the morning.'

Seth doesn't respond and I think he's lost it completely, but then he nods and rolls out of the duvet. Somehow, I manage to fit it back on the bed, with him underneath it, and I get back in too. He reaches over to switch off the light, and I gather him into my arms in the darkness. I stroke his back and make soothing noises like he's a small child. 'Don't worry. It'll be OK. I won't let anything happen to you.' He heaves a big shuddering sigh and curls into me. I've never seen Seth like this before, vulnerable and afraid. He's usually so in control. Even more bizarre is the fact that not too long ago, he was giving me a rip-roaring orgasm that nearly shook me senseless. But I'm too far gone; I want him, all facets of him, the weak and the strong.

I must have fallen asleep at some stage because when I next open my eyes, it's daylight, and Seth is fully dressed and sitting on the edge of the bed next to me.

'Hey,' I say and reach for his hand. It feels kind of special that we spent the night together, even though it was under peculiar circumstances. By the way he's typing flat out on his phone, I can tell the problem with Gabe is still uppermost in his mind.

'Hey,' he leans down to kiss me distractedly on the cheek.

'Did you sleep?' I ask, sitting up.

'A little,' he says.

'Who are you messaging?'

'No one, I'm just writing some notes about what happened, so I can refer to them when I talk to Dad. I know he's going to want details.'

'Ah,' I say, 'are you going to mention me?'

'I kind of have to since we're at your place, and he'll want to know why I was naked. But I won't mention any specifics about that side of it.'

'Thank God.' I don't particularly want Seth's father getting a blow-by-blow account about what his son was doing to me beforehand.

'I was also thinking I should meet up with Calypso,' he adds. 'Her Dad's a lawyer, and she's picked up a lot of stuff through osmosis over the years. Plus, she's been involved in a few litigious disputes herself, so she's pretty clued up. She'll know what to do.'

My heart sinks. Great, now he's being thrown together with Calypso. They'll be spending a lot of time together, talking about the case if it ever gets to that stage. Bloody

Violet, I could strangle her for telling Gabe I was here. It's causing so many problems. But I don't say anything, just press my lips together into a thin line and fold my arms across my chest.

Seth glances at me. I know I'm coming across as a jealous girlfriend. 'I don't want to see her, but she's here, and she has my best interests at heart,' he says.

I feel like wailing, *What about me? I care about your best interests and your heart!*

But I nod, and he kisses me gently on the forehead. 'Go back to sleep. I'll message you later.'

He gets up and heads towards the door but a jolt of panic shoots through me. If he goes off with this thing hanging between us, Calypso could somehow turn him against me. Then he'll ditch me, and I'll never see him again. He'll start going out with Calypso because she's saved his reputation from certain ruin. They'll lie in bed naked together, and she'll say, "thank fuck you didn't get involved with that Jenna girl, I knew she was bad news for you and the band." And then he'll agree and start kissing her...

'Seth—wait!' I screech.

He pauses by the door and looks back. 'What?'

'Don't go. I can fix this.'

CHAPTER TWENTY-FIVE

My palms are slick with sweat as Seth and I sit outside, under an umbrella, at the appointed café near the Duomo. It's hot and I'm nervous, so I keep wiping them on my short-sleeved yellow sundress. The meeting with Gabe was ridiculously easy to arrange. I simply texted Violet saying I needed his number and she sent it through. Then I texted him saying Violet told me he was in Florence and asked whether he fancied catching up for lunch. His affirmative reply came through shortly after, when Seth and I were munching on cereal in our spot on the window seat.

My plan to fix things, which I brainstormed in the space of ten seconds to stop Seth walking out the door, is actually pretty good. As I said to him in the kitchen before I sent the text, 'You're forgetting a vital piece of information—I'm Gabe's ex-girlfriend, and he wants me back. All we have to do is meet up with him for lunch and don't let on that we know he was outside and he's got the photo. Knowing Gabe, he won't do anything with it straight away. He'll sit on it. I'll make it clear during lunch that you and I are just friends in case he's thinking of using it for blackmail purposes to break us up.'

'Why would he believe we're only friends when I was naked in your bedroom?' Seth asks flatly, following me into the lounge. I think about this for a minute.

'Ah, he didn't see me and he doesn't know which apartment is mine, so I'll mention you hooked up with Antonella next door.'

'Go on.' Seth sounds unconvinced.

'Anyway,' I continue hopping up on the window seat, 'Then, I'll suggest we go for a stroll along the Arno and, during that, I'll offer to take a photo of him for Facebook. Once his phone is in my hot little hand, I delete your photo from his camera roll, and *bam!* Problem solved.'

'What happens if he tries it on with you?' Seth asks, sitting down opposite me.

'Er, I'll say I'm flattered, but all the reasons I had for breaking up with him are still there. Then I wish him well, and hope we can remain friends. Job done.'

'Is he attractive? I didn't get a proper look at him last night.'

I shrug. 'Why is that relevant?'

'I'm just curious since you were with him for five years.'

'He's cute but not devastatingly sexy,' I say.

'Oh.' He gives me the side-eye. 'Am I?'

I shrug.

Seth lowers his cereal bowl to his lap and runs a finger down the sole of my bare foot. I jerk my leg up, but he grasps my ankle more firmly, so I can't pull away. He tickles my foot until I'm squawking with laughter.

'Yes! You are!' I gasp, practically flinging my cereal at him, 'You're so fucking sexy it hurts my eyes to look at you!'

Seth releases my foot and picks up his cereal bowl again. 'That's good to know,' he smirks.

'Humph. I'm not sure that extracting the truth by tickling is good-boyfriend behaviour,' I pout, poking him with my big toe.

'As long as you don't forget I am your boyfriend.'

Ooh, Seth's getting a little territorial, I kind of like that. 'You have absolutely nothing to worry about,' I reassure him picking up my phone to text Gabe. 'This is purely a transactional meeting, designed to save your arse. Literally.'

Now I'm wishing this transactional meeting would hurry up and be over with. I look down at the tiny white daisies on my dress and remember the time I wore it for an outing with Gabe to Hyde Park. It was a scorcher of a day, much like this one. We lay on sunloungers and drank Pimms. I had on a big straw hat, and he said I looked like a sunflower, which I took as a compliment.

That's part of the reason I decided to wear the dress today, as a nod to our past. I've even resorted to putting my hair in pigtail buns, which he always found cute. Yet, I've added sunglasses, heels and Antonella's black Gucci bag to make it look more sophisticated. Well, we are in Italy, and I don't want to look like a twelve-year-old.

At the last minute, Seth decided to invite Calypso along as well, which I wasn't too happy about. He said it was to kill two birds with one stone since she wanted to hang out. But I suspect he wants her on-site just in case my idea backfires, and we have to resort to lawyer speak or something.

So not only are we waiting at the café for Gabe to turn up, we're also waiting for Calypso. Oh, joy.

They're both late.

'Should we order some drinks?' I say to Seth, 'I'm dying of thirst.'

'Yeah, I'm dying as well. It's not a good day to be wearing black.'

'But you will insist. Maybe we should get you a pink shirt and a pair of tight crotch-hugging blue jeans, like the Italian guys wear. I could go for that,' I tease and Seth shudders. 'There's probably a shop nearby...'

Twisting around to look for one, I catch sight of Gabe who's approaching the café. Oddly enough, he is wearing a pink shirt, but he's paired it with white shorts and brown boat shoes without socks. He looks like a dapper young gentleman about to play a round of golf. I swallow nervously. 'Showtime. He's here.'

Seth swivels to check him out silently, and his eyes narrow. I'm not sure why he's so threatened by Gabe. I guess the fact that he's my ex-boyfriend could be part of the reason, but I did dump him a year ago, and I hardly talk about him in glowing terms. It's probably more about him holding all the cards with that explicit photo of Seth's dangly bits he managed to snap. I still can't believe he did that.

Gabe stops abruptly when he sees me sitting at the table and gives a small wave. I nod at him and he comes over. I get up to greet him, unsure if I should proffer my cheek or not. In the end I do, and he kisses it lightly. The scent of his familiar musky aftershave wafts over me.

'Hey Jenna,' he says gruffly. 'It's been a while.'

'Hi Gabe, this is Seth, a friend of mine,' I say, emphasising the word friend. Seth gets up too, and while they shake hands politely, they look at each other warily. 'We're expecting someone else, but we were going to order anyway,' I say.

'I'll grab some menus,' Seth mutters and leaves the table to go inside.

Gabe sits down next to me. I see him checking out the pigtail buns, dress and heels. 'You look nice,' he says.

'Thanks,' I reply brusquely. 'You look… the same.' He actually looks older, but I'm not going to say that. I want him sweet and pliable, so I can get hold of his phone.

Seth comes back with the menus. His presence makes me relax a little.

'So this is strange, meeting here like this. How come you're in Florence?' I ask Gabe.

'Just a little break,' he says. 'I'm suffering from burnout since I worked all summer.'

He avoids my eyes and grabs a menu.

'Right.' So that's the story he's giving.

Calypso arrives just then, so he doesn't expound on it.

'Sorry I'm late!' she says striding over to us in another white-on-white outfit; a high-rise pencil skirt and a short sleeve crop top. What is it with her and Seth and their monochrome clothes? She stops when she sees Gabe, looking confused. A flicker of panic crosses her face, and weirdly, I know exactly what she's thinking: they're trying to set me up with him, so I'm not a third wheel. Even more weirdly, I feel a bit sorry for her.

'Calypso, this is Gabe, my ex-boyfriend. We're having a catch-up,' I explain.

'Oh, right.' She sounds a bit surprised but nods at Seth and sits down next to him, directly across from Gabe. 'Hi,' she says, and he responds with, 'Hi,' back.

'Calypso and Seth are friends from home,' I tell Gabe.

Seth has been keeping quiet until now, perusing the menu. 'So, anyway, now that's all out of the way, let's order, I'm starving,' he says looking around for a waiter. He sounds like I feel: *let's get this charade over with.*

What follows after we order, is probably the most

awkward lunch I've ever had. It starts as soon as Calypso says forthrightly, 'So Gabe, what brings you to Florence?'

I think he's going to stick with the work burnout story, but he sits up straighter under her piercing blue gaze like he's under cross-examination and he can't lie. 'I've had a major overhaul in my life, and I came to see if Jenna wants to give it another go.'

I start in surprise. I wasn't expecting that!

'Aw, that's so sweet!' exclaims Calypso. 'But I thought...' she glances at Seth and I.

'We're just friends,' I say hastily. Out of the corner of my eye I see Gabe smirk, so I say, 'Seth actually fancies my next-door neighbour, he was round at her place last night.' I force myself to look pained.

'Oh!' Calypso smiles broadly. 'Well, how romantic of you Gabe. Tell me more.'

I cringe, thinking, *Oh God,* then feel Seth's hand creep onto my knee and squeeze it slightly as if to say, *You can do this.*

So I have to sit there in silence and listen to Gabe proceed to spill his guts over what a twat he was when we were together and how he regrets it. He says he's been doing mindful meditations and even visited a life guru in Brixton for advice on how to attain greater fulfillment. It was during one of these sessions that he had the epiphany to get in touch with me, while a further session gave him the strength to

follow through with his conviction that we're meant to be together. I don't know why he's so convinced that we are. It's beginning to sound more like he's terribly lonely and internet dating isn't going well for him. Whatever the reason, it's excruciating to hear his twaddle.

I daren't risk looking at Seth during his speech. He's eating his pepperoni pizza silently but keeps his hand on my knee under the table, out of sight of Calypso the entire time, like he knows that I want to take flight.

As for Calypso, I can tell she's enjoying Gabe's monologue thoroughly, topping up his water and passing him the Parmesan cheese, so he can sprinkle it liberally on his pasta alfredo.

'That's fascinating,' she says. 'Maybe you should go to this guru in Brixton, Seth. Might give you some clarity on a few things.' Whether she means about his songwriting or their relationship, is unclear. Seth grunts.

I nibble on my asparagus risotto, feeling a bit sick. I ordered a large white wine spritzer, which went down like water, so I ordered another. Now I'm nauseous and my brain is befuddled. Gabe's phone is lying on the table, right there, in plain view. I could just reach over right now, nab it and get this over with, but I don't know his PIN code. Then I realise Gabe is looking at me expectantly, 'What?' I ask.

'So are you going to take it?'

Oh no, is it that obvious what I'm thinking?

'Take what?'

'Jenna, I'm offering you my job. If you want it. I'm leaving to go freelance. To be my own boss.'

'Oh.' But that's what I've been doing. *Badly*. I take another gulp of wine spritzer.

'I've built up a solid client base on the side, and I've got a foothold in Mayfair,' he continues.

Fuck. *Mayfair*. He'll be raking it in. That's what I could've done if he hadn't forced me out of my job before I was ready. My blood starts boiling, and I take another large swallow of wine spritzer. Seth interjects before I say something that ruins our ruse. 'Sounds like you're doing well, Gabe. Congrats.'

'Thanks. What do you do?' he asks Seth nonchalantly. But by the way he's smirking again, I can tell he already knows. It's not too hard to type "Seth Carver" into Google and bring up the Sublime Misery website. I clench my teeth.

'I'm a poet,' says Seth. 'It doesn't pay much at the moment, but I'm hoping to publish a collection quite soon. There's been interest from a few publishers.'

Calypso snorts. 'Poet? That's one way of putting it. Seth's actually a talented…' but before she can say anything I knock my wine spritzer over deliberately, 'Shit, sorry!' I exclaim and grab a handful of napkins to mop up the liquid. I stand and realise that my sundress now has a big damp patch on the crotch like I've wet myself. Fantastic.

CHAPTER TWENTY-SIX

'So, ah, maybe we should go for a walk by the Arno, Gabe, and let this dry off?' I suggest. But he wrinkles his nose at my dress as if he doesn't want to be seen with a girl who's peed herself.

'It might be better to dry it in the bathroom,' he says. 'Besides, I'm still eating my lunch.'

I give Seth a shrug, and he does a slight eye roll. There's nothing for it but to slope off to the bathroom and attempt to waft hot air down from the hand dryer onto my dress. While I'm doing so, Calypso comes in and washes her hands.

'You alright there?' she says, watching me thrust my hips valiantly at the hand dryer.

'Yup,' I say. But it's doing nothing. I give up and use the loo so we're not elbow-to-elbow in the small space. When I come out, she's checking her eyebrows in the mirror. She turns around and leans against the counter while I wash my hands.

'So, you and Seth aren't together then?' She sounds hopeful.

Here we go. I knew that was the reason she followed me

in.

'No,' I mutter, 'Irreconcilable differences.'

'Shame. But you are quite different people.'

I give a non-committal 'Mmm.'

'Did he give you the flick for your neighbour?' she presses. 'I'm not surprised. Seth's not really interested in a serious relationship. With him it's all about the music and making it big as I found out.'

I don't say anything, just wipe my hands on a paper towel.

Taking my silence for depression, Calypso pats my shoulder. 'He's a heartbreaker, isn't he? But you can still be friends. Plus, now you've got Gabe wanting you back. There's always a silver lining to these things. I'll see you out there.'

She goes into one of the stalls and, as I leave, I hear her doing a trying-to-be-discrete fart.

Grrr, I know Calypso is inherently a bitch, but what she said about Seth is drilling into my insecurity like a jackhammer. I *am* terrified that once he finishes writing, he'll dump me, and the next time I see him it will be smouldering sexily from the cover of Rolling Stone. It makes me flinch even thinking about it. I suspect the pain would be worse than a root canal without anaesthetic.

When I get back outside, there's no Seth or Gabe in sight. The table has been cleared of our glasses and plates, and there's a gaggle of older Italian women sitting there with small dogs lapping from bowls. Confused, I leave the café but, not too far away, I spy Gabe taking photos of the Duomo while Seth slouches against the side of a building with his sunglasses on, watching him with an annoyed expression.

'Hey, how come you guys left?'

'We got kicked off the table for a group reservation,' he replies, 'And now this…' He nods at Gabe who's busily snapping away. 'I asked him if he wanted one with him in, but he said "no thanks, mate". He's not stupid.'

I sigh. 'OK, I'll try the walk along the Arno again and see if that works. For someone who wants to give it another go, he's not being particularly attentive,' I grumble.

'Come to the hotel later. I'll show you what attentive looks like,' Seth whispers in my ear and hooks his little finger through mine. But then quickly moves it away as Calypso comes out of the café. At least it reassures me that he's still interested, even if it's for a quickie at the hotel.

'What's going on?' Calypso asks, shouldering her handbag.

'We got kicked off the table, so I sorted the bill,' Seth tells her, shoving his hands in his pockets. 'Now we're thinking of going for a walk along the Arno.'

'I've got a bunch of free tickets to the Uffizi Gallery through a journalist friend of mine,' she says, scrolling on her phone. 'Anyone interested?'

Seth looks at me and widens his eyes. 'Would lover-boy be keen to see some Renaissance art?'

'I'm sure he would be. And if not, I'll make him,' I say, resolutely.

Gabe is extremely keen since the tickets are free, so we all head down to the Uffizi, which is apparently on the banks of the Arno, near the Ponte Vecchio. Since I'm his renewed love interest, I'm walking alongside Gabe, while Seth and Calypso are in front leading the way. I'm trying to keep calm, but I'm feeling the pressure to undertake the task at hand. Maybe I can try and get a photo of him by the river and delete the photo of Seth before we go in. Then, I can just relax and enjoy myself. I'm clueless about this Renaissance art, but if it's naked men that look like David, I'm happy to check it out. Come to think of it, the Uffizi was on Cathy's must-do list, somewhere near the bottom.

Calypso is nattering away to Seth about their mutual friends in Hampstead and, since her voice is so loud, I can't help but overhear. 'Oh, and Dahlia has a cute new puppy,' I hear her say, 'We'll have to go over one day so you can meet him. Just adorable!'

Seth replies briefly, with something that sounds like 'if I'm not recording.'

It feels like Calypso is in Try-Again-With Seth mode, even though she told me all that stuff in the loo about him not being interested in a relationship. My instincts are telling me I shouldn't believe a word out of her sly-tongued mouth.

What's making me feel really grumpy and left out is that they actually do have a shared history. My mood is sliding into a dangerously low ebb, so when Gabe asks me a question, I just nod automatically like a roboton. Then I realise I have no idea what I've nodded to. 'Sorry, what did you say?'

'I asked if things were going OK with your freelancing?'

That's a question that deserves more of a shake of the head than a nod, but I say 'Yes, it is. I'm getting loads of clients through word of mouth. So I'm not sure if I want to go back to the agency.' I sense my nose growing longer the instant I say it.

I wait for Gabe to say, 'We should join forces' or something like that, but he doesn't. I forgot he's competitive when it comes to clients. Besides if he's raking it in in Mayfair, he won't need my piddly pool of people who want new beige carpet.

He just says, 'When I spoke to your friend Violet, she mentioned you'd been staying with her, so I thought you might be finding it tough out there.'

Dammit, thanks Violet.

'She also mentioned you were still single. That's when I went to my guru for guidance and what she said made me hope...'

'What exactly did she say?'

'She said you might have grown up a bit and be ready to settle down.'

I bristle. Who the hell is this guru? She doesn't know me or what I want. And why is he going to her for advice on his lovelife? But I can't lose it, for Seth's sake, so I bite back my words, again, like I've been doing this entire afternoon.

We walk through an imposing archway into a colonnaded courtyard thronging with tourists and street artists. Calypso twists around and says to us. 'We're here. Keep together, and we'll go through as a group.'

Shit. I've missed my chance to take the photo. It's going to have to be inside.

A line of people snakes down the entire length of the portico and squiggles across the courtyard. My jaw drops. 'Is this the queue to get in?' I ask dumbfounded. Wow, these must be spectacular paintings if people are willing to stand in a queue this long to see them.

'Yes. But only if you don't have a ticket. Luckily we do, so no queuing for us,' answers Calypso smugly.

Even though she isn't my favourite person, she does have her uses. It feels like we're VIPs as she flashes a card and shows her phone to the guard on the door, and we're waved through without any hassle. 'Is the art really famous or something?' I ask, surprised at the airport type security in the entrance. My handbag has to go through the scanner.

Calypso gives me a withering look. 'You could say that. All the big names from the Renaissance are here—Giotto, Botticelli, Da Vinci, Raphael, Michelangelo.'

'Cool,' I say. *OK, there's no need to be a bitch about it.*

'Though, the art in the Uffizi does range from the twelfth to the seventeenth century, while the Italian Renaissance started in the fourteenth century,' she intones in an art history teacher's voice.

Whether she's attempting to educate thicko me or impress Seth, I'm not sure, but it's incredibly annoying nonetheless. I suppose she thinks it's weird that an interior decorator doesn't know about Renaissance art.

'Oh right. I'm actually more into Surrealism,' I say airily, 'You know—Dali, Picasso, Magritte, Chagall.'

That shuts her up.

After climbing a set of stairs, we reach a main corridor that stretches as far as the eye can see. According to the handy map I've been given, we're on one arm of a horseshoe-shaped building. On the left-hand side of the corridor, a row of marble statues on plinths adorn the walls. The other side has tall picture windows that run along the length letting in streams of light. Looking up, I see the wooden ceiling is covered with finely drawn, vividly coloured frescoes; animals, cupids and nymphs frolicking. Even with all the people milling about, the place glows with calming energy, and a feeling of peace flows over me.

'It's lovely,' I comment and Seth smiles.

'This is one of my favourite places in Florence,' he says.

I smile back at him fondly. *Then I'm sure I'll like it.*

'Seth can be our guide,' says Calypso, 'he's an Uffizi expert.'

But he looks embarrassed and shakes his head. 'I'm not. Maybe it's best if we split up and just wander,' he says, giving me a meaningful glance. For a moment I get hopeful, thinking he wants to hold hands and stroll around together, but then I realise he's referring to Operation Gabe, and he's giving me space to execute my plan.

'Yes,' I say in an overly confident tone. 'Great idea.'

'Fine with me,' echoes Gabe immediately. He seems keen to not spend any more time with Seth than he has to. I consult my map. 'Gabe and I will start here with the Giotto room, and we'll meet you guys a bit later.'

I grip Gabe's elbow and guide him to a doorway on the left, while Seth takes his cue saying to Calypso, 'Come on, we'll find an Italian tour group to listen in on. I'll translate.' Calypso doesn't protest and follows Seth down the corridor like an eager puppy. I wish it was me going with him, not her. But no, I'm left with Gabe to sort out this freaking nightmare of a photo. Lucky me.

Gabe and I wander around the Giotto room which is full of religious paintings featuring an abundance of gold leaf. They're pretty, but there are only so many variations of Madonna and Child you can handle without them all blurring into one. We move into the Early Renaissance Room, and I'm still trying to figure out how to suggest taking a photo with his phone without being obvious. I'm just going to have to bite the bullet and hope he doesn't see through me. I take a deep breath. 'Shall we take a selfie together for Insta?' I enquire, pretending to look in my bag for my phone.

'Hmm?' he says, reading the placard of a work called The Duke and Duchess of Urbino; a grim-faced couple in profile staring at each other within a ornate gold frame. Suddenly, I get a brainwave.

'Actually, let's take a photo of us standing in front of the Duke and Duchess. You do mine in front of her, and I'll do yours in front of him, and we can join them together. It'll be fun.'

Gabe grins. 'OK. We'll use my phone, and I'll do the stitch.' I knew he'd go for it. He loves that kind of thing. Once he made us dress up for a Halloween party as a PB&J sandwich; he was the peanut butter and I was the jam. Then, he had us pose for what felt like a hundred photos set on timer. Half a dozen of the best went up on Facebook in a collage. Cringe.

'I'll go first,' I say and arrange myself in front of the painting. I tuck my hair behind my ears and press my lips together to mimic the woman's po-faced expression.

'Move back slightly, now towards me. Got it! Perfect.' He looks at the photo and laughs.

'Now your turn,' I say, holding out my hand for his phone.

'I'll just edit it a bit.' He starts a series of adjustments to the photo, while I tap my foot impatiently. Gabe is obsessive about photo edits too, which is why Seth has a right to be worried. The photo he's taken of him has probably been cropped, brightened, sharpened and vibrance-enhanced, until it's newspaper-worthy. There's no way Gabe will want to be credited for a sub-par photo. The adjustments continue until I'm ready to explode with frustration. Then, he switches his phone to camera mode and hands it to me. I let out the lung-pinching breath I've been holding. Finally! The moment I've been waiting for. But I still have to go through the motions.

Gabe gets into position in front of the Duke of Urbino, a haughty fellow with a hooked nose and a red jacket and hat. I take a couple of random photos, then flip through his camera feed while he's not looking. I've got a few seconds before he realises what I'm up to. I flick past the Duomo shots from today, and, oh my God, the photo of Seth is there all right, and it's a doozy. He's standing in the window, peering out with a frown, and his bits are clearly in focus. He puts David to shame, I must say. I feel like a voyeur looking at a naked photo of him, but I can't help gawping. The Goth groupies would be shrieking in ecstasy at seeing that. Poor Seth.

I click on the trash can button to delete it, then go into the Recently Deleted folder to permanently erase it from there, congratulating myself on my foresight. Imagine how much I'd be kicking myself if I forgot that step!

'Have you finished?' says Gabe impatiently, still holding the pose.

'Almost,' I say. 'I'm not as good at this as you are. Can you just move forward a bit, now tilt your head down.'

He does what I say, and I hold the phone up, but really I'm checking his Recents folder to double check the photo is definitely gone. However, when I do, I get the shock of my life. There are a whole series of the same bloody photo, like it's sprouted evil children. He must've copied it or taken a photo burst or something. Panicking, I start selecting all the photos in quick succession so I can delete them. But a hand closes around mine before I have a chance to do it.

CHAPTER TWENTY-SEVEN

'What are you doing, Jenna?'

I raise my eyes slowly to find Gabe glaring at me. He carefully removes the phone out of my grasp, and I have no choice but to let him. Oh no, *no!*

'I was checking the photos I took…'

'No, you're not. You're looking at *him*. Seth Carver,' he growls, nostrils flaring. His cheeks are lobster red and clashing terribly with his pink shirt.

I try to stay calm and focused. I'm going to have to get his phone off him again somehow. 'Why are you getting pissy with me? You're the one who took a bunch of nude photos of him,' I state evenly, 'What are you, some kind of pervert?'

Gabe huffs and his cheeks glow redder. 'Whatever. I was looking for you, then he appeared at the window. It was a knee jerk reaction. I didn't know exactly what I'd taken until later, and then, I had a right laugh.'

Ugh. Prat. More like he was crying because Seth is so gorgeous. 'Why didn't you message me instead of hanging around outside the apartment?'

'Because you'd just ignore it. So I was hoping to catch you

face-to-face.'

Huh, he knows that about me at least. 'So what are you going to do with them now?'

'I'm not sure.'

'You know who he is, don't you?'

'Yes, I know who he is. The *poet* of Sublime Misery. Not a household name just yet but famous enough to warrant these photos being worth something to interested parties. But why do you care so much anyway? I thought you were *just friends...*' He suddenly smacks his forehead with his hand. 'Duh, I'm an idiot. You were there with him, weren't you? He wasn't next door with the neighbour, that was bullshit to throw me off the scent. It's friends with benefits.'

'No, it's not. It's... deeper,' I say biting my lip, unwilling to reveal too much. 'Besides, even if he was just my friend, I'd try to help him out. He doesn't deserve his photo splashed all over the tabloids. What has he ever done to you?'

Gabe is holding his phone lightly in his hand, which is down by his side. If only there was some kind of distraction... Perhaps, I can just push him over and grab it...

But Gabe's got that dog-with-a-bone look on his face. He ignores my question and says suspiciously, 'What do you mean—deeper?'

I blush and look away, but it's probably written all over my face since I'm more readable than I thought I was.

'Oh... I see,' he says slowly. 'You're in love with him. And he's sent you to do his dirty work.'

I don't deny the former, but I do have to correct him about the latter. I fold my arms and try to look imposing which, at five-four, is not an easy feat. 'Actually, it was my idea to try and delete the photo. I just didn't realise there would be so many.'

He shrugs. 'As I said, it was a spur of the moment thing. So, you and Seth Carver, huh? Now I know why you're clearly not interested in giving it another go.' He leans in and searches my face looking for some kind of reaction, but I don't give him one. 'Maybe I'll make it worth my while and see if I can get something for them. It would reimburse me for the money I wasted on this trip anyway. I'm sure there are quite a few papers or online sites who'd like to publish them. Pretty well hung, isn't he?'

'Fuck you, Gabe.'

I turn to leave, sick of being goaded, and he tugs on my arm, 'Wait, Jenna.' But I yank it back sharply. However, the action makes me overbalance and step on the tip of his boat shoe, just as he steps back. Since he's heavier than me and not wearing any socks, he slips out of it and the momentum sends him tipping backwards. His hands whip up into the air doing wheelies to keep his balance, but he falls on his arse with a grunt and his phone scoots across the highly polished floor like an ice hockey puck. A guy wearing a New York Yankees t-shirt and cargo shorts, stops it with his trainer and bends to pick it up.

Leaving Gabe sprawled on the floor, I beat a hasty retreat to collect the phone.

'Oh, thank you for that,' I say, breathlessly, snatching it out of the guy's hand. 'My boyfriend's. He slipped. Accident.'

'Does he need some help?' He nods at Gabe who's sitting up and looking around dazedly, minus one boat shoe. Gabe sees I have his phone in my hand and starts clambering to his feet.

'Ah, no, looks like he'll live, but thanks again!' I start hoofing it towards the doorway, leaving the guy to make his own assumptions about why I'm hurrying away like a cold-hearted bitch and not assisting my boyfriend.

Walking rapidly down the corridor, I tuck Gabe's phone into my bra for safekeeping—women always do that in action movies and it makes good sense. If Gabe catches me, he's not going to go rummaging around in my bra. I'm pumped with adrenaline at finally having his phone, I can feel it jiggling, cool and comforting, against my boob as I trot down the corridor. I did it! But I can't celebrate just yet. The Uffizi is a sizeable art museum. Seth could be anywhere. I fish in my handbag for my phone so I can text him, but I discover the battery has died. Great. With all the hoo haa last night and this morning, I've forgotten to charge it. Now what? I'm just going to have to find him. Easier said than done since I have no idea where he could be.

I try to clear my mind and focus on his face. *Seth, I need you*. Strangely, I start feeling his presence flow into my brain, like he's thinking about me too, willing me to find him. With each room I pass, I send out feelers, to sense if he's in there, all the while knowing Gabe can't be too far behind. *Where the hell are you?* As I pass a tour group, a word is spoken clearly by the guide "Primavera". It doesn't mean anything to me, so I ignore it and keep moving, but suddenly, I hear it again, and then again, from different people walking past me. It's too insistent to be a coincidence. *Is it a painting?* I check my handbag for the map, but it's not there. Damn, I must've dropped it.

A woman in a green dress is standing alone by a statue, wearing audio guide earphones and gazing up at the frescoed ceiling. She looks like she knows stuff so I veer over to her. 'Excuse me, where's the Primavera?'

She takes an earphone out, smiles and points to the room on the left, 'That way. But no rush, love, he's there, you've got time.'

'Thanks.' It's only when I'm walking away do I realise what she's said, and a shiver goes through me. What the? Maybe I misheard and she meant *it's there*.

I stand in the doorway, scanning the room for a glimpse of Seth, but it's chokka with people, as if everyone in the queue has made a beeline here. Then the crowd parts like the red sea and Seth's there, alone, with his back to me in front of a large intricate painting of several golden-haired women frolicking in a flowered forest. He turns as if sensing me, and we lock eyes. My heart soars like a bird over the terracotta rooftops of the city and I know without a doubt that I'm in love. I'd run to the ends of the earth on bleeding feet for him if I had to. But there's no time to tell him any of that; I'm being pursued.

The distress I'm feeling must be palpable because he instantly makes his way over.

'What is it?'

I draw Gabe's phone part way out of my bra to show him. 'There isn't just one photo. There's a whole Seth Carver porno exhibition on there. I didn't have time to delete them, he caught me in the middle of it.'

Seth sucks in his breath. 'Shit.'

'Where's Calypso?'

'She went to the loo, something didn't agree with her at lunch.'

'I'll delete them now.'

But Seth has other ideas. 'No, keep it hidden. Let's leave.'

'Huh, but what about Calypso?'

'I'll text her. This way.'

He grabs my hand, and we start weaving through the crowd, back towards the painting. My eyes are drawn to it. I slow down and hang back. 'Is that the Primavera?'

'Yeah.'

'It's so beautiful,' I say wistfully.

Seth tightens his grasp on my hand. 'I know, it is. We'll come back another time.'

I guess he's not taking any chances with Gabe on the loose. We peer cautiously into the corridor, but there's no sign of him. 'If he's smart, he'll be waiting at the exit,' I say.

'Then we'll be smarter and go to the entrance.'

'Can we get out that way though?'

'No, but I've got an idea. It may work.'

I feel a bit bad that we're leaving Calypso in the loo dealing with whatever bowel issues she's having. Perhaps, I should offer to check in on her? But I can't make myself say the words out loud. I'm a nice person, but maybe not that nice.

When we get to the ground floor, it's a one-way system as I suspected. They're only letting people in.

'What now?'

'This way.' Seth leads the way down another corridor until we arrive at the edge of a small group of people. A bespectacled older man with a comb-over, who barely comes up to Seth's chest, breaks away from a conversation and speaks up in a sing-songy voice.

'Hello, this is a special tour. Have you both got tickets?' He sounds Irish to my ears, which is completely incongruous to the setting.

'Yes,' says Seth confidently. 'We have.'

I stare at him. This is news to me.

'Can I see them please?'

'Of course.' Seth proffers his phone to the man who looks down his glasses at it.

'These are for tomorrow's time slot at ten o'clock,' he says, and hands it back. 'You're a day early.'

'I'm aware of that,' says Seth patiently. 'But my girlfriend here has to fly back to London for a family emergency tomorrow, so I was hoping we could do it today instead?'

'Sorry, no, that's not how it works,' says the man, who according to his name badge, is called Iarlaithe. *Definitely Irish,* I think. I'm not even sure how to pronounce that. 'You'll have to apply for a refund,' he tells Seth.

'The tour is for twelve people and you've only got eight. Surely you can fit us in?' says Seth in a tone bordering on annoyance.

The man's lips tighten. He doesn't look pleased at being told what to do.

I put on my best sad face. 'Oh, pretty please, Arlathe,' I plead, going for the phonetic pronunciation of his name. 'We'll post a five-star review of... the tour... and mention you specifically. And I'd be so grateful. I've been really looking forward to this... tour.' I'm not even sure what the tour is, so I don't want to put my foot in it.

'Fine,' the man sighs. 'You can join us. And my name is pronounced EAR-lah, for future reference.'

'Sorry,' I say contritely, 'what a great name. So unusual.'

'Thank you, yes, it was my great-grandfather's,' he says, sounding more accommodating.

'Gosh. It really suits you...' I trail off, noticing too late that he does actually have rather large ears. I feel a burble of hysteria threaten but stamp on it quickly. *Shut up, Jenna.*

'The tour starts in five minutes,' he says, moving away to answer a question from someone else in the group.

'Are you going to tell me what this tour is?' I mutter to Seth as we wait. I lean against the wall to try and take some weight off my feet, which are starting to hurt like the dickens.

'It's the Vasari Corridor.'

I stare at him blankly. 'You know, the secret corridor that runs over the Ponte Vecchio that I showed you? It starts here at the Uffizi.'

'Oh, wow!'

'I was going to surprise you tomorrow but—surprise! We're doing it today instead.'

'That's so cool.'

He grins. 'I know. I've been wanting to do it for ages, but it's been closed for renovations.'

I squeeze his arm. 'Thank you. For booking it.'

'Looks like the Uffizi is killing a lot of birds with one stone.' He nods at my boobs where Gabe's phone is still lying hidden.

'Yeah. Slight problem with that. I forgot I don't have his

PIN code, so I can't get into his phone to delete the photos.'

'We'll think of something.'

'We could take out the SIM card but that means he's going to lose all his contacts and photos.' I squirm. That includes the Mayfair clients that he's worked so hard to build up.

'Maybe we can take it to a phone hacker and get them to open it. Or meet with him and say he needs to give us the PIN code or we'll take the SIM card and he'll lose his contacts.'

I sigh. 'This is getting convoluted. Now we're resorting to blackmail. Next thing, the Mafia will be involved.'

Seth leans towards me. 'Sssh, I wouldn't mention the Mafia here,' he whispers.

'Why not?'

'They bombed the Uffizi in 1993. It's a bit of a sensitive subject.'

'Oh, right, good to know,' I say, making a zipping motion across my lips.

CHAPTER TWENTY-EIGHT

I assume that the corridor finishes over the Ponte Vecchio but, when the tour starts, I remember that it's actually a kilometre long and ends up in the Palazzo Pitti on the other side of the river. At any other time, I wouldn't mind that distance, but after all the walking I've done today, my feet are killing me. Why did I decide to wear heels? Now I'm wishing I tucked flip-flops in my handbag. I know I said I'd walk on bleeding feet for Seth, but I didn't think the bleeding would start quite so soon.

However, I try to forget about my aching arches and listen to the history of Cosimo Medici's secret corridor, which is actually pretty interesting. There's a section that shows the damage from the bomb, and we get to peek out of the small round windows that look across the Arno and down onto the streets.

'It feels like we're spying on people. Is this what Cosimo wanted to build it for?'

'I don't think so. Not like in a big brother sense,' says Seth. 'It was more so he and his family could move around discretely and not be bothered by the riff-raff. But it was also supposed to be an escape route when things got iffy at the palace.'

I say a prayer of grateful thanks for Cosimo's foresight, and that four hundred and fifty years later, we're able to use the corridor as an escape route of our own.

When we reach the series of windows overlooking the Ponte Vecchio, the tour stops briefly while Iarlaithe explains how the windows are a more recent addition, installed by Mussolini in 1939 so Hitler could have a view of the Arno. Seth points out the window. 'Look, that's the exact spot where we were on the bikes.'

'Hah, yes. When Stefano was being an ass. It feels like ages ago.'

Seth puts his arm around me and kisses the top of my head.

'What was that for?'

'A thank you for getting the phone off Gabe. You're so amazing.'

Warmth spreads through me at his praise, and I lean into him. 'You are too, with your quick thinking to get us on the tour.'

'We make a good team.'

'And we haven't even pissed off the tour guide.'

'Don't speak too soon. It's not over yet,' Seth says deadpan.

The corridor meanders endlessly. I wonder if the Medicis

even used it that much since it takes so long to get to the other side. But I guess they didn't have an Irish tour guide who stopped them every ten minutes to blather on. Finally, we make it to the Pitti Palace and pop out onto a courtyard by a grotto. The light is muted and the shadows are long. It feels like we've been in there for four hundred and fifty years. By this time, I'm hobbling quite badly, and Seth is propping me up on his arm.

'We can get a taxi to the hotel if you want,' he says.

'I need to go to the apartment first and sort Filippo out as we're so close anyway. I'll also change into flip-flops. Then, I should be OK to walk.'

'Brave soldier. I'll give you a foot massage later.'

I groan. 'Oooh, yes, please.'

'I can massage some other bits too.'

'That's even more motivating,' I say, speeding up despite the pain. Seth laughs.

When we reach the apartment after much complaining from me, Seth waits outside while I kick off my heels, change into my red sundress and race around dealing with Filippo.

Seeing that Seth's left behind his purple toothbrush in the bathroom, I stuff it into my handbag, and add my own. Then, after considering, I put in a few bits of makeup, my hairbrush, deodorant and a fresh pair of knickers. I don't want to make it look too obvious that I'm planning on staying the night since he hasn't actually suggested it. But there's nothing wrong with being prepared—and hopeful—is there?

Slipping my poor bruised feet into flip-flops feels so heavenly, I almost cry. 'I am not wearing heels ever again,' I tell Filippo who's ripping into his fish like he hasn't been fed for a week. 'In fact, I think I'll invest in some Crocs. Pink ones.'

When I get outside, Seth is finishing up a conversation on his phone. 'Calypso,' he says at my enquiring look. 'I had to find out how she was and tell her we had to leave.'

'What did she say?'

'She apologised for abandoning us and said she was feeling better. And since she's leaving early tomorrow for Rome, she'll probably see me back in London.'

'So she's been in the loo the entire time?'

'Apparently.'

'Yikes, I wonder what she ate.' I can't even remember what she had, I was so focused on Operation Gabe. Seth and I head towards the Ponte Vecchio with our fingers laced.

'I think it was something with prosciutto. That can be dodgy. Me and one of the guys from the band were in Spain once, and he ate a whole load of cured meats the afternoon before we flew back to London. Let's just say, no one else got to use that toilet for the entire flight. And, they probably had the plane fumigated afterwards.'

I stifle a laugh. 'Oh no, poor guy.'

'Anyway, changing the subject to something much nicer. I

was thinking you should stay over tonight since Gabe now knows exactly where you're based. He'll be on the warpath looking for his phone. You did bring it?'

I pat my boob, 'Still in here for safekeeping. And, um, thanks for the invite. I did happen to pack a few essentials while I was in the apartment, including your toothbrush.'

'Oh, did you?'

I nod. 'Not that I was expecting to stay. If it happened, cool, but if you wanted an early night, that's OK too.'

Seth snorts. 'An early night? What am I, eighty?' He stops on the corner of the bridge and glances down at me. 'If I'm going to bed, you're going to be in there too. I'm getting withdrawal symptoms from not kissing you.'

My lips tingle, while other parts of me are doing a samba at the thought of spending the night with him. 'Ah. Luckily neither of us ate a whole load of cured meats then,' I say brightly.

'Indeed.'

We join the river of people crossing the Ponte Vecchio and I'm about to ask if we can stop off for gelato before the hotel, when I spot Gabe idly peering in a jewellery shop window directly up ahead. I tug on Seth's hand to attract his attention. But he's already seen him and pulls me into the nearest jewellery shop to hide. I breathe a sigh of relief. That was close!

'Buona sera. Can I help you, sir, madam?' purrs a woman

with a rich Italian accent. We turn to see an impeccably groomed woman behind the counter. She's wearing a tight navy dress with a double stripe of white piping around the waistline and a heart-shaped neckline. My eyes are first drawn to the scary amount of gold chains nestling in the crease of her ample bosom, then to her fingers, which have an equally crazy amount of gold rings. She's a walking advertisement for the shop! But the thing that's even more scary is her chestnut hairdo with gently flipped ends. It's so lacquered with hairspray, it's immovable, like plastic Lego hair.

Seth recovers first.

'Yes, please, I'm after some jewellery for my girlfriend.'

The woman twinkles at him. 'Ah, si, lovely. Something similar to what she has on...' She eyes my seahorse earrings, 'Or something more classic? Like pearls or diamonds?'

'No, actually I was thinking of rings...'

The woman's eyes light up, 'Oh, si!' She starts whipping out trays of what look like engagement rings, and I groan inwardly. This is getting a bit much. He could've just said we're tourists and wanted a photo for Insta, so we can get out. Now we've got to pretend we're engaged.

Seth doesn't seem too phased, however. 'These are very nice, thank you,' he says politely. 'But, actually, I was thinking more along the lines of nipple rings.' My face instantly goes bright red, and I wish I could sink through the floor and drop into the Arno. I'm going to kill him. To her credit, the woman doesn't bat an eyelid. She reaches beneath the counter and pulls out a tray of small gold rings. 'Would any of these be suitable?'

'Ah, yes. Jenna, what do you think?' asks Seth, twisting to see where I am.

Oh my God, he is such dead meat. Since I have no choice in the matter, and we're talking about my nipples, I might as well go along with it and pretend to check them out.

'Um, yeah, maybe those,' I say pointing randomly at a pair that each have a fine filigree drop chain interspersed with gold stars. I could actually imagine wearing them as earrings.

'Si, the chains are detachable,' says the woman helpfully. 'You can dress the rings up or down, depending on the... occasion.'

'Yes, good choice. I think those would look great on you, Jenna.' Seth's voice has a gravelly undertone, which I've noticed appears when he's turned on. I kick his foot under the counter. This isn't the time to be fantasising about my breasts adorned with nipple rings.

'We'll take them,' he says matter-of-factly.

I stare at him agog and grind my flip-flop onto his foot, but he ignores me and pulls out his wallet. A few minutes later, and I'm the proud owner of a pair of gold nipple rings, ensconced in a black jewellery box. Seth checks the way is clear, and we exit the shop. I feel slightly dazed.

He grins at me. 'Well, that was a fun detour.'

There's no way I'm going to get it done. I can always make up some excuse. *I talked to my nipples, and they said they weren't keen.*

I shake my head at him, 'You… You're …', but whatever I'm about to call Seth is lost forever when Gabe materialises in front of us.

He's been under the shady portico, next to a small market stall of tourist tat. 'Hello, Jenna. I think you've got something of mine.' He eyes my handbag. 'Is it in there?' The three of us are stones in a stream with people flowing around us like water.

'She's not giving it to you,' Seth says through gritted teeth.

'I was talking to Jenna,' retorts Gabe. 'Give me my phone, and I'll delete the photos as soon as I get back to my hotel.'

'No,' I say. 'I don't trust that you will.'

'Give it to me. Now.' He starts advancing towards me, and I dodge around him and run to the side of the bridge. There's a clear view of the river from this spot. Not knowing what else to do, I take his phone out of my bra, draw back my arm and throw as hard as I can. The phone travels in a high arc over the Arno, falls with a plop and sinks out of sight. Good riddance, now I don't have to deal with it any more. Having it on me was starting to make my skin crawl.

'Fuck you, Jenna. You owe me an iPhone 8,' growls Gabe from behind me. I turn around and see him with his fists clenched looking murderous. 'You're lucky I backed up my client deets in the Cloud last week.'

I roll my eyes. I knew it, it's not even the latest model. I can't believe I put up with him for all those years. His stinginess and self-righteousness totally got on my wick. His interior decorating skills aren't even that good, he copied a lot of his ideas from me. Suddenly I'm hit with startling clarity. It hasn't taken me a year to get over him. It's taken me a year to find myself again.

'Go home, Gabe. I don't know why you bothered coming here in the first place. You've just caused a whole lot of trouble. I don't want you, and I don't want my old job back. I'm happier without any of it. Just fuck off, and leave me alone!'

In the background, I see Seth give me a silent whoop and a fist pump, and I feel quite proud of myself for standing up to him. Even in front of a crowd of rubbernecking tourists. Gabe doesn't really have a comeback apart from another, 'Fuck you.' He jerks his head like an offended chicken, says, 'Fuck you' again and stalks off down the bridge.

It's too much drama for me. I sink down on the low wall of the bridge as the crowd of onlookers disperses and bury my face in my hands. Seth sits next to me. 'Well done, corporal. For the phone and for telling him to fuck off.'

I lean against him, and he puts his arm around me. 'I can't believe I said that. Even when I dumped him, I gave him the 'it's not you, it's me' speech when really, it was all him. I should've told the truth, I just didn't want to hurt his feelings.'

'Understandable. You're a nice person.'

'It feels good to finally say it though.'

'I bet.'

'Now I feel zonked.'

'It's been quite a day. Shall we get some gelato on the way back to the hotel?'

I nod, 'Yes, please.'

'And discuss your impending nipple piercings?'

'No!'

CHAPTER TWENTY-NINE

I say it in a joking tone, but firmly enough, that Seth doesn't bring it up again while we're walking to get gelato. Although, when we're waiting in line, he says, 'I hope you're not mad that I bought those rings for you. After what you said last night, I thought you may be on board, and since we were in the shop I figured, why not? But I can see I may have jumped the gun a little. Sorry.'

'I was a bit surprised, but I'm not mad,' I reply, staring down at my red varnished toes.

'So you're not totally anti?'

'I guess not. I just didn't have nipple piercings high on my list of priorities. But still, thank you, you didn't have to.'

'I wanted to. To say thanks for helping me with the writing.' He sounds concerned that I'm not happy about it, and I soften. So what if we have different ideas when it comes to jewellery? It's still a romantic gesture. Also the rings weren't cheap. I squeeze his forearm.

'I love them, really, thank you. I can always use them as earrings.'

'You could. Though, you know, sometimes the best way

to tackle scary things is to take a deep breath and just do it.'

'Noted,' I say dryly.

We spend some time looking at the glass cabinet, deliberating over gelato flavours. Well, I do. Seth wants cioccolato, but I get overwhelmed by all the flavours again, and I can't decide. So he buys me a medium-sized cup with fragola (strawberry), bacio (hazelnut and chocolate) and frutti di bosco (fruit of the forest).

'So, what's the scariest thing you've ever done?' I say, continuing our conversation as we stroll towards the hotel with our gelato cups.

'Singing a song I'd written in front of a bunch of people at Dad's office. It was terrifying,' Seth says, digging out a chunk of creamy cioccolato with a little wooden spoon.

'Oh,' I say, surprised at this piece of backstory. He's been pretty reticent until now about the origins of the band. 'What were you doing before that?'

'We mucked around in my mate's basement doing covers of other Goth bands. But then I started writing my own stuff, and I showed Kyle, so we started experimenting. When we had a song ready, I plucked up my courage and asked Dad if he could have a listen. He said, "Right, let's hear it then. Come into the office."' Seth sucks on his spoon and takes a while digging out more gelato.

'So, what happened?' I ask, impatient to know.

'I thought it was just going to be him, but unbeknownst

to me, he'd set up a meeting with a few of the execs, as well as some of the admin staff to see what they thought.'

'Fuck,' I say taken aback. 'That's harsh.'

'I know, trial by fire. Either he was confident I'd be good or he was trying to traumatise me so I'd never ask him again.'

'Had he heard you sing before?'

'Possibly once at a karaoke night. Anyway, I was pissing myself. It was me and Kyle with his acoustic guitar doing the unplugged version. Luckily, we had a couple of days before the meeting, so we practised hard out to make sure it didn't sound completely amateurish.'

'And?' I ask wide-eyed.

Seth smiles modestly. 'Everyone was blown away. I don't think I've ever seen Dad look so gobsmacked, it was pretty satisfying. When he found out I had a backlog of material, he signed us on the spot and not long after, we started recording the EP. It was all kind of surreal. I was on a high for about a week afterwards.'

I can picture the scene perfectly. A crowded room, no one expecting much. His friend strumming away while Seth, looking every inch the angsty Goth muso, wows everyone, even the tea lady, with his velvety vocals. I get shivers down my spine, like I'm hearing a history in the making story firsthand. 'Wow, so that was your discovery?'

'Yeah. Not really that impressive since my Dad's a producer.'

'But he wouldn't have signed you if you were shit.'

Seth laughs. 'No, he's not that kind. He said we needed a new band name as well. We did have one, but it was pretty bad.'

'What was it?'

He grimaces. 'The Dogs of Woe.'

I giggle. 'Not great.'

'Yeah. *Sublime Misery* was the name of the song we performed, so we just used that. I've got some of the lyrics on me.' He pulls up his t-shirt and points at the tattoo on his abs. 'I figured it was a good luck charm.'

'Ah, I was trying to read that last night, but I got distracted,' I say, unable to help staring. He does have the most amazing set of abs. I can't help thinking of him lying in front of me naked and erect, that's a vision I'm not going to forget in a hurry.

'You're welcome to have another look tonight,' Seth says cheekily and somehow, I don't think he's talking about the tattoo. I avert my eyes and take a mouthful of strawberry gelato as heat courses through me.

'What about you? What's the scariest thing you've ever done?' he asks, dropping his t-shirt.

'Nothing in your league, I can tell you now.' I lick my spoon, considering. 'Leaving my job without having anything else to go to was pretty bad. I had a few panic attacks after that. And I guess... Knocking on your door and inviting you to dinner. I had to psyche myself up quite a bit to do that. But curiosity won over fear. I was intrigued, and I wanted to meet you.' I wait for him to scoff and say "Seriously? That doesn't count as scary", but he nods.

'Yeah, I was impressed you did that. You went in totally blind. I didn't make it easy for you either. I'm not exactly an extrovert as you may have noticed.'

'It was worse waiting for you to show up that evening. I had no idea what to expect.'

Seth grins. 'Did you get a shock?'

'You could say that. But I'd been expecting an overweight, bearded gamer with acne, so it was a pleasant shock.'

He laughs and deposits his empty cup and spoon into a nearby bin, then pulls me unexpectedly into a hug. I'm still eating my gelato, so I have to hold one of my hands up in the air behind his back, so I don't spill it on him. 'The day you knocked on my door was the day everything changed. If you hadn't, I'd still be in London with writer's block. Actually,' he says thoughtfully, resting his chin on my head, 'I think I'll dedicate this next album to you.'

I choke a little on my mouthful of frutti di bosco and swallow quickly. 'What? You can't do that!'

'I can, and I will. You're my muse. You made it happen.'

I'm even more curious to see these songs now. What the hell has he been writing?

I feel relaxed and happy when we get to the hotel. The photos have been dealt with, the early evening sun is warming my face, I'm holding hands with the hottest guy in the world and we're about to spend the night together. PLUS, I'm going to have an album dedicated to me! I don't think my life can get any better at this point unless I score a fabulous interior decorating job.

But the day from hell has one last stinger waiting in store. Calypso. As soon as we walk into the hotel lobby, she launches herself at us from a side chair with an icy expression. I note that she seems fully recovered from her bowel problem, whatever that was.

'There you are. I've been waiting bloody ages.'

'Are you OK?' I ask her, trying to divert her from causing a scene.

'What? Yes, I'm fine,' she snaps. 'I hope you both enjoyed your free Uffizi tour?'

'We did, thanks,' says Seth pleasantly. 'Sorry we had to leave, but something came up. I thought you were going to your Airbnb?'

'I was, but I ran into Gabe outside after I spoke to you.' She folds her arms and looks at me with an accusing glare. 'He told me that Jenna had stolen his phone, and you'd both taken off. He was livid. What are you playing at?'

'Let's go outside,' Seth says, with a nervous glance at Giacomo, whose ears are flapping. We all troop outside to the parking area.

'Gabe took naked photos of me while I was at Jenna's place last night. We were attempting to delete them off his phone,' Seth says without any preamble.

'He did what!' Calypso's mouth drops open. 'What the hell were you doing, having a threesome?'

'He was outside the apartment!' says Seth hurriedly. 'Jenna saw him lurking around. I went over to the window to check and he got a photo. Several photos actually.'

'Oh my God,' Calypso covers her mouth with her hand. 'Are you mental? If those got leaked...'

'I know, I was an idiot.'

She turns to me. 'Why did you let him near the window? Don't you know how damaging photos like that are?'

'I didn't know Gabe was going to do that!' I feel a bit disgruntled that she's putting the blame on me.

'It's not Jenna's fault,' Seth interjects. 'Besides, she was the one who saved the day. She managed to get his phone off him at the Uffizi, and we escaped through the Vasari Corridor. Then we had a showdown with him on the Ponte Vecchio, and Jenna chucked his phone in the Arno. She was brilliant.' He stops to draw breath, and I note his eyes are bright and his cheeks are pinkened. Now that his reputation is safe, I think Seth is quite enjoying the drama.

'So that whole thing about you hooking up with the neighbour was bullshit?'

'Yeah, I was hooking up with Jenna. If you want to use an unromantic term.' He smiles at me and winks; I blush. *Hooking up indeed.*

Calypso's face is unreadable. She's extremely good at keeping her emotions in check. I can't tell if she's jealous or if she's just concerned for him as a friend. Her interrogation in the café loo had me convinced she was after him, but I'm not sure now. Maybe she's more worried that if Seth's name gets trashed, as the band photographer, she'll be out of a job.

'Oh, well, it's good you got that sorted out,' she says to Seth, 'Because you won't be here much longer.'

'What's that supposed to mean?'

'I mean,' she says smugly, 'that I told your Dad the true state of things. That you're writing off brand, getting distracted,' she narrows her eyes at me, 'and generally not keeping up your end of the bargain. He wasn't happy.'

Seth inhales deeply. I think he's going to tell her off for interfering, but he says in an overly polite tone, 'Have a good time in Rome, Calypso.' Then he turns to me, 'Come on Jenna, let's go and make use of the facilities while we can.'

He turns and walks back into the hotel, leaving me alone with Calypso. We eye each other warily. Her looking sleek and classy in her white-on-white outfit and me, in my sundress, flip-flops and pigtail buns. 'Well, bye, I guess,' I say awkwardly. 'And thanks for the Uffizi tickets.'

She sniffs and says 'Bye. Enjoy it while it lasts.'

Which makes me feel like I've been pigeon-holed as a summer fling.

My heart sinks as we take the lift up to 312. 'It may not happen,' Seth says, reading my thoughts. 'But it probably will as I've written ten songs. That was the deal. So now, there's no reason for me to be here.' He sounds resigned to going home.

'Am I not reason enough?' I ask in a small voice.

He glances at me. 'Of course, you are. To me. But not to my Dad. He doesn't know you. Bloody Calypso. I knew she'd tell him something like this.'

I feel bad for saying it, but I have to, it's what I'm feeling. 'I'm not sure I like her that much.'

Seth grunts. 'She used to be nicer when she was younger— I think boarding school ruined her. That's the problem when someone's a family friend. They're ingrained in your life, and you can't get rid of them.'

Suddenly, the girl in the photo that I thought was his sister… It makes sense. The gangly boy with teenage acne. Calypso in the pink party dress.

'Did you ever go to Brighton with Calypso when you were kids?'

'Yeah, Dad and I used to go every year with her and her parents. How did you know about that?'

'I saw a photo at the house. You didn't look happy.'

'I hated it.'

'So her Dad took the photo, and her mum...'

'Is India's sister.'

'Right.' I'm trying to get my head around the family connections. 'So if India is Calypso's aunt, then she's your step-cousin?'

'Yeah. Another reason why I didn't want to get involved with her as anything more than a friend. We're not blood related, but still, it felt incestuous and could be construed that way.'

'But why is India with your Dad? Where's your mum?'

There's a heavy silence, and Seth's face hardens. 'I'll tell you in the room,' he says gruffly.

Oh God, it's bad. As soon as I saw that photo, I knew something awful had happened with his family. I shouldn't have asked.

In his room, I perch on the couch while he leans on the desk. He hangs his head, appearing reluctant to talk about it. But it's too late now, I've asked the question.

Is it scenario six, the one where India had a steamy affair with Drew, the wife walked in on them and India threatened to kill her unless Drew married her? Or is it worse?

'Is your mum... Is she dead?' I whisper, steeling myself for scenario seven. India did actually kill her, then stole her husband.

Seth sighs. 'No. But she may as well be. She's living in

Skegness with a loser, who's an alcoholic and a gambler. She left when I was thirteen. I haven't heard from her in years.'

Skegness? OK, that didn't feature in any of my scenarios.

'Dad was devastated at first, but he started dating again a few years after they got a divorce. He already knew India through Portia, Calypso's mum, so I guess it was a natural progression to start seeing her. It took me a while to get used to the idea. That was just puberty rage though, now I can see they're perfect for each other.'

Wait, what? India's the good guy in this?

'But the first night we met you gave me the impression you didn't like India?'

'Did I?'

'Yes! I was imagining all sorts of things.'

'Ah, no, we get along OK. I was probably just grumpy at her because she'd organised a house sitter when I'd said I could look after Sephy. She never trusts I'll remember to feed her.'

'So I was the reason you were in a bad mood?'

'Yeah. But I cheered up when we chatted.'

'Oh, good. I couldn't tell,' I say teasingly.

He grins. 'Anyway, now you know the ugly truth about my family history, do you fancy using the rooftop Jacuzzi? I'll book it out for our private use.'

'Tempting, but I haven't got a swimming costume.'

'We've got our underwear.' Seth's eyes glint

mischievously. 'There are robes too.'

Getting up close and personal with Seth in a Jacuzzi sounds heavenly, so I don't take too much convincing.

'OK,' I say happily.

While he talks to Giacomo on the hotel landline about booking the Jacuzzi, I collect a white towelling robe from the wardrobe and head to the bathroom. When I come out with it tied tightly around my middle, Seth's waiting by the door donned in his. 'What?' he asks, catching sight of my bemused expression.

'I've never seen you wear anything other than black. It's a bit of a shock.'

He grunts. 'I might suggest anonymously that the hotel provides black robes for Goth guests.'

CHAPTER THIRTY

We take the lift up to the roof, and Seth punches in a code beside a glass swing door. We walk through an ante room with a turquoise tiled floor and wooden lockers, then through another glass door out onto a small terrace. There's a square hot tub on a raised platform, set back under the tiled roof overhang and a couple of white sun loungers placed nearby. But what's really amazing is that the terrace provides an unfettered panoramic view of Florence.

'Woah,' I say walking to the edge, which has a waist-high wall. The sun is setting over the city, bathing it in golden light. The Duomo rises stately in the distance, with the terracotta roofs of the buildings spread out beneath. A flock of birds fly overhead and dip down to settle and rustle the branches of a tree in the hotel garden beneath us.

I hear a small splash and turn to see Seth's robe lying on a sun lounger and him in the Jacuzzi with his arms outstretched, fingertips resting on the edge. He tilts his head back slightly and sighs. 'It's just the right temperature.' My stomach flips. Seeing Seth's body, even half-naked, is always electrifying. It's the combination of his raven hair, pale skin and the inky swirls snaking over his chest and shoulder; it lights a fire in my belly. My eyes drop to the still water. Is he even wearing underwear…? I inch closer, but before I can get a good look, he presses a button with his right hand and bubbles erupt obscuring my view. He scratches his chest lazily and catches me trying to gawp at his bits. 'Are you coming in? I could only book half an hour unfortunately.'

'Oh, yes,' I say, blushing. 'I'm just checking for CCTV cameras. After the photo incident, you can't be too careful.'

'I don't think they're in the Jacuzzi.'

'Well, they might be… underwater cameras.'

He smiles at me. 'I did a check. I think we're good.'

'Right. I'll, er, take this off then.' Suddenly, I'm as shy as I was last night, but this time, I don't have a towel for protection. I'm baring it all. Well, I'm wearing my bra and knickers, but it feels like I'm baring it all under his watchful gaze.

'Can you close your eyes?' I know I'm being silly, but he's intimidating me. His mouth quirks, but he obeys, scrunching his eyes shut tight.

I fling off my robe, step up onto the platform and put one foot in next to him, only to find him gazing at my navel. He runs his hand up the back of my thigh.

'Cheat,' I say.

'You didn't say how long for,' he murmurs. I gingerly put in my other leg and sink down into the warm frothing water.

Seth puts his hands on my waist positioning me, so I'm straddling his thighs facing him. I find out then, when my hand accidentally brushes his crotch, that he isn't wearing any underwear.

'I think you've lured me in here under false pretences,' I say, exploring his impressive length.

'There's nothing false about it,' he replies in a gravelly tone, his half-lidded eyes locked on mine. 'As you can tell, it's very real.'

I touch the tip with the barbell piercing and manipulate it with my fingers, not really sure what I'm doing, but Seth's breathing quickens, and he gently removes my fingers. 'I wouldn't do that.'

'Oh, does it hurt?'

'No, it feels extremely nice, and there are people using the Jacuzzi after us. Not exactly manners, if you get my drift.'

He probably shouldn't have said that because now I'm intrigued. It's like telling a kid to stay away from the cookie jar. Not going to happen. We start kissing and my hand drops down and strokes him, then moves up to fiddle with the barbell. He lets me for a bit, then studiously removes my hand. This goes on backwards and forwards like it's a game. But after a while it must get too much, because he pushes my fingers away and groans, 'Torture.'

Part of me feels gleeful that I've worked him into such a state. But also a bit bad that I aroused him with no chance of release.

'Sorry.'

'It's OK. Time's nearly up anyway. We could continue in my room?' he says expectantly. In my mind's eye, I see myself in the apartment last night taking the three condoms from his jeans pocket and placing them in the nightstand. Then fast forward to this afternoon, me racing around putting toiletries in my handbag, and completely forgetting about them.

I lean back in the water. 'There are no condoms.'

'Yes there are. In my pocket.'

'I took them out last night. And forgot to bring them.'

'Oh. OK. We'll just have to… improvise.'

I'm not sure what he means by that, but now there's an air of disappointment, on my part too. I was looking forward to having sex with him. I get out of the Jacuzzi first and put on my robe. I hand him his but then just before he ties it, I gesture to the lounger and say, 'Lie down.'

'What for?'

'Humour me.'

He lies down, and I flip his robe open.

'What are you doing?'

'Worshipping you under the Tuscan sun.'

He glances at the sky. 'The sun's already set… Ahhhh, OK,' he says, as I lick up his length and start sucking. Then he goes completely quiet apart from some low-level guttural moaning. After about two minutes, he grips my pigtail buns, and I reach up and give his nipple piercing a decent twist like a tap. He practically bounces off the lounger as he comes, and I drink the nectar of the Gods.

The lift dings and wiping my mouth, I hastily tie his robe. There's chatter and a couple come out onto the terrace in robes, with two kiddies trailing behind, wearing water wings. The scene before them is the picture of innocence. I'm standing at the wall looking out at the view, and Seth is lying on the lounger with his eyes closed like he's having a nap.

'Evening. Lovely night for a spa,' says the husband, nodding at the view while the wife helps the kids up the platform into the water.

Seth rouses himself off the lounger and stands up unsteadily. 'It is indeed,' he says, sounding a bit wheezy, 'We'll let you enjoy it and go and grab some dinner.'

I smile at the parents and wave at the kids. 'Have fun!'

Seth grabs my hand and yanks me through the door and into the lift. He leans against the lift wall and covers his eyes. 'Oh my God, that was astounding. But… the children! If it had been a minute later!'

'Lucky you were quick,' I say, inspecting my fingernails nonchalantly.

All the way down in the lift, he keeps groaning and laughing. I think for once I've actually managed to shock the hell out of him. Perhaps I am a risk taker after all.

'We can grab dinner in the restaurant or order room service.

Which do you prefer?' Seth asks when we get back to his room.

'I think room service,' I say, kicking off my flip-flops in the lounge area. 'Do you mind if I take a shower?'

'No, help yourself. There may be some shower gel left,' he says with a roguish grin, picking up his phone from the desk.

'Haha.'

I think from that smile he might suggest washing my back but he's frowning at his phone instead.

'What is it?'

'A missed call from Dad. He hasn't left a message.'

We look at each other.

'That's not good,' I say, tucking my hands up into the sleeves of my oversized robe, so it looks like they've been chopped off.

Seth sighs and sits down at the desk. 'Not after what Calypso said. I guess I should ring him back.'

'I'll leave you to it then,' I say, not wanting to get in the way of their father-son chat. I give him a good luck kiss on the temple and a shoulder squeeze on the way past to the shower. I'm dreading what his Dad will say. Even if he's peeved that Seth appears to be running amok in Florence, surely he'll understand about me being a creative influence, rather than a hindrance. The fact that he's written ten songs is testament. Besides, their deal was that he could stay here for two weeks, so wouldn't he keep to that?

After spending twenty minutes in the shower and having

washed and conditioned my hair, I judge that it's been long enough. I was half expecting Seth to poke his head in the door and ask if he could join me, but he didn't, which is feeding my anxiety that something has gone down with his Dad.

I put on my sundress and clean knickers, then dry my hair off with the hotel hairdryer so it's damp rather than sopping. I wring out my wet underwear and drape it over the heated towel rail. Seth's not in the lounge when I come out. I find him fully dressed and lying on the bed with his hands behind his head, contemplating the ceiling. Uh oh.

'Hey,' I say, hopping up and crawling over to him.

'Hey.' He puts an arm around me and I snuggle into his chest.

'So what did your Dad say?'

'In a nutshell—playtime's over. I need to get my arse home and start recording.'

'Oh. But you've got a few more days?'

'No, I'm leaving tomorrow afternoon. He's booked the flight,' he replies flatly.

I prop myself up on my elbow and stare at him in shock. 'That soon.' Oh no!

Seth grunts. 'Yeah. It's the nature of the beast unfortunately.'

I struggle to keep my emotions in check and act as cool as he is about it, but I feel like my heart is being shredded by a grater. 'So, that's it then,' I say, with a slight voice wobble.

He frowns. 'Huh?'

I wave a hand generally in his direction. 'You and me.'

I've been dreading having this conversation. I know what's coming. In Florence, we've been on an equal footing because we're both tourists, and this is the city where we've gotten to know each other. In London, we're just strangers that met one night in a kitchen in Hampstead. I'm expecting the 'of course, we'll see each other' reassurance, which will tide me over in hopeful expectation until I get back. Once I'm there, we may exchange a few texts, and even endure an awkward café meet-up, where he admits that our lives are too different to make it work and our time in Florence is best shelved as an extraordinary memory.

But I've forgotten this is Seth, and he tends to have a different take on things to me.

'Actually,' he says, pulling the strap of my sundress down. 'I think playtime's just beginning. What do you say to a night of no holds barred, hedonistic fun?' He licks my bare shoulder and rolls me back on the bed, kissing his way down to my breast where my erect nipple suddenly becomes the starter course. 'Mmm,' he breathes, flicking it with his tongue. 'Fruitily delicious.'

I inhale and let out a long, slow breath; anxiety falling away and arousal kicking in. I have no idea what he has in mind, but if this is the last night I ever have with Seth Carver, then I'm going to make it count. Calypso's words are coming back to haunt me, *Enjoy it while it lasts.*

CHAPTER THIRTY-ONE

'Seth,' I whisper in his ear. 'I have to go.' I peer over to see if he's awake. He's lying on his front, head buried in the pillow, hair mussed, and with what looks like a smear of strawberry on his cheek. He cracks open an eye and croaks, 'Morning. My head hurts.'

'Mine too, but I have to feed Filippo. And you have to... pack.' The word spits out of my mouth like a smoker's cough.

He rolls over and gathers me naked into his arms. 'Uh uh, the cat and the packing can wait. I'm not letting you go.'

I nestle in and lick off the smear of strawberry on his cheek. I do vaguely remember feeding him strawberries. Last night is mostly blurry, thanks to two large bottles of Prosecco shared between us. But I can still piece together fragments of what we got up to. I bury my head in his chest feeling morning after abashment. *Jesus, Jenna.*

'Are you having flashbacks?' he asks.

'Yeah,' I say in a muffled voice.

'Mmm, me too. It was great.' Seth takes my hand and glides it down his smooth stomach, but I snatch it away.

'No, I can't.'

'Oh.'

Last night was crazy, good crazy, but I need strong boundaries this morning to make things easier.

'You're leaving,' I say by way of explanation.

'Yes, but not for a few hours.'

I roll away from him onto my back and he sighs. 'Don't act like this.'

'Like what?'

'Like it's the last time I'm ever going to see you. We both live in London.'

There it is, I think. The 'of course we'll see each other' reassurance.

'It just feels like it,' I mutter. 'Things get in the way. People change on home ground. This isn't reality, it's fantasy.'

He tilts my chin towards him and kisses my lips. 'A pretty nice fantasy. One that I want to keep going for a bit longer. Especially since we haven't perfected the trifecta of pleasure. Close but not quite.'

I giggle a little. 'Ah, yes, that.' Since we didn't have condoms, there were several different contortions last night, one of which I'm pretty sure involved a vigorous sixty-nine. I blink as the memory surfaces. Bloody hell. I run my tongue over my teeth to check they're all still there. Thank God, they feel intact.

'Sure you don't want to practise now?' he offers. 'I could run out to a chemist.'

'Seth, I'm being serious.'

'So am I. I'm not going to forget about you.'

'Easy to say that when I'm lying right here,' I grumble. 'Harder when you're in Hampstead, busy recording, and I'm in Putney doing… whatever I'm doing.'

'Do you know how close Hampstead and Putney are?'

'No.'

'Count.' He kisses each of the fingers on my left hand, then each on the right.

'Ten miles?'

'Correct. That's fifty minutes in a taxi or fifty minutes on the District and Overground or walkable in three hours.'

'Did you look that up on Google Maps?'

'I did.'

'Oh.'

The fact that he's been thinking practically about transport options makes it feel more real, like it could actually work.

'So just relax and stop worrying about it. In a bit, I'll order us a hearty breakfast involving bacon and eggs, a large jug of orange juice, one of water, and possibly the Italian equivalent of paracetamol. Meanwhile…' his hand moves down between my legs, where I'm already slippery from his sexy voice reverberating in my ear. He nuzzles my earlobe as he gently teases my clit awake with his fingers.

'While we're on the subject though, probably best not to

walk it,' he murmurs, continuing to stimulate me.

'No?' I shift onto my side so I can stroke his erection.

'Mmm, especially not in heels.'

'I may not be in Putney anyway.'

'Oh?' He twirls a finger inside me and rubs my clit with his thumb. I moan softly.

'Hello, we're having a serious logistical discussion here, Jenna,' he teases.

'I can't think straight when you do that.' He starts rubbing against my hand, breathing harder. 'Or that.'

'Maybe we should shelve it…' But I can't answer because what he's doing with his fingers is making me groan in bliss.

An hour later, I'm walking along the Arno, back to the apartment in the sun, dragging my heels and feeling spacey after our night of hedonism and not much sleep. Leaving was a trying-not-to-cry affair on my part. Seth hugged me tightly at the door and said 'Whatever happens, I'll see you again,' and that he'd ring me when he got to the airport. I think if he'd said "We'll always have Florence", I would've hit him. As it is, his parting statement is a sentence of two halves that I'm now chewing over. The "whatever happens" suggests he's blasé, but the "I'll see you again" is a solid promise. Like it's possible we're going to be torn apart but that also our relationship is somewhat in our control if both of us want it. So my mood is yo-yoing between depression and hope.

Unfortunately, everything at the apartment reminds me of him. The kitchen where we sort of confessed how we felt about each other and he cooked me a twelve-egg omelette. Our spot on the window seat in the lounge where he wrote a song with his hand on my leg. The bedroom where the duvet he wrapped himself in is rumpled on the bed. Worst of all, are the three unused condoms lying in the bedside table. I'm trying not to take it as a sign of doom.

After moping around, I feed Filippo, who's meowing like crazy. Then, for want of something better to do, go out to the Mercato Centrale to replace the eggs, buy some more fish and other food items that I'm running low on. The lunch time atmosphere at the market is cheerful and bustling but it only serves to make me feel more bereft. I've got another week of this. How am I going to cope?

I feel angry that I've been cut off from him, like I'm some kind of bad influence. He was the one who tracked me down, so he could feel inspired enough to write again. Maybe I should've charged him muse energy rights or something. It's not nice of me to think it, but perhaps Calypso's right about his motivations. That he's more interested in the music and making it big than in me.

But the logical part of my brain knows he wouldn't have come to Florence, spent so much time or have been so intimate in bed with me if it was only that. Plus, he bought me nipple-earrings. Buying jewellery is a definite sign, it's always in the *How To Tell If A Guy Is Serious About You* articles.

Maybe I need some female advice. Violet is out of the question. After the whole Gabe debacle, she's persona non grata with me at the moment. Stacey has no clue what's going on apart from the fact I'm in Florence. My mother is completely out of the loop, and doesn't even know I'm here, unless Stacey's told her. I can't imagine what she'd say if I rang and said I'd fallen in love with a Goth musician.

Antonella is the only one who's actually seen me with Seth, so at least she'll have context of what I'm dealing with. When I'm near the apartment, I message her to see if she's home and say I've got her clothes and handbag, which I assume she wants back?

She texts back immediately with: *Come over for lunch!*

Instantly, I feel uplifted. This is what I need, a supportive girly chat!

I race around flinging all her clothes into a hessian carrier bag and upending the Gucci handbag on the bed. My makeup, toiletries and damp knickers fall out. Pity, I was getting used to having a designer handbag. Seth's purple toothbrush lands on top of the pile. For some reason, this really upsets me, and I nearly burst into tears. I forgot to give it to him. Now, he can't clean his teeth! What if he's on the train, annoyed, because his teeth are all furry?

Stop being ridiculous, I tell myself sternly, *he'll buy*

another one. Unfortunately, it means I now have three unused condoms and a used toothbrush as a reminder. I can picture myself as an eighty-year-old woman taking them out of my jewellery box with a shaky hand to show my middle-aged daughters, and saying in a wavering voice—'This is all I have left to remind me of him. I never saw Seth Carver again. The album he dedicated to me made him a superstar and life got in the way so there was no continuation of our romance in London. But I'll always remember our time in Florence, it's as real to me as if it was yesterday…' Oh God, I'm spiralling. I need to talk to Antonella pronto.

I thought I might have to lead into it, but I needn't have worried. As soon as I'm ushered into her apartment, which is a replica of Cathy's but the pre-refurbed version, she exclaims, 'I can see why you wanted to go all out for the hotel meeting. Seth is smoking! I'm not usually into Goths, but I'd definitely put out for him.'

Hearing that brings back my worst fears, namely, he's going to forget all about me in favour of someone more attractive and cool, and my face crumples like a concertina.

'Oh no, what happened?'

'Nothing. Everything. He's gone,' I mumble.

'Come through to the kitchen. I'll cobble together some lunch.'

Silently, I give her a jar of olives and a wedge of Pecorino cheese from the market.

'Thanks!'

I slump onto a barstool while she bustles around the kitchen. It's weird being in the exact same apartment but with no Seth imprint. Maybe I'll ask her if she wants to swap. She hands me a glass of red wine. 'Drink. It will help.'

I'm not sure I should be drinking anything after last night, but I obediently take a sip, then another, larger one. It tastes a bit like cherries and, before I know it, I've drunk three-quarters of the glass.

Antonella places a neatly arranged antipasti board on the counter along with a bowl of green salad, then pulls up another bar stool. 'So what's been going on?' she asks, doling out the food onto a couple of plates.

'I've fallen in love with a Goth musician,' I blurt, somewhat drunkenly. 'He said I was his muse and bought me nipple rings to use as earrings. Then his record-producer father marked me as a bad influence, so we had one last night of hedonistic fun. Now he's gone back to London to record an album, so I'm never going to see him again. *And I forgot to give him his purple toothbrush!*' This last bit comes out as an anguished wail as if it's the most important takeaway from the story.

Antonella's eyebrows shoot upward, and she pauses with the salad tongs in the air staring at me in awe. 'Fan-fucking-tastic!' she says. 'This is better than a viral TikTok. Start from the beginning, and tell me everything!'

Offloading to Antonella does make me feel better, especially since she's hanging on every word. She loves the story about the e-biking detour ('Oh, he's a rebel!') and hoots about us being caught making out in the storeroom during the cooking class ('Awkward!'). I move onto Calypso turning up, then Gabe, the naked photos, me running off with his phone in the Uffizi, then the escape through the Vasari Corridor. When I tell her about Seth spontaneously buying me jewellery, the showdown on the Ponte Vecchio and throwing Gabe's phone in the Arno, she's on the edge of her seat wide-eyed. 'No wonder I haven't heard from you. Your life is like a movie. Go on!'

'There's nothing much more to tell. Calypso said I should enjoy my time with Seth while it lasted, intimating that I'm a summer fling, Seth and I had a nice Jacuzzi…'—I blush a bit at that—'His Dad told him he had to go back and start recording, then we got shitfaced on Prosecco, and well… the next morning when I left, he said 'Whatever happens, I'll see you again'.'

Antonella sucks in a lungful of air and sits back on her seat.

'Well, I'm not an expert on men or anything, but I'd say after hearing all that, he's pretty into you. I told you from the start it's never just business when a guy hops on a plane to see a girl. No matter how much he says it is. Buying you jewellery is also a dead giveaway. Actions speak louder than words.'

'I thought so.'

'Then why are you worried that he's going to suddenly ghost you?'

'We're so different.'

'But that's why he likes you. You intrigue him.'

'I can't imagine why. Surely, he'd go for someone like Calypso.'

Antonella snorts derisively. 'I don't think so. And she knows it. That's why she's telling you all that bullshit about enjoying it while it lasts. It sounds like she's trying to muck with your head so you get all insecure and self-sabotage it.'

'Oh.' She could have a point there.

'So is he really gone? If he has to leave the hotel, I'm sure Cathy wouldn't mind if he stayed with you at hers.'

'I think it's too late, he'll be on his way to Pisa by now.'

'You could ring him?'

I shake my head quickly. 'Thanks for listening though. Just maybe keep it on the down low.'

'You're welcome, and don't worry, I won't tell a soul.'

I feel exhausted from the wine and the rehashing of our adventures, so I say I'm going to head off and have a lie down.

Antonella sees me to the door and gives me a hug. 'Chin up. He'll call you.'

When I'm back next door, I check my phone, but there are

no messages. I crawl under the duvet, fully-clothed, and move over to his side of the bed. There's a faint scent of him on the pillow. I imagine, but it's probably just wishful thinking, that I can even feel a slight indentation in the mattress where he was lying. *I miss you, call me*, I think intently, waiting, but there's nothing.

By the late afternoon, I'm still lying there, unable to sleep, now holding onto his toothbrush. This actually feels quite comforting. Filippo pads in and meows in my ear. Not quite the conversation I was looking for, but I pat his head, and he purrs. 'Dinnertime, huh?'

I'm in the kitchen with the pink rubber gloves on, and just given Filippo his fish, when my phone lights up on the counter. My heart jumps into my mouth when I see it's Seth. I stare at it frozen, then rip off the rubber gloves, take a few deep breaths and answer normally.

'Hey!'

'Hi, it's me.' Hearing his voice makes me want to cry.

'Hey,' I repeat again, not knowing what else to say.

There's a pause, and I can hear ambient chatter in the background. He must be at the airport.

'So I've been thinking. About London... There could be a problem.'

My heart sinks like a lead weight. Oh, no. He's giving me the flick. *We're too different. This was fun but I need to concentrate on my music.*

'Right,' I say stiffly, not wanting to hear his excuses. 'I get it. You don't have to explain.'

'Yeah I do. I'm not going to be in London.'

'Oh. A band tour?'

'No.'

Suddenly, I get a strong feeling that he's right next to me.

'Where are you?'

'Where do you think?'

Slowly, I walk into the lounge and look out the window. But there's no one on the wall.

'Seth, stop playing games.'

'I'm not.'

If he's freaking messing with me, I'm going to kill him. My nerves can't take it. I open the apartment door and walk to the top of the stairs, keeping my phone to my ear. But I can't stand the suspense, so I go racing down the stairs and fling open the front door. Seth's standing there with his phone, and a bag slung over his shoulder.

'Surprise,' he says into his phone.

'Oh my God. What the hell are you doing?' I say into mine, then realise it's redundant because he's right in front of me.

'I missed my flight.'

'Did you go to the airport?'

'Yes, but then I got on the next train and came back again.'

I open my mouth to say something about that not being

very eco-friendly and then shut it again. *He missed it on purpose, for you, Jenna.*

'Was there a reason for all this train travel?' I ask.

Seth gazes at me and I melt, wanting to touch him, kiss him and never let him go. 'You're the reason.'

'Oh?' My heart is pounding.

Seth licks his lips nervously and puts his bag down. 'You're going to make me say it, aren't you?'

I nod, tears already starting to form.

Then, in a doorway in Florence, the boy I met by pure chance on a house sit in Hampstead, takes me in his arms and utters the words I've been longing to hear.

'I love you, Jenna. You're like sunlight in the darkness. Being without you, even for a minute, is utter agony.'

Well, he is a Goth poet. I wouldn't expect anything less.

CHAPTER THIRTY-TWO

By unspoken mutual agreement, we head straight to the bedroom where Seth dumps his bag, grabs me to him and we fall onto the bed, kissing and clinging to each other. 'I love you, I love you,' I gasp, wrapping my arms around his neck and breathing him in. 'I can't believe you're here.'

Seth kisses me deeply, and I lose myself in the feeling of his hard body on mine and his tongue swirling sensually in my mouth. He sucks softly on my bottom lip and my back arches as electricity zaps straight to my groin.

'You taste delicious,' I tell him. 'Like caramel.'

'I had a Mars Bar,' he says smiling. I trace down his nose and across his lips with my finger.

'You're so crazy doing this. I love you.' I can't stop saying it now. I tug his head down to kiss me again. My dress is ruched around my waist and as we kiss, he trails his cool hand up and down the hot skin of my bare thigh. His fingers move over the material of my g-string, pressing and rubbing, and I push against his hand wantonly.

'What are you going to do?' I ask, panting, trying not to get carried away. We have to talk about stuff, don't we?

'I'm going to take your knickers off for a start,' he says gruffly.

'No, about your Dad, and the band.'

'Don't worry about that. I'll sort it.' He pulls my g-string round my thighs and strokes a finger in my wetness, tracing around my clit, making me shiver with desire.

I unzip his jeans and shove my hand down his pants, wanting to feel him. He's as hard as a broom handle but missing a vital element on the end. 'Where is it?'

Seth sucks in his breath as I run my fingers over his moist but bare tip. 'I took it out for the metal detector at security. But then I never went through.'

'Oh. And these?' I pull up his t-shirt. No nipple piercings either. I do a double take. I'm so used to them now, it's strange to see him without his hardware. He's like a snail without its shell.

'I can put everything back in if you want,' he says, sounding amused. 'But it depends.'

'On what?'

'On whether you want the first time to be a vanilla latte or a triple-shot espresso.'

I don't know what to say.

Seth kisses me and says, 'I'll let you think about it. But just for reference, so you know what you're in for…'

Before I can react, his head is between my legs. He spreads me open and licks my clit with the tip of his tongue. The feather-light strokes feel amazing and I groan and open my legs wider. His tongue flicks me like a snake, then there's a pause, and something different starts happening. The pleasure verges on pain, and I realise he's using his tongue stud to massage my clit, the hard metal rubbing on my sensitive flesh is almost unbearable, but excruciatingly enjoyable.

'Ohh yes, ohh yes,' I pant, starting to build towards climax.

But he lifts his head and places his hand on my mound, so I'm throbbing in neutral but not going anywhere.

'I want the hardware,' I say eagerly, taking off my dress, my bra and toeing off my knickers which are hanging round one ankle. 'Give me everything you've got.'

Seth inhales and lets out a breath. 'Going straight for the good stuff, huh? You're a brave woman.'

'No, thanks to what you just did, an extremely horny woman.'

He smirks. 'OK. I'll be back in a sec.'

He heads to the bathroom with his toiletry bag, and I crawl under the duvet in anticipation.

When Seth walks out naked with his piercings back in, my body instantly responds with a visceral yearning, like I'm hard wired for him. I don't know why I find him so freaking hot. But I do. And he knows it by the way my tongue is practically lolling out of my mouth. He grins at my expression. 'I love the way you get so turned on.'

'Get in here.'

He dives underneath the covers and I instantly zero in on his piercings, knowing exactly how to manipulate them to make him squirm. 'You're getting good at that.' He closes his eyes as I suck on a nipple and stroke him at the same time. 'Oh, God.' His voice contorts in pleasure. 'Let's do it, I'm not going to last long.'

My fingers are shaking so much, I can't open the condom. 'Let me,' he says, and I avert my eyes as he rolls it on.

'This is going to be intense,' he warns.

'Good,' I say, and he slides into my hot wet opening with expert precision.

I groan, wrapping my legs around him and taking him deeper, so he's hitting all the right spots of the alphabet. He starts thrusting so fast the friction sets me alight, and I thrust back like a woman possessed. I'm making all kinds of animalistic sounds; grinding my hips, gripping his hair and raking my nails across his back which seems to make him speed up even more. Then he slows, and we're tense, holding onto each other, almost there, swaying on a tightrope. He moves his hips languidly, and whispers 'I love you' in my ear. The pleasure is too much to handle, and I let go of the wire, shuddering hard just as he comes hot and pulsing in my chasm.

I lie in his arms as our breathing slows. He kisses my

sweaty forehead and murmurs, 'And that wasn't even the trifecta.'

'Arrrgh, you've ruined me,' I whimper.

'In a good way though?'

'In the best way possible.'

I'm tempted not to tell Cathy that Seth is staying, after all, it's only for a week. Antonella checked in with me the next day, and I gave her the good news. She whooped so loudly, I think the tourists on the Ponte Vecchio heard her.

Anyway, I don't want to get into trouble with Cathy if Antonella lets it slip, so I email her, saying someone I know is visiting from London unexpectedly and ask whether it would be OK if they stayed for the last week of the house sit. I attach a couple of photos of Filippo sunning himself to let her know that he's well and happy. I've been a bit lax on that account. Half an hour later, I get a reply:

Hi Jenna,

Thanks for the photos, glad to see Filippo is AOK. Yes, that's fine as long as she doesn't mind sharing a bed or there's the couch?

Damn. I'm going to have to come clean. Honesty is the best

policy after all. Also, I don't want her to blacklist me as a dodgy house sitter.

Thanks, Cathy. "She" is actually a "He" as it's my boyfriend. I hope that's still OK?

Oh! I see. I didn't realise you were with someone. Yes, I don't mind. Thanks for checking with me. Hope you're having a wonderful time! I'm missing the sun, London is all drizzle and grey skies. Talk soon, Cathy

She sounds totally fine about it rather than simply being polite. I sigh in relief and walk through to the lounge where Seth is on the window seat with Filippo on his lap, looking out at the Arno. I put my arms around him. 'You're in. Cathy said it's fine.'

He presses his cheek against mine. 'Fantastic. Thanks, I know me turning up like this makes it awkward for you.'

'Not at all. I'm just glad she's OK with it.'

'So, I need to sort out what's happening my end, but we've got another whole week in Florence. What are we going to do?'

I shrug. 'More tours?'

'Hmm, maybe we should do some self-guided ones.'

I rub the front of his t-shirt, feeling his nipple piercing, 'We could start with Jenna's self-guided tour of the apartment.'

'I'm all EARS,' he says in an Irish accent, and I giggle. He moves Filippo to the side and pulls me down onto his lap. 'What does it entail?'

'Well, it starts in the bedroom, clothing optional. Then it moves to the kitchen to refuel with the gelato that's still in the freezer.'

He kisses me. 'Sounds good, then what?'

'Then it heads to the bathroom where we get nice and clean in the tub, and I scrub your back and any other parts you want me to.'

'How much does this tour cost?'

'Oh, it's free, but you can give me a big tip afterwards.'

He guides my hand to his crotch. 'I might give you a big tip beforehand.'

Impromptu self-guided tours aside, planning our week in Florence beats thinking about what the hell I'm going to do about my living arrangements in London. But I'm forced to face it, so I swallow my pride and ask Violet if I can stay with her for a bit until I sort myself out. She messages back after many hours with a curt: *Yes, that's fine. What day are you arriving?*

It feels like cracks have started appearing in our friendship that I can't ignore. Part of it is my fault, for trusting her with information in the first place. But I also think that if she's a good friend, I should be able to trust her, and if I can't, then there's a big problem. Yet, typical me, I've stuck my head in the sand and didn't confront her about it. However, sticking up to Gabe and telling him what I thought of him was quite cathartic, so maybe I'll take the bull by the horns with Violet too.

The job situation is even more shaky, and I'm dreading having to drum up business. The Instagram posts have garnered a lot of attention but nothing concrete in terms of interior decorating opportunities. I'm thinking now that applying for Gabe's job would be a smart move as at least I'd have money. Or perhaps I can bypass Gabe's job and go grovelling to my old boss. At the time, he said he wanted to stay well out of our domestic issues, but as long as Gabe hasn't been poisoning the well, he might be open to rehiring me for another position.

Seth's also been busy, smoothing over cracks of his own. His Dad apparently hit the roof when he found out he missed his flight and was staying another week. But Seth calmly told him that he's aware he's under contract, the songs are done and that he'll send through the lyrics to the band so they can start working on the music. Plus, he'll have some sessions with them via Zoom. I didn't know you could work remotely when you're in a band, but Seth said it was done all the time. He also said that he told the rest of the band about me. 'They were going to find out anyway when we get back.'

'What did you say?' I ask, pushing down my misgivings

about being seen as a bad influence. *Yoko Ono, here we go.*

'I said I'd met someone, we were in Florence and that you'd been a big inspiration for the album.'

I glow at that.

'What did they say?'

Seth grins. 'There was a bit of surprise. They wanted to know if you were Italian. I had to explain that I'd actually met you in London.'

'Right.'

'Then they wanted to know how it was possible that I'd met someone since I'm such a recluse.'

'Haha.'

'They wanted to know if you were a Goth fan that had tracked me down and seduced me… I said you weren't, a Goth I mean,' he adds quickly.

'How did they take that?'

'With even bigger surprise. They really want to meet you now.'

'Is me not being a Goth a big deal?'

'No. They just can't imagine anyone who's not, being into me.'

'Ah.' I think about Antonella's comment about how hot she thought he was. Seth definitely has the power to turn non-Goth women into gibbering idiots, but I might just keep that piece of information to myself.

CHAPTER THIRTY-THREE

The next week passes in a flurry of sightseeing, gelato and more sex than is humanly decent, and before I know it, we're sitting on an EasyJet flight at Pisa Airport, taxiing down the runway. Seth holds my hand for the entire journey, only letting go to visit the toilet and when we're eating lunch.

It's bittersweet leaving Florence. For me, it's forever going to be the place where Seth and I fell in love. But I'm not too upset, since the man in question is sitting next to me, happily munching away on a ham and cheddar cheese toastie, and swigging from a can of Sprite. We came, we saw, we conquered. And we came quite a few more times after that.

We managed to fit quite a lot of things in during the afternoons, after Seth had finished his band meetings and before our nighttime activities. The Palazzo Vecchio and Boboli Gardens were a no-brainer since they were near the apartment. We also went to the Accademia Gallery to see the real David (who I still don't think holds a candle to Seth). Then there were drinks at SESTO, an amazing rooftop bar with views of the Arno and on the last day, we went back to the Uffizi Gallery to have another gawk at the Primavera. I raved about it so much that Seth bought me a poster, which I'm going to have framed and hang up (when I get a flat).

After around two hours of flying, neat rows of London houses come into view out the plane window. It looks grey and cold, which the captain reinforces with his pre-landing announcement that we can expect a temperature of thirteen and drizzle. I already miss the warmth and sun of Florence. After we land, Seth and I catch the Gatwick Express to Victoria station then, it's time to part ways. He's heading north to Hampstead and I'm going south-west to Putney. As much as I crave it, there's going to be no romantic meet-up later. For one thing, he doesn't actually know Violet's address.

Seth hugs me tightly in the noisy chaos of Victoria station and says simply, 'Thank you for Florence.'

'It was just… wonderful,' I reply, unable to put into words what I'm feeling; he's the poet, not me.

I must sound glum, because Seth pulls back and frowns. 'Are you sure you'll be OK at Violet's?'

I told him I wasn't exactly looking forward to seeing her, but that I felt I needed to. 'Yeah. It'll be fine. We've got stuff to talk about.'

'I'll message you tonight. I'm not sure what my schedule's like during the next few days, but I want to see you.'

I snuggle back into his arms. 'I want to see you too.'

'Then it's settled.' He kisses the top of my head. 'Now go

and make peace with Violent Violet,' he says, and I giggle. Oops, I forgot I told him I call her that, he's got a memory like an elephant.

It's rush hour, so the Tube is packed, and I have to stand all the way. Rattling through dark tunnels with my head thrusting against someone's armpit is a bit of a shock to the system after strolling the sunlit streets of Florence with gelato. I'm relieved when I get out at East Putney station. There's a fine drizzle coming down and, as I'm only wearing shorts and a thin top with a light cardigan, by the time I reach Violet's flat, I'm completely drenched and miserable. The thought of a night on her back-breaking couch, when I've gotten used to being cosied up with Seth in a double bed, is lowering my mood further.

The Sainbury's below her flat is beckoning me to buy something, so I don't turn up empty handed. But I'll go up first to check whether there's anything she needs. I don't want to arrive armed with cereal and eggs if she needs milk and bread. I'm tempted to buy a couple of bottles of Chianti so I can reminisce about Italy and endure the night.

Violet opens the door and eyes me warily.

'Hi,' she says bluntly. 'Come in. I'm just about to make a chicken curry.' Why do I get the feeling this isn't going to go well? She's wearing black jeans and a blue-and-green checked shirt with a black tank underneath; toenails and fingernails painted a garish purple.

'Do you want me to nip down to the shop and get anything?' I offer.

'Nope, you're all good.'

There's no movement towards a hug exchange so I wheel my bag into the lounge. Everything looks exactly the same as when I left two weeks ago, even down to the magazines on the coffee table. There's a stale smell of damp.

'Nice tan,' says Violet, leaning against the door jamb, watching me get changed into a hoodie and jeans.

'Thanks,' I say, not biting at the opening. 'Want any help with dinner?'

She shrugs. 'Sure.'

It's not until I'm chopping a courgette that's bordering on its use-by date, and she's frying chicken, that Violet broaches the subject in a direct manner. She must be dying to know what's happened.

'So did Gabe catch up with you?'

'He did,' I say evenly.

'Oh, great. So did you guys manage to sort stuff out?' I don't know why she's so keen for me to get back together with him. But it's now or never to state my case.

'No, Violet, we didn't. Gabe being there caused a big problem for me and Seth. To be honest, I'm pretty pissed off you told Gabe I was there with him when I asked you specifically not to tell anyone.'

There's a silence and she flips the chicken pieces in the pan so they sizzle and spit.

'Sorry,' Violet says tightly. 'I was just trying to help. Gabe seems to genuinely care about you.'

'He doesn't. He's a selfish prick. I should know, I went out with him for five years. Besides, Seth and I are together…'

'You don't honestly think Seth Carver is going to bother about you once he gets back here?' she scoffs. 'Wake up, Jenna, he lives in a different world to us.'

I push the chopped courgette aside and stick the point of my knife in the board. 'You don't know him, he's not up himself or a user just because he's in a band. He loves me. We love each other.'

Violet shakes her head pityingly and makes a grunting noise.

I'm starting to get annoyed. 'Is it so hard to believe that he feels that way about me?'

'Yes. You're not exactly the type a Goth would go for,' she says under her breath, dumping the courgette into the frying pan.

'Seriously? I thought you of all people would be more open-minded about us. Seth doesn't care that I'm not a Goth, he sees me for who I am.'

Violet doesn't say anything, just moves the chicken around in the pan moodily.

Then I realise why she's acting like this. It's so obvious I don't know why I didn't see it before. Violet is harbouring a major Goth groupie crush on Seth and is jealous of me being with him. I thought her attitude was based on concern about me getting hurt but her motivations for telling Gabe I was in Florence are becoming clearer. She probably guessed it would cause havoc if he showed up on the scene.

I let out a breath. 'Violet, I'm sorry you're not happy about me being with Seth. But I'm not about to break up with him just to make you feel better.'

'You're delusional if you think it's going to last,' she mutters. 'Don't expect me to pick up the pieces when he dumps you.'

Then we continue making the curry in silence because, really, what else is there to say after that?

After a tense dinner, where we hardly speak, Violet says she's going to watch a movie in her room and leaves me to make up the couch. Seth messages to ask how things are going and I reply with OK, not wanting to reveal the true state of things. He says he'll message me tomorrow when he knows what he's doing.

The fact that he's contacting me and using plenty of XXXs is reassuring. I can't let Violet's negativity about our relationship get to me. But doubts are already starting to creep in again. Why does he want me? Is he just interested in sex? Is he going to dump me? Was he just using me in Florence?

I wake early, thanks to a terrible night's sleep, and reality finally sinks in—Violet's flat is no longer a viable option. But what's the alternative? Living with my parents in Camberley or going up to Edinburgh and staying with Stacey in her tiny one-bedroom flat in Fountainbridge? Just when she's started dating again, and I owe her money. I'm not sure which is the lesser of the two evils. If Violet's trying to break me and Seth up, she might just achieve it.

I hear her bustling around in the kitchen, making tea and toast. I can hear footsteps getting closer to the lounge. They seem to stop in the doorway, and I decide to pretend to be asleep. I don't really feel like talking to her. I've said everything I want to say. What Violet doesn't seem to realise is that Seth gives me the good stuff, the stuff that life is about. What we have is healthy, and it's real. I wish she could just get over herself and be happy for me. But I know Violet and she probably won't ever be happy about it.

When she leaves for work, I lie there thinking, trying to come up with a plan. But I can't seem to get my brain to focus on anything except that I don't want to be here.

Around mid-morning, I heave myself off the couch, tidy up, have a shower and some breakfast. I then sit in the lounge again, not knowing what to do. Seth hasn't messaged, so I'm not sure if we're meeting up or not. Fuck it, I'm just going to take my stuff and go… somewhere else. Maybe if I ride the Tube around for a bit, I'll get a brilliant brainwave.

I let myself out of the flat and walk to East Putney station, wheeling my bag behind me. It's raining quite heavily, so I shelter under a tree and fish out my windbreaker. I put on a pink beanie because I don't have an umbrella. Tucked behind the netting of the inner pocket, I spot the small black box with the nipple-earrings. A jolt of rebellion goes through me, the kind I haven't felt since I was a teenager. Why not? It's turning out to be a "fuck it" kind of day, and I've got nothing better to do.

I'm in Fulham when Seth messages:

Hey, want to meet in Hampstead Heath for lunch, 12.30? Redemption Roasters.

OK *xxx*

Remember fifty minutes, District and Overland XXX

I head for Fulham Broadway station, feeling slightly nauseous but also triumphant, despite my two aching nipples. What's got into me? Whatever it is, it feels refreshing and freeing, like I'm breaking away from my old life. The life I didn't actually choose for myself. The further I travel from Putney and Violet's presence, the more my mood lifts. When I get to Hampstead Heath, I cheer up even more, knowing I'm about to see Seth.

Redemption Roasters is an airy, industrial space with a

black frontage, wood-look lino and pine tables and chairs. There's a cabinet full of glossy pastries. I discover Seth ensconced in a corner table, reading a book. As soon as I see him, my heart rate kicks up a notch. It feels odd seeing him in a public place outside the Hampstead house. He's wearing a long-sleeve black t-shirt and black jeans, his hair is standing up in spikes. I haven't seen it look like that for a while, it's usually all over the place once my hands have been in it. I tug my beanie down over my wet hair, feeling like a starstruck teenager.

Seth is absorbed in his book, but looks up and smiles when I approach the table. I notice there's a pink-and-white striped golf umbrella propped up next to the table. It looks like a large candy cane.

'Hello, beautiful,' he says gazing at me, which makes me feel a bit emotional, knowing this might be the last time I see him for a while. I smile thinly, and sit down without saying anything. He follows it with 'Hey, what's up?' when he realises I'm near tears.

My boobs are starting to sting like crazy now the numbing cream has worn off, and I almost tell him what I've done, but I focus on the bigger problem that's making me upset. 'I think I'm going to have to leave London.'

'Right…' he says slowly. 'How come?'

'I can't stay with Violet. Things aren't good between us, and I'm not sure what else to…'

'Stay with me,' Seth says instantly.

'You don't have to put me up,' I reply quickly, not wanting to be a burden. 'I can stay with my parents in Camberley or my sister in Edinburgh. It just makes things difficult for... us.'

'Jenna, don't be silly. You put me up in Florence. Besides, I miss you. Last night, I hardly got any sleep because you weren't there.'

'Really?' I breathe. 'Me too.'

'So, please. Stay. You've seen the setup. It's a bit of a boys' grotto, but it'll be fun.'

'But what about your Dad and India?'

Seth shrugs and closes his book, some high fantasy novel. 'I'll tell them, but they won't care. I can do what I want.'

'It'll just be until I can sort out job stuff...'

'Stay for as long as you want. Stay forever,' he says lightly.

My head is swimming. He wants me to live with him. This definitely isn't a summer fling.

'I'm going to be recording soon, but Dad and India are going away next week, so it's perfect,' he continues, 'I'll say you can look after Sephy and that you'll be in with me, instead of up at the house. You can sort things out with work, relax and use the pool or whatever.' He looks out the window at the bullet-grey sky. 'Though it's not exactly pool weather. You might want to scratch that idea.'

When he looks back at me, I'm crying silent tears. 'I love you.'

He kisses me full on the lips and doesn't care if anyone sees him. 'I love you more. Now, what would you like? A coffee or a hot chocolate? And they do really good toasties or you could go for a pastry. Fuck it, just have everything.'

I give a watery giggle, wiping my eyes. 'I knew you were rubbing off on me.'

CHAPTER THIRTY-FOUR

Since it's still raining, we're in no particular hurry to leave the warm, snug café. So much so, that we stay there for ages—reminiscing about Florence, chatting about all sorts of things, holding hands and just enjoying being with each other.

Seth tells me stories about his school days and the gap year in Italy (minus the woofing) and I, in turn, tentatively tell him about working at the design agency in Islington, some of the funny house sits I've had and my family. I don't think he'll be interested, but he listens intently, asks questions and laughs in the right places. The lovely thing about Seth is that even though he's an introvert and appears standoffish when you first meet him, once he knows you and trusts you, he opens up like a flower. He's also a great conversationalist. I love talking to him.

We're there for so long, I think the café staff might chuck us out, but there are plenty of people on their laptops and it seems like a hub for freelancers. Seth also keeps buying us drinks and treats from the cabinet, so we're not freeloading too much.

Eventually, he says, 'We should go and get you settled in.

If I drink any more Kombucha, I'm going to explode.'

We leave the café and walk up past the station en route to the house. Seth covers us with the umbrella and wheels my bag for me.

'Why have you got a pink umbrella?'

Seth chuckles. 'It's India's. It was pouring, and I raced up to the house to get an umbrella from the hallway, but India and Dad had nabbed the black ones. It was either this or get soaked. It matches your hat, at least.'

Speaking of India, it's getting on for tea time, so she's probably home. I tug my beanie down further over my ears feeling nervous about the reception I'm going to get. The last time India saw me, she was doling out house sitting instructions and casually mentioning her stepson who lived in the garden. Now, here I am, moving in with him.

'So we're going to waltz through the front door?'

'Not exactly,' says Seth. 'We'll go in the back way, through the gate. They don't need to know anything tonight. We'll keep it to ourselves.'

The whole thing feels a bit clandestine, but I'm relieved not to have to face India's raised eyebrows or meet his Dad. Especially since I look and feel worse for wear, and my nipples are rubbing against my bra and driving me barmy. I'm hoping when Seth sees them, they're a turn on and not a swollen mess.

Seth reads my silence as nerves and tries to reassure me. 'You can have a shower and relax, and we'll order some dinner. What about Italian?'

I smile to myself. 'From Luigi's?'

Seth glances at me. 'How did you know I order from there?'

I touch my nose with my finger. 'A house sitter knows everything.' *You can also learn a lot if you rummage through the rubbish bins.* 'I'm also interested to hear more about your green M&M's obsession. Did you know they're considered an aphrodisiac?'

It's so strange to slip through the side gate and see the shipping container, the pool and garden. Up the path is the outline of the main house. My perception is skewed. I half expect to see the other version of myself peering down from the upstairs window. The version who was longing for the boy in the garden. I'm not sure exactly what I did to get him, but the boy is very much, wholeheartedly mine. I'm not going to question it. I've waited for so long to find a guy that I love and truly want to be with, that I intend to savour every second.

Seth seems almost shy when we're inside. He bustles around tidying, turning on lights, asking if I want the heating on and finding me a blanket when I say I don't. He shows me the bathroom and says, 'Use anything you like. There are clean towels and toothpaste in the cabinet.'

I almost reply with 'I know' seeing as I looked in it, but bite my tongue. There are some things a girl should keep private. Plus, I don't want him to think I have stalker tendencies.

He leaves me alone to have a warm shower, which feels heavenly. I try not to put my sore chest under the full force of the spray but splash a bit of soothing water over my boobs and inspect the nipple jewellery. It's just the rings minus the detachable chain—but wow. I really did do it. They're a bit red, but that's to be expected according to Toni, the piercing woman. She also gave me some stuff to clean them with and said they wouldn't be healed fully for four to six weeks. I'm not sure I'm going to be able to keep them under wraps for that long, so Seth will probably find out. If not tonight, then tomorrow. I know he's going to flip. In a good way.

The reveal comes sooner than I expect, however, when we're lying on his bed replete, full of Luigi's lasagne, garlic bread, green salad, and a couple of celebratory tiramisus, to mark the occasion of my moving in.

'My stomach is telling me I'm going to have to go for jogs on the Heath if we eat too much Luigi's,' I say, patting it. 'Along with all the gelato in Florence, I think I've put on a stone.'

Seth props himself up next to me and runs an eye over my white t-shirt and pink shortie pyjama bottoms. 'I think you're perfectly…' he begins, then stops, peering closely at my chest. I look down and, shit, the nipple rings are clearly visible through my t-shirt since I'm not wearing a bra. Uh oh. I look at him and he's staring at them wide-eyed. 'Did you do what I think you did?'

'I did,' I say, holding my breath.

'Can I see?' he asks somewhat eagerly.

I nod and he lifts my t-shirt up and inspects them.

'Sore?' He prods near the piercing and I wince.

'Yes! Maybe don't touch my boobs under any circumstance for the next week or so. The piercing woman said it would be four to six weeks before they're healed properly.'

'We'll be really careful.'

I assume he means when we're having sex. Then I notice Seth's eyes are shining like obsidian, his glee barely containable. 'Fuck, Jenna! I can't believe you did it. I thought the next time I saw those, they'd be in your ears.'

'I can't believe I did it either,' I say, delicately pulling my t-shirt back down.

'You should've said, and I would've come with you. Brave girl.' He kisses me tenderly, and I roll towards him, wanting the comfort of his body against mine and the passion, which is starting to stir.

But even hugging is painful, and I pull back with an 'Ouch.'

'Hmm, this is going to take a rethink on positions,' he says, easing down my pyjama bottoms and dipping his head to kiss across my stomach. 'Why don't you just lie back, relax and let me do all the work?'

And that, ladies and gentlemen, is the real Seth Carver, I think with a sigh as his tongue starts flicking between my thighs; a truly thoughtful, selfless human being.

Two weeks later, my nipples are on the mend, and I've pretty much settled into life in the shipping container. It feels like being on holiday, so I have to remind myself it is actually real life. India and Drew found out that I was there the day after I moved in. Seth rang his Dad at work. They had a chat while I chewed my fingernails, but it turned out fine. He invited us up to the main house for dinner that night. I was horribly nervous but Drew turned out to be really nice, and not the ogre I was picturing at all. He clearly thinks the world of Seth, and it's uncanny how alike they are. It's as if I was seeing how Seth was going to look in thirty or so years' time, without the piercings and tattoos, of course. Drew is very much the clean-cut version.

India was there cooking up a storm. If you can call it "cooking", it seemed to mostly involve her sitting at the table and fiddling with the app. Whatever she thought about me living in the back garden with Seth, she kept under wraps. All she said was, 'Well, this is a surprise!', and 'Can you look after Sephy when we go away next week to Morocco?' But we had a nice meal. Drew asked about Florence, so I showed him the photos I'd posted on Instagram. He said I had a good eye, which led to Seth waxing lyrical about my abilities as a brilliant interior decorator. I ended up showing them photos of an upmarket house I'd worked on in Muswell Hill when I was at the design agency. At first, I felt a bit embarrassed but then that "fuck it" feeling came over me again. Why shouldn't I feel proud of myself? I'm good at what I do. Not being hugely successful right now is not an indicator of my underlying ability or talent. So I let Seth praise me to the hilt and bathed in the spotlight for once. It worked out in his favour. I was feeling on such a high afterwards, that his apadravya got quite a lot of attention in bed that night.

Though, in reality, things in the job arena aren't going too well. Once I knew that Gabe was no longer working at the Islington agency, I approached my old boss with the slight hope of getting another job. But I was too late. There had been a position but he'd already hired someone for it. 'I'm sorry, Jenna. If I knew you were looking to work here again, I definitely would've had you top of the list. I'm surprised that Gabe didn't mention he'd been in touch with you.' In between shopping for the latest iPhone and throwing darts at a cutout of Seth, I have the feeling Gabe probably won't be mentioning my name ever again.

As for Calypso, she actually came over with her friend Dahlia and a dachshund puppy called Daisy, not too long after I moved in with Seth. He was recording, so it was up to me to entertain them. Since it was a nice day, we sat out by the pool, chatted about her time in Rome and threw a ball for the puppy, trying to stop it from jumping in the water. I still don't trust her completely where Seth is concerned, but she seems to have accepted that I'm important to him, and I'm not going anywhere in a hurry. As she's India's niece and the band photographer, I can't exactly throw my weight around where she's concerned. Seth knows she's not my favourite person and that I'll be polite to her, but also that we're not going to be BFFs anytime soon.

At least the other members of Sublime Misery aren't trying

to sabotage us. I met them when Seth invited me to one of their recording sessions at a studio in Hammersmith. It was spine-tingling seeing him in Goth muso action. I even dressed hipster for the occasion; beanie, baggie jumper, ripped jeans and hair in plaits. However, it may have looked more cutesy than grungy.

That day, they were recording an additional song for the album, called *Tortuous Love* which, from some of the lyrics, I suspect is loosely based on our time in the rooftop Jacuzzi. Bloody Seth. He kept winking at me, and I didn't know where to look. I still haven't read all of the songs he's written. He says I'll be the first to hear them when the album's finished, which is cool but nerve-wracking. I can't shake the feeling that our private time in Florence is going to be on display for public consumption. But I know Seth wouldn't do that. I asked him about it, and he said he hadn't written songs about me baring my boobs under the moonlight or anything like that.

After the recording session, we all went to a nearby pub for drinks. It was bizarre hanging out with four Goth guys, who had so many body piercings between them, they could open their own jewellery store on the Ponte Vecchio. But, thanks to Seth making me feel at ease, I relaxed and chatted away to them, even though they didn't smile much. I think they could tell we were loved up by the hand holding and Seth whispering sweet nothings in my ear. As Kyle remarked dolefully when we were leaving, 'You two are like heads and tails of the same coin'. I thought that was quite profound. It made me feel like they saw we fit well together and didn't consider me a threat. There's nothing I'd hate more than to give the impression I'm against him being in the band. I want him to take it as far as he can. Whether that's a UK presence or worldwide fame, I'm totally behind it.

My friendship with Violet is at an impasse. I messaged her on the first night to say I was staying with Seth, so at least she knew where I was. But she never replied. Probably even reading that was too difficult for her to accept. The ironic thing is that she wanted to meet Seth Carver, but when she actually could, she decided to turn on me!

Her attitude is annoying as hell. Yet, I can't do anything about it, and I'm not sure I want to. I miss her as a friend but also a part of me is over her toxicity. I need to be around people that are supportive of my relationship with him. Like Antonella, who I've been messaging with. She's going to come to London to visit us when she's finished her semester in Florence. I can't wait. I'm going to take her up St Paul's. There are five hundred and twenty-eight steps to the Golden Gallery, hah!

Just before India and Drew are due back from Morocco, I return from a client's house one afternoon (another boring beige carpet consult) to find Seth's journal open on the bed. There's message in his handwriting which says: *I'm in the zoo room if you want to see it.*

It gives me telepathy tingles because I was going to ask him about that exact thing. When I was up there this morning feeding Sephy, I had a bit of a poke around the house, including another look at the Disney bedroom. I still love it, but I'd rather be in the studio with Seth as it's more private, and we can make a bit of noise or go skinny dipping in the pool at night without anyone getting embarrassed. Anyway, out of curiosity, I tried the handle of the zoo room and listened at the door, but it was still locked, which made me frustrated. I really wanted to see it.

So now I race up there and try the handle again. This time it opens easily but when I enter, it's a shock. The whole room is stuffed full of plants and trees reaching up to the ceiling. I can't see anything.

'Seth?' I call out, feeling a bit overwhelmed.

'I'm in the middle.'

I push my way through to get to him. The leaves, which brush against my face, feel like they're made out of some kind of waxy eco-friendly plastic. When I reach the centre of the room, it's a clearing in a forest, and I find Seth lying on his side on a green chaise longue surrounded by oversized stuffed animals—of the toy variety. I spy a tiger, a giraffe, a gorilla and a zebra.

His black shirt is unbuttoned to mid-chest, and he has a roguish look on his face that suggests he's been waiting for me and thinking sexy thoughts. 'Welcome to Pandora,' he says sultrily.

'Oh my God. You weren't joking,' I reply, probably looking startled as I feel. 'This is a greenhouse on steroids. How did you get in here, by the way?'

'This used to be my room, remember? So I've got a key.'

He pats the chaise longue and I lie on my back beside him.

'But why does India keep it locked?'

'Sephy's pretty good at opening door handles. She gets in here, jumps on the animals and claws out their glass eyes. India got sick of replacing them.' He brushes my hair from my cheek and kisses my forehead. Hmm, somehow I don't think he's invited me in here for a friendly chat.

Above our heads, branches, leaves and flowers intertwine. It doesn't feel like we're in a house anymore. 'This is so cool. Crazy but cool. I'd love to do something like this.'

'Well, funny you should say that.' Seth shifts closer, resting a hand on my thigh. 'India messaged me from Morocco.'

'Oh?'

'Apparently, she's decided that she wants to redecorate. She's over the whole Avatar meets Amazon theme and wants an interior decorator with impeccable taste to give the room an overhaul. Of course, after my recommendation of your talents the other night, she was keen for you to take on the job.'

'Wow, really?' I say surprised. 'What kind of thing is she looking for?'

'She's leaving it completely up to you. Oh, and you've got a budget of twenty thousand.'

I hit his arm in disbelief. 'No freaking way!'

'Yes, you just have to work out your commission.'

'Commission?' I rapidly try to work out what I could

feasibly charge, seeing she's Seth's stepmother, and I'm living rent-free on the property.

'It gets better. If you do a good job, then she'll recommend you to her bevy of Hampstead housewives who are suckers for themed rooms and they have incredibly deep pockets.'

I lie there taking in what's he's saying, the glassy eyes of the tiger boring into mine. If I want a foothold into the Hampstead market, then this is it, India is willing to unlock the door for me. I can see the tagline of my website now—Jenna Freeborn: Reinventing Your Hampstead Home, and a whole load of glowing reviews. It's slightly overwhelming.

'I'm not sure. Your family is so generous. Letting me live here, and now, this…' I say doubtfully, 'It's too much.'

'It's not a handout, Jenna, you've got to put in the work. But it's a chance to do what you love. We'd still be banging out Goth covers in Kyle's basement if Dad wasn't a producer. But luckily, he is, and we're making the most of him being one, we'd be stupid not to.'

I guess he has a point. The best jobs aren't advertised, it's all about knowing the right people. And I still have to prove myself.

'So, really,' Seth continues 'the only question you should be asking yourself is: what am I going to do with this room?'

'A Renaissance theme,' I say immediately. 'A nod to the Uffizi but with a modern, liveable twist.'

'Sounds awesome, I'd definitely hang out in that room. Will it feature the Primavera?' Seth teases.

'Of course. I'd have to plan it all, and then, there's the

issue with sourcing the materials. I might have to ship some from Italy if she wants the real deal.'

'This is India. She wants the real deal,' says Seth dryly.

'We could go back to Florence and source them personally,' I suggest, getting a tad ahead of myself.

'I'm sure that can be arranged,' he chuckles. 'Meanwhile, since you're still in the planning stages, can I interest you in some afternoon jungle delight?'

Seth stealthily undoes the bottom button of my shirt and then the next one, sliding a cool hand up over my hot skin which is now flushed with excitement, from his touch and the future. Thanks to him, I am starting to believe good things can happen if you do scary things. So, I'm just going take a deep breath, jump in feet first and try my luck. Everything will probably work out just fine. And if it doesn't? Well... It'll inspire one heck of an angsty Goth song.

The End

PICK UP A FREEBIE

Thank you for reading *I'll Meet You in Florence,*
I hope you enjoyed it! If so, I'd be thrilled if you left a
review or star rating on Amazon and/or Goodreads.

Want more of Jenna and Seth?

Join my mailing list using the QR code below and get an
exclusive bonus chapter.

KEEP READING

If you liked *I'll Meet You in Florence,* check out my new co-authored rom-com *You Had Me at Ice Cream.*

Oliver is keen to lose his Covid kilos so he hires personal trainer Zara to get him back on track. Despite the potential for a budding gym romance between the two of them, things take an interesting turn when Oliver's newly toned physique starts attracting female attention.

Available on Amazon and Kindle Unlimited

ACKNOWLEDGEMENTS

I'm so grateful for having a team of people to help me on this publishing journey. My beta readers: Aimee Ferro, Kylo Kotze and Lauryn Lambert, thank you for your insightful and honest feedback. A special thanks to Lauryn for her developmental editing.

More thanks go to Katerina Hristova for her beta reading and copyediting, Tania Courtine for her proofreading and Kostis Pavlou for his wonderful cover art. I'm also super grateful for the encouragement from the indie author community, plus my friends and family who've bought and read my books. I appreciate your support!

Last but not least, thanks to Chris Lambert, for sharing his music biz knowledge on this one.

Angela Xx

To receive alerts about new releases,
sign up to my newsletter at:

➜ angelapearse.pub

ABOUT THE AUTHOR

ANGELA PEARSE writes quirky romantic comedies which capture the humour of everyday life. A freelance editor with an MA in English, Angela enjoys travelling, hiking, cooking, binge-watching Netflix, and reading copious amounts of chick lit. Originally from New Zealand, Angela currently lives in Edinburgh with her partner. Visit angelapearse.pub.